What they're saying about The Goldberg Variations 1:

"Jonathan A. Taylor's The Rites of Passage is marketed as the first in a series of novels; it also ably stands on its own. The story follows Jamie Goldberg from elementary school to college, as he grows from an abused boy into a self- possessed young man. His life is a symphony of pain, humor, filth, and beauty as he struggles to come to terms with his identity in homophobic America."
— *Foreward Reviews*

"Heartbreaking and hilarious, provocative and roman-tic—in The Rites of Passage, the first book in The Goldberg Variations, debut novelist Jonathan Taylor drills down till it hurts in a coming-of-age and coming out story tailored to our times."
—Linda Watanabe McFerrin, author of *Namako, Dead Love* and *The Hand of Buddha*

"When I read the searing tale of Jamie's journey from childhood through adolescence and young adulthood, I lived it as if it were my own. It chronicles his anguish as he finds himself on the outside, increasingly isolated from family, school and college, his coming to terms with transgressive fantasies and his authentic self ... set against the backdrop of political upheaval that defined the Seventies."
—Kunal Mukherjee, author of *My Magical Palace*

"The Rites of Passage is like encountering a gay Portnoy's Complaint in its distinctive blend of Jewishness, sex, moral panic, and maternal dominance. And it's painfully realistic in its depiction of what 'coming out' is, its alternation of moments of euphoric liberation with moments of renewed shame and sorrow, as if life were a coin God is flipping and can never be better than half right, but not always the same half. I've spent many pages and many hours with Jamie, and I still want to know what happens to him.

—Patrick Mulcahey, seven-time Emmy Award-winning screenwriter of *The Bold and the Beautiful*

"Reading The Rites of Passage reminded me of the fragile time in one's youth when one may or may not mistakenly believe that all information is somehow related to one's self. So, rather irrationally and hilariously, I started to assume the book was about me and was frankly upset about that. This is when the genius of the author's trick hit me. Through Jonathan's writing style and his character's problematic self-driven gay psychosis, he managed to bring me back to that most vulnerable part of myself: youth. Reading it then became addicting. If The Rites of Passage doesn't remind you of yourself, it will certainly remind you of someone you love."

—Rene Capone, gay figure painter and author of many graphic novels including *The Legend of Hedgehog Boy*

THE GOLDBERG VARIATIONS:

THE REDEMPTION OF THE DAMNED

THE GOLDBERG VARIATIONS:

THE REDEMPTION OF THE DAMNED

Jonathan A. Taylor

ArnoLand Press, LLC, Publishers
74 Pond Street, San Francisco, CA 94114 USA

CATALOGING DATA:
The Redemption of the Damned
By Jonathan A. Taylor
Library of Congress Control Number: 2020934880
ISBN: 978-1-7342957-0-2

Cover design: Michael Arent
Cover illustration: "Sex & Melancholy Flowers" by René Capone

Excerpts from the song, "Gretchen am den Spinrade" by Goethe; and opera librettos Tristan und Isolde and Parsifal by Richard Wagner; and Don Giovanni by Lorenzo da Ponte, are translated by the author but are intended to reflect the main character's state of mind and not a literal translation.
Excerpts from Hamlet by William Shake-speare are reprinted by kind permission of Edward de Vere, 17th Earl of Oxford.

Dedication

In Memory of

Morris Lyle Taylor,

Arthur Athanason,

& Harold G. Marcus

When fighting monsters, make sure you don't become one in the process. And if you gaze long enough into an abyss, the abyss will gaze back into you.

—Friedrich Nietzsche, *Beyond Good and Evil*

Variation: Forced Gaiety

Late Fall 1980

I. Stürmisch Bewegt
(Stormy Movement)

Chapter 1: Pyrrhic Victory

Thanksgiving Weekend, Detroit, Michigan

I just wanted acceptance, even if I had trouble accepting myself. I vainly searched everywhere for it, including every inch of my mind. Until September 17, 1980, I feared I had not a prayer to ever achieve this ambition. But on that rainy afternoon, sequestered in a secret corner of a library, I read this unexpected paragraph in a history book:

> *In the entire New Testament, Jesus never concerned himself with nor ever uttered a word about homosexuals or homosexual behavior except by inference for calm acceptance of all people outside the norm.*

Strangely, what Judaism's most infamous Jew, our *enfant terrible*, did not say about homosexuality meant a great deal to me. For me the passage destroyed the premise for much of the hatred of homosexuality, which was most vocally done by Christians. I felt a mental paperweight was removed freeing my self-conception. My mind was given the power to both embrace new thoughts of the heretofore unacceptable; and reject any claims, Christian or otherwise, to the contrary.

I could look myself in the mirror of my dorm room

and say out loud: "I am a homosexual. How is it possible? But it is deliciously true. I have become me." I played the musical redemption themes from *Tannhauser,* a Wagner opera. The sound vibrated through my body and my dorm room, much to the chagrin of my floor-mates. I had triumphed ... round one.

Round two took place on Detroit's northwest side the weekend after Thanksgiving. There I assumed my bleeding-heart liberal family (we were proud of that title) would rejoice in my self-discovery. My parents, who worried and fretted about me, could finally be enlightened and unburdened.

That Sunday dinner started like all other Sunday dinners in my parents' small kitchen. My mother stood there, her fiery red hair, sturdy body, and everyday fierceness that made her appear more imposing than her five-foot-one frame would otherwise suggest. Her passions spilled over into her cooking as she shook chicken pieces in a Shake 'n Bake bag as if the chicken parts were Republicans needing to be battered into submission. Then she would take the coated chicken pieces and placing them on a cookie sheet on our Formica countertop.

All the while, in the back at the kitchen table, my father sat perched in front of the TV news. His attention to world affairs enabled his ignorance of the immediate family affairs around him. All seemed normal—well, for us anyway—until I said it.

My mother was happily recounting her trials and tribulations fighting for civil rights as a member of the

Wayne County Democratic Central Committee—that's right, the one and only WCDCC. Her election to this organization signaled and legitimatized her fight for the poor, the racially discriminated against, and the otherwise downtrodden—most of them, anyway.

When she paused for a breath, I wasted the hours devoted to planning my subtle and crafty soliloquy and instead just blurted out:

"Mom, I'm gay."

She said nothing. But I did get her attention, so I tried to soften it a bit.

"I think I might be—I actually know I think I might be … gay," I stammered.

"You're what?" my mother shrieked in utter disbelief. "How can you possibly think you're a *faygeleh!*"

I was shocked, *faygeleh* was Yiddish for 'faggot.' From one of the leaders of the WCDCC, this must be a misunderstanding.

"Mom, you don't understand—I thought we were always so liberal—"

"Don't give me that bullshit. I know all about this *mishegoss;* I saw what your cousin Harold—may he rest in peace—did to your poor Aunt Louise. And am I gonna stop and watch you degenerate in front of my eyes? Next you're going to tell me you'll commit suicide?"

She had to mention Harold, the sad specter of our family. Harold came out of the closet most publicly when his fey-clad dead body appeared in a photo in the local newspaper. I was twelve at the time. Harold died of a drug overdose. Recalling that horror, my mother now looked at me with disgust, an image. Suddenly all the ferocity aimed at Republicans, bigots, and other bad people was aimed at me. I had just one Plan B.

"Look, Mom, if you just read this book, you will see … Here, I just want you to read this." I handed her the book, *Now That You Know Your Son is Gay.*

She impulsively grabbed it and gawked at it as if someone had just given her a handful of dog shit. Then, she blanched as the enormity of having a gay son began to sink in. She put one hand to her mouth, staring in revulsion at the book in her other hand. I withered, as I felt as if I'd stabbed a dagger through her heart. The person I loved most I had just destroyed. Then suddenly, she seemed to be studying the book as if she were going to read it. But instead of opening it, she flung the book into the living room. Glass crashed as her Diego Rivera farm laborer print fell to the ground. She was horrified because she had destroyed her beloved painting and repulsed her faggot son. She began to cry.

Meanwhile, my father's decisive moment had arrived. He got up from his chair.

"You better settle down, Ruth," my father said, putting his hand tenderly on my mother's shoulder, a rare moment of open physical intimacy between them. He turned to me. His voice trembled with quiet emotion. "Leave us alone. Don't come back until you're cured. Go, before you give your mother a heart attack."

I felt guilty of the crime of the century: daring to be a *faygeleh* and thinking my parents would be relieved.

Instead, their own son stabbed them through the heart.

Numb, I stood there like an idiot. They were silently embraced in a circle where I no longer belonged. Mulling over the last thing I was told, "Go, before you give your mother a heart attack." I realized they were expecting me to leave home—for good. Impulsively, I ran to my bedroom and grabbed a book, *The Nietzsche Reader*. I threw the book into my backpack and stuffed in an extra sweater that was on the dresser. Then I pulled on my coat, not realizing this was about to be the sum total of my possessions. Amid the broken glass and the torn print, I picked up the thrown library book that was meant to soften the blow. I looked at it; blood smeared the cover as I'd cut my hand on the broken glass.

I lumbered, bleeding, to a bus stop to go back to my Detroit State University dormitory.

My father's words haunted me. They were a stark contrast to my therapist's pronouncement, "You are not a disease." But all I heard now was, "Don't come back until you're cured."

From a revelation to the crime of the century— coming out suddenly weighed heavily on my mind.

Back in the security of my dorm room, the realization of my situation came crashing down on me. I had no money, no protector, and when the term ended in a few weeks, no place to live. I had precious few people to turn to.

At least I had my roommate, Tim; he was quickly becoming my only friend. At least, I knew we could count on each other. We were alike in so many ways;

undernourished and emotionally starved, we clung to each other as friends. Unlike me, he was a music student. He spoke in a calmingly deep gravelly voice. His short black Gothic hair framing his mild Roman features. He wasn't exactly attractive but, like me, he was vulnerable, which gave him a natural allure. He supported me, though he didn't know exactly what was going on. I decided with Tim to be friendly but kept at a distance. Nice though he was, I didn't want to tell him too much. The last thing I wanted to be was the victim of another attack of homosexual panic, and although Tim was an unlikely candidate for that, I'd also thought my mom wouldn't be. Besides, if I needed any emotional support, I knew I could rely on the one gay friend I had, my former teaching assistant, Jack Devlin.

I was adrift at sea, and my life preserver had been ripped away from me. How could I keep from drowning? Tim and Jack. Yet, at the same time, both frightened me. Tim seemed so pure, asexual, like a child. Jack was the polar opposite. He had the exterior of a genteel Southern gentleman encased in a rattling pressure cooker. Perhaps the safest place for me was just being alone.

Chapter 2: The Magical Disappearing Act

Back in my college dormitory, I consoled myself that at least I didn't have to tell my parents I was no longer studying pre-law—their precondition for covering my college expenses. Lost my parents, gained myself.

Remembering my cousin Harold's death some ten years before, which my mother had so cruelly thrown in my face, didn't make me feel any better. *Was he my future?* I wondered.

The day we found out, I came home and saw my mother sitting uncharacteristically vulnerable. She was hunched over the dining room table. She looked blankly at her hands. With a clumsy cheerfulness, I whispered, "Hello."

When she looked up, I could see a face full of agony, all her customary ferocity gone.

"Mom, are you okay?" I asked.

She turned to me. Her eyes were tired and bloodshot. Tears streaked her face.

"Jamie, dear … yesterday …" My mother's voice retreating deeper and deeper into her throat, "your poor Aunt Louise … your cousin Harold … died."

My childhood hope seemed to vanish along with Harold. Harold was the only person who seemed to know I was suffering. The rest of my family was oblivious to it. Once Harold said, "Jamie, look at me. You'll be all right. Things are tough now, but you will be fine." I looked into his caring blue eyes. I felt his concern, but I felt embarrassed by it. "Maybe I understand you better than you know," he said. "Give me a call sometime."

I never did call him. Now I longed to have had one last conversation with him. It turns out we were the two fags in the family. We could have helped each other. Maybe I could have saved his life. Perhaps *my* company, *my* support was all he had needed. I certainly desperately needed him now. Had I had his support, how different my coming out might have been. Maybe he could have been there to protect me. Now we were both alone: him dead, me hardly alive.

But that was not where my mind was at the time of Harold's death. I remember the mysterious shame I felt at his funeral when I was whisked away by my parents when one of Harold's friends, dressed in women's clothes and makeup, began to cry hysterically. I recalled the terrible sight, especially the black-gray streak of mascara and tears falling down a pained face. Like everyone else, I am ashamed to say, I acceded to the judgment of *revolting behavior from an offensive faggot*, and I acceded that my aunt was right for having him physically removed. Only now I finally understood how heartless that was.

Harold went from favorite cousin to nonexistent. No one ever spoke of him. No one reminisced about him. He ceased to be. It was as if he never had been. Was that

now my fate with the Goldbergs?
    My demons would not leave me alone.
    Your cousin Harold is dead.
    Don't come back until you're cured.

Chapter 3: A Real Pro

There was another impetus in my desire to accept being gay. Earlier in the school year I fell in love with a man, Casper. He was so profoundly beautiful that it was at first oppressively intimidating.

Then, there was this fear of longing to see him and what that might portend. Even if I did meet him, I didn't dare approach him. In the name of normalcy, I foreswore my greedy lust in holy reverence for a sublime, selfless and romantic love the depth of which I had never known. I hoped just to behold such beauty was blessing enough to feel an unknown height of tender fulfillment.

Eventually, my earthly longing overpowered my romanticism. I was mastered by the need to touch him, the desire to cuddle him from the world's evil, and the jealousy of not learning from him the lessons of life that I could not even fathom. I twisted my life to the singular goal of meeting him. Even to the point of changing majors to theater just to see him. When I learned his name was Casper Tyres, I wondered how to pronounce his last name, whether it would presage my own tears or the tires to carry me away. Then, I could no longer escape admitting I was gay.

Still, in loving him from afar even with an

overflowing lust, love still seemed so lofty, so romantic that I imagined myself as the young Werther or some other equally literary or operatic character.

The rude reality came when we met. I offered to assist him in the tech booth for a performance of *Long Day's Journey into Night*. After the play, in the dark, the encounter degenerated into a long night's descent into shame. I remember, standing in the dark with him; I thought it was scintillating and promising. There was Casper the cute blond love of my life, I thought.

"Come here." He had beckoned with a leer. A leer punctuated by this cute little twitch he had in his eyes. He seemed full of requited desire. But not exactly the kind I had in mind. The power of his beauty overwhelming my apprehension. He was going to kiss me, I just knew it. I prepared myself to follow his lead.

I walked over to him. Heart pounding, I savored every step I took. I had never felt the power of a presence like his in my life. Casper seemed omnipotent.

"I am so glad you came, Jamie. Thanks for helping me out."

"I loved it, Casper. I am so glad to see you, and I have to say something, Casper." I loved the sound of my voice saying his name aloud. "I just wanted to tell you .... that ..."

"Could you help me?" he interrupted.

"Of course, Casper."

"My jogging pants ... are tied in a knot." He looked

at me with an irresistible shyness. But something felt wrong. "Can you untie them?"

With overwhelming naiveté, I knelt in front of him. My entire world seem to change on my knees. I looked up at him. He loomed larger than my small existence. He seemed to be a towering being. I felt a rush, submitting to him, to his presence, his being, his desire for me. I untied the knot. His pants fell to the ground, his cock pointing at me. I looked up at his face. He was looking down, smiling at me. My heart was pounding, no longer in excitement but in fear.

"Yes," he said in an intense whisper, like an order.

Suddenly a jabbing unpleasant feeling of *deja vu* ruined the moment. I had no idea what to do, but somehow I knew exactly what to do. I felt an uncontrollable sadness. It welled up and flooded into my throat. Tears started leaking from my eyes.

This powerful perverse self-hatred invaded my being. An inner voice said, *This is all you are good for.* My mouth dropped wide open. I closed my eyes. And it all came flowing to me, like a wave at first, then a gulf; it was a warm humid flush of the deepest love I have ever felt turned into slimy semen in my mouth.

"That was great; you're a real pro," Casper said as he pulled up his pants and left me alone.

After that one act, he didn't want to have anything to do with me. It made no sense … until I remembered: "They care more about the penis than the person," a terrible sex education book had said about homosexuals. My love for Casper was meant to prove it wrong, and instead it proved that book right.

I'd thought Casper and I would make love. But that wasn't what happened, and I shrank back into being the unredeemed, unclean pervert doing what all unsalvageable perverts do: caring about the penis not the person. But I also had this hope he would save me from something I didn't want to face some ugly vision or memory.

I resisted the vision of my life being just about the penis, for despite it all—I had to remind myself—I was full of hope ... and yes, even joy of coming out. In spite of everyone trying to spoil my happiness, I was grimly determined to find someone as interested in love as I was. But where to find this person? It had to be Casper I had to make him realize what he was missing. But for some reason I didn't understand, he wouldn't talk to me no matter how hard I tried.

Your cousin Harold is dead.
Don't come back until you're cured.
That was great; you're a real pro.

Chapter 4: Purgatory

On the Sunday before finals week, I sought refuge in my favorite spot: the Student Union lobby with its mixture of faded Bauhaus beauty and utter neglect. I went there seeking peace as I knew almost no one who went there. I optimistically walked up to the free buffet (student ID required). Although, as usual, there was just a skeleton of a steam table. Next to the skeleton was a tin box with an assortment of cookie crumbs. I never did see an actual cookie no matter how early I arrived. At the end of the buffet, there were 2 large stainless steel thermoses labelled: 'Coffee' and (over-confidently) 'Black Tea.' Next to the thermoses was a battlefield of wounded sugar packets and a half empty coffee scarred black-and-white canister marked "coffee whitener." A red plastic scoop stuck out of the beige-singed white powder. The supply of university mugs had vanished for the day, so I took a large paper cup and filled it with coffee, the lesser of two evils. The coffee whitener turned it into a light beige liquid.

Coffee in hand, I scoped out the lobby, quickly rejecting the cubicles near the buffet. These cubicles with desks were the object of fierce territorial warfare. Only students were supposed to use them, but their possession usually degenerated into a form of social Darwinism with the scariest occupier winning. The homeless were usually the winners, camping out and putting their heads down sleeping.

This left the couches strewn about the main lobby for studying. I got the last unoccupied couch, and I soon learned why it was the last. It was a bit sticky for reasons better left uncontemplated. At least it finally gave me a use for the tepid tea. I went back to the buffet and poured a half cup of the translucent 'black' tea and took a few napkins. Dipping the napkins in the tea, I wiped down a place to sit on the couch. The couch was riddled with cracks and holes, the armrests with cigarette burns. Overall a true creature comfort.

I set down my textbooks, class notes, and copy of Harold Pinter's *The Caretaker.* I was all set. The couch was officially occupied, my stuff spread out deep enough to prevent the varied undesirables from sitting in my proximity: people attempting to sell me something, take something from me, or blow smoke in my face.

I hunkered down for the afternoon until it was as late as I could stand it. The leather made my back sweat. The overheated lobby didn't help matters. The lobby's warmth carried with it a musty human stench, the tawdry smell of cigarettes and their concomitant cloud of smoke, which hung over the entire lobby despite its nonsmoker's section. The smoke was so thick, that not even my problems could find me there. I studied in peace.

The other denizens of the Student Union were primarily those similarly impervious to the building's obvious shortcomings. They fell into roughly three categories: foreign students, the homeless, and perverts.

Foreign students because they often had little money or little inclination to engage in the Western society bustling beyond those walls. The homeless needed a warm place to stay during the bitter Detroit winter. As long as there weren't too many and they didn't stink too much, they were tolerated. As an added bonus for them, the homeless intimidated the security staff into rarely taking any action against them. The perverts hung out at the Union mainly because of the lewd things happening on the second-floor men's room. The security staff was clearly not intimidated by this group. In fact, these wannabe police officers often helped the real police stage entrapment operations to catch those who lingered in the men's room too long.

As a psychological alien, a soon-to-be-homeless person, and a reluctant pervert, I was in my element. Oh, I had come out of the closet all right, but I felt more an outsider than ever before. It was bad enough being a Jew. As a homosexual I was three times an outsider: a white liberal in Reagan-era Michigan, a Jew in a Christian country, and a queer throughout the world. As for being homeless, I had until the end of the term—twelve days and counting—to find a new place and a job. As for the men's room, I was still in love and more felt the need to celebrate that. Consequently, I did not wish to go from fêtes and fireworks to farts and feces. In contrast to my friend, Jack, who often came to the Union building for sex, I was not yet convinced there was no alternative.

As for a job, I had just landed a low-paying but nevertheless paying job at the Brooklyn Bagel Factory not far from school.

I was studying my copy of *The Caretaker*, the play for which I was to audition next term. I wanted the role to get to a chance to maintain contact with Casper, who was working on the set design. While he wouldn't talk to me, I was still hoping I could use the role as a way of proving myself worthy of more than just a one-night stand.

Actually, theater seemed to be attracting me in more ways than I anticipated. The play was an awkward read yet it seemed oddly moving to me. A British play written in English slang, *The Caretaker* is about a man, Davies, trying to manipulate his way into a place he does not belong. I now thought of myself as this Davies, the homeless drifter trying to take over a house. However, Mr. Nathan, the theater professor, and Dwight Griss, the slimy director, both insisted I try out for the role of Aston. Aston was the mentally disturbed, eternally naive victim in the play. I couldn't imagine why Mr. Nathan thought I had something in common with that. But the more I read, the more into the character I got. Theater had started out as a lark to get to know Casper, but it was quickly proving a way into my hard to navigate psyche. Getting into it, I muttered my lines half-aloud, which had the welcomed side effect of making my Student Union couch even more unattractive to all comers.

Chapter 5: If That's Your Story

"What … do you … want to do … to my brain?"
I recited my lines in the halting, pause-strewn language for which both Pinter and the insane are notorious.

With greater confidence, I put the book down and closed my eyes and entered Aston's world of bewilderment.

"What … do you … want to do—"

"Jamie!"

"Huh—oh." I couldn't believe my anonymity was suddenly intruded upon. My initial frustration at being interrupted was replaced with a ray of cautious glee. Standing above my couch was Eula. She was the only other student I knew who was out of the closet. But once in a theater class, in the same breath that she admitted she was gay, she'd outed me. Which was strange because I never told her I was gay. Still, she seemed to assume it was common knowledge, which must have meant that Casper had told her. Outside of my parents—and a library checkout clerk—no one else knew I was gay. There was Jack, but he was reticent to admitting being gay himself, let alone exposing someone else.

"Didn't you hear me talking?" She cocked her austere boyish face. I detected a strain of hostility in her voice. With her short brown hair, sturdy frame, and pleasant makeup-free face, she looked like a tough—yet very cute—boy. Could this be a new Lesbian friend?

"Sorry—have you been here long?" I asked.

"No, I just got here, but I must have said your name three times," she declared. I tried to hide *The Caretaker* from her by placing it face down on the couch, just in case I didn't get the part.

"I guess I was caught up in the … moment, ha ha. Eula, how are you doing?" I asked cautiously.

"Whatever, but what's up with you?"

She didn't strike me as the friendliest of people. Still, a lesbian and a fellow tribesman, I felt I needed her. I forced a smile and cleared a spot for her on the couch. She swung her backpack down with a macho swagger. Her male mannerisms made me smile.

She sat down, and her expression turned immediately sour. "What is this? … It's a bit sticky, isn't it?" I had forgotten the couch was dirty.

"Oh, it's fine here, though," I said moving books to the floor.

"Gross." She bent to get up.

"Here, let me help," I offered. I took the cup of tea and tried to pour a little next to her and wipe off the couch, but instead my hand shook and spilled the tea on her before she could stand up.

"Jamie! What are you doing?"

"Sorry, I didn't mean to get you wet."

"You poured tea on me."

"Let me get some napkins. Sorry, I was just trying to

make it less sticky." I ran to the buffet and grabbed the last of the cocktail napkins.

When I walked back, Eula was sitting in my place holding *The Caretaker.* I wiped down the other side of the couch with my tea dampened napkins while she blotted the wet spots on her jeans. She placed the book back on the newly dried spot.

"Good for you, learning your lines like a diligent little boy." She gave me an odd wink.

I heard something sarcastic in her voice. I couldn't piece it together. She seemed mean but acted friendly, as if her mind did one thing and her body another. I felt another flash of paranoia. What did she know? She seemed to already know I was trying out for the play and I thought just Dwight and Prof. Nathan knew. And she outted me in class when only Casper knew I was gay. I wondered if Casper had spoken to her and if so, what he said. Maybe Dwight told Casper? But all this byzantine theorizing was making me paranoid like there is some bizarre conspiracy against me, so I decided to change the subject in order to find more agreeable territory.

"Did you finish reading *The First Breeze of Summer* for Mr. Nathan's class?" I asked.

"Oh, yes, it was totally awesome."

"I loved it too; I want to write my final on it," I remarked.

"You don't have to write a final." The challenge in her voice was unmistakable. I had to wonder if we'd somehow gotten off on the wrong foot, but this was the first time we'd ever really spoken to each other outside of class.

"I don't? Doesn't everyone have to?"

"It's your first class with Arthur, isn't it?"

"Yes," I admitted. Calling Mr. Nathan 'Arthur' seemed as presumptuous as calling my mother 'Ruth.'

"Don't sweat it; the final is totally optional, and it's not even expected—at least not from us, you know theater majors."

"Really?"

"You know he is a bit of an unusual teacher, so he has to give a final for those jerks in our class like that prissy Cindy Prite. He makes those guys write a final to prove they deserve the grade they got."

"I don't have to write anything?"

"Of course not. Everyone in the Theater Department knows that."

"The other teachers know this too?"

"Not every one, every student. Get with it."

"Too bad. My idea for the final was going to be interesting." I was eager to somehow steer the conversation back to a clever theory about racism in *The First Breeze of Summer*, but Eula had a different agenda.

"You know what Cindy's problem is, and people like her—they object to Arthur being real." Eula tried to imitate one of Mr. Nathan's dramatic reading voices. "Why don't we have a little game? Let's pretend that we're human beings, and that we're actually alive." Then back to her own voice, "Shit like that scares the daylights out of Miss Suburbia Prite. Why she doesn't go to Wayne

Community College or something like that, I don't know."

"His readings are amazing, and he can always get right to the core. But Mr. Nathan can be unnerving."

"Unnerving?" she exclaimed. "You can be unnerving, which is great teaching everyone a lesson."

"What do you mean, Eula?"

"You can get around you know what you do—"

"What?" frustration seeping into my voice.

"Oh, come on, you're a bit of a ... how do I say it?"

"A what?" I asked a little too sharply.

"Don't bite my head off. Why are you so touchy?"

"But a what, Eula? ... Let me just ask you: What are you getting at?"

"What am I getting at?" She suddenly got defensive. She clearly knew something, and I didn't know how or what. I was afraid Casper must have told her all the embarrassing details of what I had done, as if I sucked people off in darkened rooms all the time. Finally, she just looked at me coldly and said, "Well, let's just say you have a bit of a reputation."

Her words broadsided me like a speeding truck. Casper, the one I loved, clearly did not love me. He was telling the worst about me.

"Who did you hear this from?" I demanded losing my temper and my friendship. "What is my reputation?"

"Come on."

"How do you know, then—about my reputation?" I tried to calm down.

Eula did not want to answer; she looked away.

"Honestly, Jamie? After the way you read the role of Alan Strang in *Equus?* That was bare naked, dude."

I blushed in shame. I wondered what was I telegraphing and if everyone could read me like an open book? We had been studying Peter Schaffer's play, *Equus,* and Mr. Nathan asked me to read a very disturbing scene where Alan describes to his therapist his rather warped sexuality.

"I gave a … good reading of it, but nothing horrible, right?" I said defensively.

"Don't be ashamed; it was awesome. It shook everyone up."

"But I was just following Mr. Nathan's lead."

"Don't blame him for our perversions."

"I am not." I no longer knew what we were talking about.

"Touchy."

"I am not!" I had to calm down. I took a deep breath, "You know, speaking of that class, there was something I'd been meaning to ask you. How did you know I'm gay? And why tell the class?"

"Oh yeah, that."

"There was this day in class, remember, when you said I was gay in front of everyone."

"I didn't say *that.*"

"Still, you knew. I mean, you know what I am talking about, right?" I waited until she finally nodded her head. She softened her posture, which kept me from getting angry. "I never told you. How did you know?"

"Uh …"

"Is it tattooed all over me? Can anyone tell?"

"No." She blew a sigh of relief. "You don't have it tattooed all over yourself. But ... I don't know, maybe it's the way you look at some students—"

"Like who?" I snapped.

"Jamie, chill out. I don't have to say; you know already—come on, relax. No one is judging you. It's not like—" She reached over and produced my copy of The Caretaker. "It's not like it's hurting your chances of getting a part in this play."

"Wha—whoa, what's that got to do with anything? I'm studying hard for this."

"Yeah, right, real hard."

"Huh? What is going on here? How did you know I was trying out for this play?"

"Jeez, don't be so paranoid, dude. I found the book here on the couch, besides, there are no secrets in the Theater Department. Jamie, will you stop it? I am sorry if you feel I forced you out of the closet but—but dude, come on, you know, everyone already knew."

"Right. Casper," leapt out of my mouth.

"No," she whined. Her sudden loss of confidence seemed to confirm it.

I felt betrayed—a sad bitter betrayal. I once thought my love for him was so splendid and sublime that it had inspired in me the courage to admit I was gay. Casper, whom I fell unconditionally in love with. I never thought I would ever dare to meet him. I quit studying pre-law and switched to theater just to see him. He is the only one who knew I was gay. Far from loving me, he hated me, and I had no idea why … sort of. I guess when I had sex with him in the back of the empty theater, he lost any respect for me. I looked at Eula and wondered why or how I got involved in all this.

"Great. Well, you get the breaking news, which you can spread all over the Theater Department. I don't even want the part anymore. I am sorry I went into theater at all. I am not going to try out for the part."

We stared at each other a moment. Then Eula got up and swung her backpack over her back.

"You're not fooling me; you're gonna get the part," she shot back.

"I will? How do you know?"

She didn't answer.

"I don't know. How do you know?" I asked.

"Let's call it my lesbo-intuition." She flashed a smile that was not exactly kind.

"Sit down?" I asked as sweetly as I could muster. "Do you know why Casper won't talk to me?"

"Jamie, forget it. I don't even know what you're talking about."

"Then who told you? Come on."

She looked at me pathetically and sank back down on the couch.

"Look, I didn't know about you and Casper. But like I said, there aren't any secrets in the Theater Department. I have heard a lot about … the others."

"What others? There are no others!" I objected, knowing full well I had others buried in the closet, but no one here could know that.

"Oh for god's sake, Jamie, let's not go into this, okay?"

"Should I quit?"

"What?"

"Should I quit? I mean, he must have told the whole school—I feel so embarrassed, Eula."

"Dude, you need to seriously chill. Look, maybe it might help if we go out together sometime. Get away from here and be more real in a different ... place, right?"

"I would like that." I was surprised by her sudden invitation, though I found what she was saying still very cryptic.

"Let's go on a date—a friend date."

"Yeah, I'd like."

"You can help me," she said. "I mean, you know the gay community."

"I'll do the best—we'll learn together."

"Yeah. But you know the places, like Dreamland, Menjo's. I know it's mainly men, but I don't mind being the fag hag for once."

"Dreamland? Menji's? What are they? I've never heard of them."

"Oh, come on, don't get coy with me, dude. You never heard of them? Like the best gay bars in the city—for guys."

"No, I never heard of them."

"Jesus, are we playing that still? What about the park?" Her insistence that I knew this just made my paranoia well up again.

"What park? Now you're gonna tell me there's a gay park?"

"Really. Never heard of the park? Never heard of the bars either?"

"Never heard of them. And bars, I can't get into bars I am not twenty-one." I asked.

"Jamie, you don't need to pretend. Okay, okay, whatever you need to do to live with yourself, if that's your story. Well … fine, dude, then how about if I show you around?" She was angry, and I was still completely confused.

"I don't know what you're talking about. But it would be great to go out sometime—maybe go to a coffee shop?"

"Right." She grimaced, then got up abruptly. "Jamie, you don't need to pretend, but if that's your story … I gotta go now. See you later."

She ran off.

Moments later I saw Dwight's thick Pillsbury Doughboy body waddling by. I ducked down on the floor. I saw him go upstairs to the infamous men's room. Now I was certain Dwight was gay. Casper was gay. These seemed to be some strange kind of connection, but it didn't make any sense.

I turned back to my books. I felt scared to study theater, but I picked up my copy of The Caretaker anyway. I stared at the cover of a man completely devastated while in the background another character furiously throws something against a wall. It seemed to sum up how I was feeling. I kept staring at it like a painting, then I opened it and began to read. I was just getting into it when Dwight surprised the hell out of me.

"Hi, Goldberg, know your lines yet?" I jumped at his contemptuous voice booming over me. "Good thing you're studying; you're gonna need it. The auditions are gonna be pretty competitive."

"Really? … No one's a shoo-in." I asked looking for some sign if I was already getting the part.

"Of course not, least of all you." Dwight looked at his watch.

"I don't have the role?"

"Of course not. You think you're just entitled? Give first, then receive, boy. Know what I mean?"

"I am studying my lines, I am giving my best."

"Right. See you around, Goldie, and study hard; you have to give it all—get it?"

"I will." I said desperately as he waddled away.

He stopped and turned, looking at me with a contempt I could only attribute to a story Casper must have told him.

"Yes, you will. Of course, you could study with me, and maybe I could help boost you up a bit."

"Is that fair?" I asked, feeling goosebumps over my skin.

"You're right," he said abruptly. "It wouldn't be fair to the others. Forget it. Just study hard."

I had this sick feeling in the pit of my stomach as my curses seemed to pile up:

Your cousin Harold is dead.

Don't come back until you're cured.

That was great; you're a real pro.

Jamie, you don't need to pretend, but if that's your story …

Chapter 6: Crumbs and Coffee

"Well, well, well, if it isn't our studious friend, just a studyin' away here at the Student Union of all places." Without looking up, I knew that southern lilt. Jack Devlin, my one and only gay male friend. My Student Union refuge was turning into a highway of people I wanted to avoid.

Jack reeked of handsome elegance and cheap cigars. The way he dressed, his starched shirt and pale blue suit, you would swear he was a debonair Southern gentleman. A full-length winter coat folded over his arms was his only concession to the Detroit winter. Yet behind those good looks and prim manners I could not help but suspect lurked a serial killer or someone equally evil. Something just didn't jibe with his appearance. It was hard to place it. His black hair, usually cut short, looked a little mussed up. His usual trim mustache was cut back to thin stubble, giving him a wicked adolescent look.

"Hi, Jack, you surprised me." *He's a good friend,* I told myself, yet I could not help but feel he was constantly hitting on me.

"I wasn't creepin' around, darlin'. You were in la-la land." He waved his hand like a magic wand.

"I was. Say what are you doing here? I've never seen

you here before."

"Never mind that, what happened last night?"

"Er … nothing—what brings you here?" I squirmed, realizing I shouldn't have said anything.

"Oh, it was something, darlin'. I know you are trying to hide something. Does it concern our Mr. Timothy, your cutie-pie roommate?"

"How do you know he's cute? You haven't even met him."

"You're dreaming about him; that's good enough."

"I am not. I mean … not the way you're thinking."

"Oh, I am sure you weren't. Don't tell me he hasn't been inside your pants yet?"

"Nothing like that."

"Oh, then you were in his pants."

"Stop it. We just stayed up listening to music."

"Really? You must have been playing Bo-leró."

"Schubert, if you must know."

I thought winsomely of the intimacy Tim and I shared listening to Schubert songs the other night. For more than a few fleeting moments, I thought Jack could be right that Tim might be gay. But I had no way of safely knowing for sure.

"Listenin' to music all night, aha! That can't be all you did?"

"Yes, of course. He's just my roommate."

"I've heard that before. You didn't cop a feel—oh, I see on your face you did. You're blushin'. Guilty as charged." Jack glanced around the lobby. "Usual motley crew here tonight. Has it been busy?" Waiting for an answer, he got impatient. "Come on, boy; don't play stupid. I know why you're here too. Been a lot of traffic … upstairs?"

"I am studying, Jack."

"I know that. What do you think I am doing?" He leered at me. I looked away. "Fine then. Mind if I study with you?"

"Okay, but I am leaving soon. I've been here all day, and I want to get back to my dorm."

"Just stayin' a minute, myself." He placed his coat next to mine on the couch, then sat down next to me. I took a sip of cold coffee from my drip-stained cup. He eyed me as I drank. "Smart boy. Drinking that slop, sooner or later you'll *just have to go upstairs.*" He nodded his head toward the stairs leading to the second-floor men's room.

"It's not like that."

"And don't be so stuck up, dear. We're all just, as your Nietzsche would say, human-all-too-human." Just then, of all unlikely people, one of my former professors walked by and Jack instantaneously switched out of his Southern lilt and stood up. "Hello, Dr. Brown. I must say I was truly impressed with your excellent article on the role of religion and farming during the Prague Spring."

"Oh, thank you, Devlin. I am glad you got to read it." The short stubby professor gazed up at him and then down at me before looking back up. "I am surprised you liked it. I didn't think that article would have meshed with your world view."

"Don't trouble yourself about that, Doctor, you'd have to go all the way back to the Civil War to mesh with my world view, professor."

They shared a laugh.

"Indeed they do, Devlin," and the professor looked down to me, "And you, young man, why aren't you in my follow-up course on Cold War policies? It's required you know."

I didn't want to tell him I had switched from political science to Theater. "I'll take it next term, professor."

"I only offer it in the fall, you're going to have to take it next year."

"Great. I look forward to that—sure do."

"I see. Well, goodbye, boys."

"Goodbye, professor," Jack said. Then waiting until he was barely out of earshot, "What a sticky stuck-up, eh? Religion and farmin', what a jerk. But he's on my committee … Don't worry, Jamie, you'll get used to the smell of kissing ass."

"I am not kissing anyone's—behind."

"Not what I hear, boy. You're telling me you're not going up there right now to kiss the good professor's? Because he is going up there for a quickie. He don't even care if I know it 'cause he knows I know."

"Just because he went up those steps, you think—"

"What else is up there?" asked Jack.

"The … the Student Travel Office."

"He's a professor. Besides, what other reason would he, or anyone else, be here? Especially someone like you, honey, sittin' here camped right below that stairway to the seven-minute heaven."

"Seven-minute?"

"No, you're right, I suppose with you it'd be almost *instantaneous*."

"Stop it. Besides, Professor Brown isn't like that."

"Well, just go on in there and find out. He'd love that you decided to take his follow-up course, after all."

I squirmed.

"I met the right guy already. Casper is the only one I care about."

"I got to teach you, boy: a cock is a cock is a cock is a cock is a cock, understand?"

"I understand."

"Then get with it and—get with me, sweetheart, for a little fun." He snuggled closer to me.

"Jack, I already met Casper. I love him more than anything, even more than myself," I said, no longer sounding convincing as I pressed myself into the corner of the couch away from Jack.

"More than me?" Jack flashed a meaningless frown. "Kiddin' aside, boy, this Casper boy is not waiting around for you. Besides, I know who you really have the hots for—it's little Timmy."

"No!"

"Bird in a hand is worth two in the bush, and that bird is eatin' it out of yours. What are you getting so defensive about, sweetie? You have the hots for him, and he does for you. There isn't anything to be ashamed of."

"Tim's just my roommate. I told you that."

"He's sweet on you."

"You haven't even met him."

"He sounds very sweet on you, Jamie."

I choked up suddenly; I could hardly talk. A strange emotionless tear rolled down my cheek.

"Oh, dear. I done put my foot in my mouth again. I am sorry," said Jack.

"Stop it, will you? We're just friends. Which … I … hope … you and I are."

"What is up with you, dear?"

"First, Casper hates me. Next, it's Tim's turn, I just know it. What am I going to do if I get thrown out of the dorm? What will I do if Tim finds out?"

"It's not that bad, Jamie. You don't know if anyone hates you. I sure don't, baby. I sure don't."

"You said we're going to hell."

"Don't listen to me. We have to make the best of the hand we're dealt. I don't like this either, but it is all we have. You might as well get used to it, baby. I can ease you into it. Besides, you really don't know how Casper feels because you never spoke to him since that night you did the nasty, right? And you are afraid to talk to Tim, aren't you? Just try to get into his pants. I think you would be surprised; I know I won't be."

"I should talk to Casper …"

"Wait a sec, isn't this the same boy who …" Jack looked around and whispered, "… just about raped you?"

"He did not."

"The way you described it, it sure sounds like it."

"It's difficult to explain. I forced myself to do it—so

it isn't rape … unless you can rape yourself."

"Honey, you mean he just unzipped his pants and you forced yourself to …"

"Please. I can't—here."

"Well, explain it to me, because I don't get it. Just speak softly and *cleanly* boy."

"I can't … well … we were alone. I thought we would talk. But Casper told me … he wanted me to untie a knot in his …" Jack began to snort a laugh. "… in his pants—jogging pants. Forget it. Forget I mentioned the whole thing," I said, embarrassed.

"Calm yourself, darlin', I am not laughing at you. Just don't be so cocksure naive. You just fell for an old one; you're new. But say, I might have a stuck zipper; can you help me with it? … Not funny?" I did not smile. Jack's smile faded. "Anyway, you untied his knot?"

"Yes, I did. I didn't have time to think. But I had dreamed about him for so long, fantasized about him, too."

"Love from afar, how romantic."

"And there he was. It was supposed to be a dream come true."

"Of course."

"It wasn't the way I wanted it to be. But I didn't want to reject him either or his … beautiful body."

"There ya go. Oh, of course he was beautiful; I am salivatin' and I never even met the boy."

"I just thought I would talk to him afterwards … and there I was on my knees in front of him, so I forced myself … I wanted to impress him."

"And impress yourself on his cock." Jack had a distant smile.

"I guess so. But when I … finished, he never stuck around for me to talk to him. It was the last time I saw him, really."

"Okay then, come on." He nodded his head toward the stairs. "One good turn deserves another. It will help you get over these things. You're fixating on that boy; time to fixate on yours truly."

"Please. I have to go home."

"Don't get defensive, sweetie. I can make you feel better. Once you realize he doesn't have the magic," then switching to a whisper, "that a cock is a cock is a cock is a cock is a cock, you'll feel better and get some perspective. Don't you want that? But you gotta let your hair down, my boy. I didn't know you were suddenly so high and mighty."

"I am not. Did you talk to Eula?"

"Who?"

"Nevermind. I want to go home."

"What home? Oh, dear … maybe that was a foot in the mouth." He caressed my back and shoulders as a kind of consolation prize.

"I just don't want to have sex in a toilet."

Jack squeezed my arm ungently.

"Angel, you just have to keep your voice down about things like that. We will all get in trouble. I don't want to do something I will regret, you know what I mean?" This last he accented with a very painful squeeze before letting go of me.

"Sorry," I said, rubbing my arm.

"Forget it, honey, didn't mean to squeeze so hard; don't know my own strength. Just don't get us in trouble, okay?" His intensity slackened but hushed, "You think you're better than it all. Oh, I've seen it, sweetie, and in a few days, you'll be the first one spending all night toodling in there. Trust me."

"It's not what I want."

"You will sooner or later. Look, it is the same there as what you've already done with Casper, isn't it?"

"That's different; I love him. By the way, have you talked about me to ... anyone?"

"What did you end up doin' when you met this love of your life?" asked Jack in a whisper. "You pulled down his pants so you could give him a class-A blow job." He smiled and then said out loud, "And then he left you faster than if his hair was on fire."

"I don't care, Jack, I'm not like you," I stopped myself.

"Not like me? I am sorry to say it," Jack said, again dropping his voice to a whisper, "but remember that book I saw you readin' in the library, sweetie? It said the same thing. We fags—"

"Can you stop saying that?"

"I said it softly. Oh, don't give me that look, honey; it's not like sayin' the word 'nigger.'"

"Christ, can you stop saying that?" I said in an intense whisper. "You know how I feel about those words." I looked around the lobby. Luckily, no one heard us.

"Oh dear, I've put my foot in my mouth again, haven't I? Sweetie, if I can't say anything around you, this won't be a fine conversation. I thought you liberals didn't go in for censorship."

"We don't."

"Well, 'you can't say this and you can't say that' sounds like censorship to me."

"It's different."

"Right. Being politically correct is allowable censorship."

"It isn't censorship."

"What do you call it? If I have to edit out the words you don't like, what is that called?"

"Being considerate. I do that all the time. Look, I better go home. I have to get ready for my theater class."

"Are you still tryin' out for that play?"

"Of course."

"I thought they rejected you."

"No, they didn't want me for the part of Davies. But the director, Dwight, wants me to try out for the role of Aston … he's a mentally disturbed guy."

"Is he?"

"I mean the character, not the director, Jack."

"Dwight? That name does sound familiar."

"I am sure it does," I said, shivering at the thought of Jack doing it to that gross director in the men's room.

"Yes, it does. I do know the boy. And I happen to know that he's queerer than a three-dollar bill, and he will probably give you the part and the clap if you just stick around here long enough and follow him upstairs."

Even though I knew it was true, I didn't want to admit it. "You think everyone I know is gay. He can't be."

"Why not?"

"Because he's ugly."

Jack laughed uproariously until he caught himself being a spectacle. "Listen, they are the worst kind. In fact, I do believe he is the worst kind, now that I recall. You better watch yourself with that one. Trust me. There's some evil ugly bitches out there."

"Great, the life story of yet another person you've never met. I'll be careful. Besides, it's Aston—the character in the play—who is mentally disturbed. He's the one who invites this old man, Davies, to live with him."

"Sounds right up your alley." He looked at me and must have noticed I was exasperated. "I mean, you'll be fine, Jamie. I like the way you read. You're a good actor. But maybe you should use some of those actin' skills to fit in just a wee bit?"

"What does that mean?"

"Keepin' a sense of decorum—and not being so loud about you-know-what."

"I'll try, Jack," I said, even though I thought he was far guiltier of it than I. "I fought so hard to come out. I thought realizing who I was would actually solve problems."

"I am sure it did, honey; it solved a lot of them. You just didn't know about the other ones it would create."

"Exactly. Problems are cropping up faster than I

know what to do with them. I used to lie to myself every day; now I have to lie to everyone else every day."

"Welcome to my world. At least we have each other."

"I gotta go," I said, and started to bundle up in my coat, gloves, hat, and scarf.

"Truth is, I gotta go, too, I'm seein' the good professor and lettin' him steal my ideas for the article he'll make me write for him. That's what graduate students are for."

I turned to leave.

"What, I don't get no hug?" he moaned.

"Here, in public?"

"No one here will care," he said as he glanced around.

He groped my waist, sliding his hands down to my butt and pinching it. I jumped. "Relax, sugar; relax and enjoy it. It won't last forever. I'll see you later."

Outside, the bitter cold hit my face with a vehemence. Walking into the night, reeling from the frosty air, I thought about Jack. I was left with the recurring feeling that I never wanted to see Jack again. But what other gay friend did I have? Maybe Eula?

After sitting there drinking coffee all day, I had to pee. With Jack safely away, I went back into the Union building. I walked upstairs to use the infamous toilet— but just for its intended purpose.

Chapter 7: Into the Men's Room

Walking into the men's room, my heart was pounding unsure of which urge was driving me there. The smell in the men's room was acrid—ammonia mixed with vinegar—and the floor was damp with a mysterious wetness. I was relieved the place was empty. But I was no sooner at the urinal unzipping my pants when a fierce-looking homeless guy stood at a urinal next to me. A flash of excitement ran through my body. His scraggly appearance did not stop him from looking dangerous, and yet he seemed more intent on my activities than his own. As I gazed at him looking at me. I felt a flash of something, I thought it was repulsion. Yet, I could see his sharp youthful features beneath that veneer of filth and poverty. He was muscled and despite—or because of—his odor, I froze. I couldn't pee anymore. An erection began to take over.

"I know what you want," he said lasciviously.

"I don't want it." I could barely speak.

"That's not what I see," he challenged. I shivered. "Don't be afraid, boy; you're gonna get just what you need."

"I don't need it," I snapped. I was sure he had some violent homophobic intentions. He meant to get me in a compromising position, and then he would strip me, hang me upside down, beat me or stab me, and take all my money—except I didn't have any money so he'd take my Jacobson's department store card and run up a bill I could never pay off. He kept looking at me. "I don't need it," I repeated lamely.

"Let me be the judge of that, little sissy boy. Don't look around; we're alone." He nodded his head in the direction of the toilet stalls. "Come on, let's go in," he commanded. My heart sank. Here it was: the moment of death or worse.

I looked toward the toilets; I thought about it for a moment. My erection had since withered. I zipped up my pants quickly.

"Are you … gay?" I asked.

"Fuck no. I ain't no faggot. You are. You sure ain't no police. I saw you get a hard-on."

This heightened my level of fear and confusion. I looked and saw the way to the doorway was clear. I dashed toward the door to make my escape. The door opened suddenly and hit me in the shoulder. Reeling away and off-balance, I slipped on the damp floor and fell. Landing on my butt, I curled my back to counterbalance my body. I didn't want to even touch the dank surface. I was now sitting on the gross moisture, which seeped into my pants. I didn't dare put my hand on the wet floor but had to in order to get back up on my feet. My right hand braved the filth on the cold damp tiles; the mystery dampness clung to my fingers. I looked up.

"Well, well, well, if this is not a surprise," said Jack.

"It's not what you think," I said from the floor.

"No, I can see it isn't. You need a little help." Jack bent over, reached out and lifted me up, he glanced at the guy standing at the urinal. "Oh, hi, Rags."

"Hi, man!"

"Rags, you suck him off?" asked Jack.

"Was about to, when you ruined it all." My heart pounded. I grabbed a paper towel to wipe my palm.

"You better come here, Jamie, or we'll get in trouble."

"Are the police here?" I asked.

"You better beat it, Rags."

"Gotcha covered; I'm outta here."

The guy ran out while Jack frog marched me—I'd almost say pushed if I didn't know better—into a toilet in the back of the men's room. He closed the stall door. It smelled even worse than the urinal. Two people standing in the stall was extremely awkward and claustrophobic.

Jack looked at me oddly. I shivered again, dreading what he was going to do. Then the door opened, and his glance shot to the direction of the door.

Someone walked in. Jack put his index finger to his mouth, telling me to be quiet. Footsteps walked toward the stalls. Tried our door. Tried to open it twice. "Do you mind?" Jack said in his best professorial voice.

"No one in there with you?"

"Of course not."

"I'll wait for you, then."

The footsteps left the bathroom; the door closed.

"What do we do?" I whispered.

"Just let me walk out. Then you count to ten and leave."

"But he'll arrest me."

"Don't worry, it's not a cop. You'll be okay. Just count to ten."

"One, two—"

"To yourself! I'm leaving. Lock it after you and start counting. Be sure to flush the toilet before you leave."

Before I could even think, Jack was out of there. I locked the door and started to count.

Footsteps returned and tried the stall door.

"Buddy, come out of there."

My heart started to pound. *I am innocent!* I pleaded to myself. Then the word innocent fell harshly on my mind. *What else could I do?* I prepared to emerge and face the unjust music.

"Got one in the bathroom," I heard the man speak into a walkie-talkie. Then, the man walked away. I heard the men's room door close

I did not flush the toilet as Jack suggested but left like a football player trying to break through a wall of defenders. There was no one in the bathroom. I swung open the door, still no sign of anyone. I looked around, slowed my gait, and straightened up. As a precaution, I walked down the hall to another stairwell. I zoomed down those stairs. I left the stairway, turned, and saw two police officers walking up the other stairs. They turned, and I knew the chase was on.

I shot outside the building into the gray, bitter Detroit winter, the blistering cold freezing my wet butt and the icy sidewalk challenging my footing. Still, nothing stopped my clumsy yet determined slip-sliding away, all the while swearing never to see Jack or the Student Union again. It was frustrating and scary trying to run on the ice. I was awkwardly sliding down the street. Finally, I got more traction as the ice turned to a grimy slush that soaked my feet. Looking back, I saw no one was chasing after me. But then a dark figure bolted out of the Student Union building, and a car drove up alongside me.

"Come on, get in!" Jack said.

For a split second, I was so relieved my savior had come, and so relieved to have escaped the police and the ice that I got into his car, and he drove off. After a moment, it started to dawn on me that this was the guy who pushed me into a toilet stall. Perhaps I wasn't in the safest place. On cue, Jack sped up.

"That was a red light!"

"Calm down, boy; it was yellow as your Detroit snow—ha ha." The snow was, in fact, a gritty gray. The beautiful white blankets of snow one associates with winter never lasted long in Detroit, where car and truck exhaust turned the snow to a crust of dark grime.

"Where are we going?" I asked.

"Let's get something to eat," Jack replied.

"You're kidding."

"No, why?"

"Well ... because—" I was at a loss and had no words to ask him to explain himself after he had the gall to push me into a toilet stall, sell me out to the police, and then run away. "We can't do this, Jack!" I demanded.

"What's the matter?"

"I still have to take a piss."

Chapter 8: Greektown

Jack ignored my plea, of course. I broke out in a sweat. My fear of arrest for being a pervert had now been replaced by the terror of Jack's maniacal driving. Most vividly, he swerved just in time to avoid hitting two shocked pedestrians.

"Damn snow." He sighed. "You Detroiters have to fix your streets, boy."

The ensuing multiple near-death experiences erased any other outrage I had with Jack.

My body pressed into the car door. My legs began to shake. Jack stared at them.

"Watch the road!" I screamed.

"I see her," Jack said calmly as he splashed a poor woman with slush as the car hit a pothole. "Look, relax, Jamie. Be a little grateful, my boy. I pulled us outta there in the nick of time. What else are we gonna do? Scream and shout to the police for mercy?"

"Why did you leave me there?" I bit my lip as the careened to the center lane. "Why did you lead me into the toilet in the first place?"

"Don't get high and mighty with me, young bugger." Jack was impossibly defensive and contemptuous. "You were already busy at it when I arrived."

"I was not." My annoyance with his presumption

was quickly displaced by the realization that Jack's boat of a car was speeding down Woodward Avenue past the dilapidated Fox Theater. "Where are we going?"

"Will you relax?" Jack screeched the car to a halt at a red light, then held my arm stiffly—stiff enough to be unsure of whether it was friendly or not. "I said we're getting a bite to eat. Okay? I am trying to be nice to you. Make up and play goodie-goodie, okay?" He released my arm and—strangely enough—caressed it. His voice turned soft. His car then took off again. "Let's get away from the university. I know a place downtown. I think we deserve it, don't you?"

"Downtown? I don't have any money!"

"Sweetie, you have to relax. It's my treat. Least I can do for you after our little kerflooey back there. Darlin', you're worth a little hush money, ha ha."

Jack turned onto the Fisher Freeway headed downtown.

"Jack … okay … but what went on back there? I was almost arrested."

"Welcome to bein' a faggot. It's our lives, baby. But, believe me, I got us out of it. Had we just marched out of there, we'd be in jail now."

Off the freeway, Jack's car sped by the empty lots and dilapidated buildings, slowly giving way to the seamy 1920s downtown grandeur.

"Just remember, Jamie child, never go back there without letting me clear it first."

"I never wanted to go there to begin with—except to pee."

"Come on, stiffen your wrists honey; we're going to Greektown."

"Stiffen your wrists?"

"That's right laddie: faggot lesson101, stiffen your wrists, meaning act straight and don't say anything queer."

"And why Greektown? I can't afford that."

"I said it was my treat. Just relax." Jack was getting testy again. Greektown was one of the few nightlife attractions of Detroit.

"And what was that all about leaving me there?"

"I said relax. I saved your butt from the police, didn't I?"

"How? It seemed like you just about threw me to them. They were coming in when I ran out."

"Were you arrested?"

"No."

"Exactly. Believe me, kid, I handled it perfectly."

"You're kidding me?" I was completely confused. I didn't know whether I should be angry, terrified, or dubiously grateful.

The film noir concrete jungle of downtown gave way to the small village-like streets of the Greek section of town.

"Just remember, Jamie boy, if you hadn't been hanging out with Rags, this would never have happened."

"Hangin' out? I just went to use the urinal."

"Right. But you didn't, did you?"

"No, I didn't, but I had to—wait I don't have to defend myself, you—"

"*I* had to protect you or you would be in jail right now. Here's the restaurant. You'll like it." What little enthusiasm I did have disappeared as we had long passed the popular Greek restaurants to arrive in a sea of mostly empty parking lots and dark warehouses.

We entered a small smoky dive where the patrons seemed more family than paying customers. Their main dish wasn't moussaka or souvlaki but, rather, hot dogs, a peculiar Detroit Greek invention—the Coney Island hot dog.

As we walked in, the sweaty-male, cigarette, and coriander stench almost knocked me over. I swore that right after dinner I would demand Jack take me home. Then I would never see him again.

At the moment, he was all smiles like he was in his element. The motley Greek crew at the back seemed happy to see Jack, who in turn lathered on the Southern charm.

"Hi, y'all!"

"Hey, it's Jack, look!"

"Hiya, Jack! Beefin' up a little, I see."

"Jack, long time no see, nice to meet—say, who is your friend?"

I didn't hear anything else. I ran for the toilet. The men's room at the restaurant was eerily similar in sight and stench to the one in the Student Union. At least it was a single-occupancy unit, and no one interrupted me as I got the relief I desperately needed.

Chapter 9: Dinner Fit for a Jack

We sat at a long horseshoe-shaped Formica counter. Union workers in construction clothes sat along the counter opposite us. Everyone was smoking, drinking beer, and minding their own business. I was particularly self-conscious being associated with Jack, who stuck out like Truman Capote in a redneck bar.

"Hey, Jack, great to see you again, buddy. What will you have, guys?" asked a gruff waiter. Jack half-bowed to me.

"I guess two Coney's with everything," I said.

"You got it."

"I'll have the same and a couple of Stroh's for us, Gus."

"Jack, come on. The kid there. How old is he?"

"Old enough to fight," said Jack with surprising vehemence. "He's off to Fort Hood in the morning." Gus's forced smile became genuine. He winked at me.

"Good enough for me, Jackie boy." Then he looked at me sympathetically. "You ain't got nothin' to worry about, son. Settle down. It's gonna make a good man outta you. I am proud of you. Serve your country! It takes guts to do what you're doing." The guy then turned to the cook in the back. "Hey! Two up, two on one!

Everything! And make 'em special for the serviceman!"

The blue-collar workers stared at me, raising their beer bottles in appreciation. I wanted to disappear. I could feel the blush on my face at receiving their undeserved affection, aware that if they really knew what I had done, they most likely would kick me out of the place—or worse. Jack, on the other hand, was thoroughly enjoying himself.

Gus reached under the counter and produced two Stroh's beers. With a bottle opener tied on a chain, he opened one beer and handed it to Jack, and then other to me.

"Here, the kid's is on the house. It'll grow hair on ya." He laughed. I pretended to laugh, too. "Say, when you bringing your girlfriend by again, Jackie?"

Girlfriend? I didn't dare ask who that could possibly be.

"Not till after winter break."

"You two getting married?"

"We're still thinking about it, Gus."

"Don't think, just do. Never know where another will come from, and she's a nice girl. Besides, if you make a mistake, you can always play around. Know what I mean?" The entire restaurant erupted in macho laughter. Gus walked away to wait on another pair of workers who'd just walked in.

I lifted my bottle in a toast: "To the lucky girl."

Jack smiled. "You will go very far, Jamie." And we clicked bottles.

I took a gulp of beer. I winced at the bitter taste and

alcoholic bite.

"What's up?" asked Jack.

"I think I hate beer."

"Ha ha, don't worry; we drink this shit for effect, not flavor. Bottoms up!"

Gus came back with the hot dogs.

"Here we are, boys!"

"Can I have a glass of water, Gus?" I asked.

"Ha ha ha, right kid." Gus winked.

He slid the two plates toward us. To the uninitiated, these Coney Island hot dogs are hideous. What lay on these plates had nothing to do with the real Coney Island in New York. In Detroit parlance, a Coney was a hot dog smothered in a mysterious brown gravy they called chili and topped with onions and mustard. It's a dish only a Detroiter could love.

Putting one of the sloppy hot dogs to my face, the mixture of sharp onions and sweet mustard reminded me of something from my childhood: a smell I knew and loved. Opening my mouth, I bit into the doughy bun. The fresh sweet flavor from the onions made a delightful crunch around the mystery meat of the chili and the rubbery hot dog. Somehow, all these unpromising ingredients came together to make a unique comfort food. I thought of my father, when he took me to the famous Lafayette Coney Island for the first time. It was just after we had gone to see a Detroit Tigers baseball game that we'd lost eight to two. It was still fun, and it's the only thing I remember doing with my father for an extended period of time. Sipping the beer, by contrast, I remembered a different childhood: one that was dirty, ugly, and unknowable.

I began to feel bad about myself—as if I was doing something wrong, but the bitter taste of the beer came in handy to wash down the spicy mess in my mouth and my mind. In the interest of getting the ordeal over with, I wolfed down the Coney's and chugged the beer, welcoming the beer's mind-clouding effects.

"Thanks for dinner, Jack." I got up to leave.

"I'm not done yet," he said, chewing his Coney. He had barely eaten one of his two hot dogs. Jack ate his Coney's with a knife and fork. He ate slowly and with what seemed like great reluctance.

"Gus, get the boy another beer." His Southern lilt disappeared. "I want to talk to you for a second."

"Yeah?" I reluctantly sat down.

"Don't pout. Or Santa won't be nice." Without his softening Southern accent, this last whispered comment had a very unpleasant edge to it. "*It* wasn't what you are thinking. I was just trying to help."

I wanted to drop the topic, not wishing to say anything in the diner. I felt ill, and I wanted to go home. But I realized I was dependent on Jack to get there.

"I'm not feeling very well, Jack."

"Don't get faggy on me," he whispered. Then he smiled and said out loud. "Come on, I don't need to finish this crap. Let's git." He got up indiscreetly, pulled out a few dollar bills, threw them on the counter, and walked swiftly to the door. "Catch ya later, Gus! I left the money on the counter."

"Oh wait, man! Wait a sec," said the waiter, rushing over to us holding something in a rolled-up fist. "Here, here—take it, take," he said, handing me a rolled up ten-dollar bill and a card. "My brother, Theo, look him up in Fort Hood. Tell him I said 'hi.' He'll look after you." I took the paper contritely, ashamed of the false pretense.

"Thank you, Gus," I said.

"Gung-ho?" Gus asked.

"Gung-ho!" I answered. Gus smiled and the workers chuckled in approval.

Chapter 10: Dodging a Bullet

Jack practically pulled me out of the place. He took the ten-dollar bill from my hand. "Sweet. That practically pays for dinner. He started walking to his car, as if not waiting for me. I thought of arguing about the ten dollars but I didn't want the ill-gotten gain anyway.

"So, where are you going now?" I called after him.

"I am going home."

"Can you drop me off at my dorm?" I asked, catching up to him.

"Really, all the way back to the campus? Can't you sleep at my house tonight? Anyway, I don't think the buses are running anymore. Lucky you, I have a couch that isn't being used."

I didn't feel good about this, something inside me said get away. "Look, Jack, haha, I need to go home. I need to study. Just use the ten bucks for gas, and take me home," I said trying desperately not to sound like I was pleading. When Jack didn't reply I added, "Shoot, I even have a test I haven't studied for."

"Nonsense, there's no test," Jack laughed.

"Just give me the ten bucks I'll get a cab. It's no big deal."

"What ten bucks, that was for dinner and you know

it. Don't get me angry and don't worry. You can sleep there safe and sound as a nickel. Yes, I said 'don't worry.' You'd think I was the Loch Ness monster. It's probably more comfortable than that dorm room anyway."

Jack was wrong. His place was far worse than the dorm. He drove his car out into the middle of nowhere, where burned-out houses stood right alongside boarded-up homes and other semi-whole buildings. Despite their dilapidated state, all of them seem to have someone or something in them. I thought I was going to have a heart attack when Jack pulled up next to one of the burned-out buildings and parked the car.

"Oh, my God! You don't live there, do you?" I panicked. "I can't go in there!"

"What? Sweetie, will you relax? Are you still upset about the Student Union kerflooey?"

"No, I can't go into that house. I know who lives there!" My panic scared me. I could swear I could see the inside of the dark building.

"I don't live in that house. Don't be loopy." I must have looked shaken because Jack stared at me for a moment. "Are you okay? We aren't going in there. Settle down. Maybe that Coney didn't agree with you, boy. Come on. My house is just a couple doors down. I prefer to park here under the street lamp." It seemed like my ridiculous panic made perfect sense to him, and his kindness calmed me down and helped re-establish our broken trust.

Next to the burned-out building, stood a row of small brick houses. I walked calmly alongside Jack. The buildings, in another era and another city, would be expensive Victorian homes. Here they were tawdry, unkempt, and dirty. Jack lived in the last house on the street. His house had a porch piled high with old junk.

"Don't mind that; it's the slumlord's junk." Jack opened the door and beckoned me in.

At first, I was grateful for the warmth. We descended into the basement, where he lived. Once there, the low ceiling and damp struck me, as did the cold draft and the stench of cheap cigars. I hoped I could hold my breath all night. The lights were dim. The floors were cement, hastily covered with cheap rugs. A small hallway to his living room was pasted with dirty yellow wallpaper with inappropriately innocent blue flowers. The paper had peeled in places revealing layers of equally hideous designs.

Once in the living room, Jack showed me the couch. It was old and lumpy. Aside from the couch, there was an old television set and a Formica table covered with a mess of papers, books, and an ashtray overfull of cigar butts. Then I noticed something on the walls much worse than the wallpaper. His living room walls were a veritable shrine to tormented depictions of Jesus Christ, assorted saints, and a joyously sneering Pope John Paul II. The Christ images were writhing in agony, wearing their crowns of blood-drawing thorns, blood dripping from graphically depicted scars. The saints were tortured with arrows, maimed, or worse. If their intention was to strike the fear of God in visitors, it worked. As I looked at the tortured Christ figures, my mind welled with sympathy—

sympathy and sadness for that tortured person. I feared that I would be next.

"You're very religious?" I asked looking at the most tormented Christ figure receiving a sadistic whipping with blood spurting from a crown of thorns.

"Not really. I was raised Catholic, but I don't go to mass any more. Just goin' to hell like everyone else. I love the art though; it makes me a little peaceful." This confirmed my worst fears: Jack was crazy. A sick feeling entered the pit of my stomach. "I need to be back early, did I tell you that? I have early classes tomorrow."

"Yes, of course. I have to teach at nine," he replied.

I was relieved. He wasn't going to kill me if he was planning to teach at nine.

"Good, I don't know where I am … exactly. Ha ha. I don't have any way of getting to the campus from here." I shuddered, thinking, *Maybe I shouldn't have admitted that.*

"Don't worry, sugar doll. Why don't you make yourself comfortable? I don't have pajamas for you, but you can just sleep in the raw. It's okay, I've seen it all." He stared at my obvious reprehension. "Oh, I know; I'll turn up the heat. Landlord won't like it one bit, but screw 'em. Ha ha. You're worth it." He got up from the couch and turned up the thermostat under a picture of some poor soul being crucified upside down. With a loud click, a roaring fan billowed warmth into the room for about twenty seconds before it clicked off, and the cold chill returned. Jack lit a cigar. The room filled with the fecal odor of a cheap stogie. He sat down in a chair opposite the couch.

"Take off your clothes," he ordered.

I nearly gagged from the cigar smoke. He stared at me. I couldn't run away; I had no idea where I was. "Go on, sweetie; I promise I won't bite. We can talk while you undress."

I tried to stall. I looked past him across the room, into the kitchen. The sink was filled with dishes. The corner of the dining table, I could see, was also stacked with dirty crockery. I felt like a cornered whore.

"I think I should go home."

"Don't be so stuck up, darlin', please. You really want to go home? Well, be my guest. I can even give you bus fare if you need it. But this isn't such a great neighborhood, honestly. Besides, it's an awful long walk to any bus stop. And they ain't runnin' anyway. I told you, I'll give you a ride tomorrow. I'll even give you breakfast if you're nice. I am kidding. Jesus. Just get ready for bed. I will, too, in a sec."

He didn't say much else. I started to unbutton my shirt. Christ and the saints seemed to judge me. The grinning face of the Pope seemed to sneer at me.

"Do you mind?" I asked trying to sound offended.

"No." Not taking the hint.

I took my shirt off. Jack stared. I was terrified. Belt off. Jack stared. Shoes off. Jack stared.

Each article of discarded clothing made me feel more and more ashamed of myself. Socks off, slowly, one at a time. Jack still stared. I went to turn around.

"Don't," he spoke softly but hard enough.

Defeated I continued to strip. Pants off. Jack smiled. He started to tremble. I left my underwear on.

"Go on. It's getting late. I have to be at work in the morning."

"What?"

"Come on, let's go."

I was determined to stiffen and not feel bad. I took off my undershirt. He looked like a hungry tiger. I was shivering. The room went cold with a drafty gust. Against my will, I started to cry. I hated myself for feeling weak and exceptionally stupid.

"Come here," Jack said.

I didn't want to, but I did anyway. I walked over to him. He put his cigar in his mouth. He put his arms around me like I thought he was going to hug me. Instead, his hands landed on my ass cheeks. I felt my sphincter tighten shut. Then his hands slid down to take off my briefs, his greedy hand sliding down my body as he peeled the underwear away from me, which fell to the floor. "Sit on the couch, sugar. You smell a bit. Don't you shower in the dorms?" he asked.

I sat down next to him, naked on the couch. He was still completely clothed. He gently grabbed me and forced me over his lap. He then held me.

"Good boy, good boy, that wasn't so hard." He seemed to enjoy comforting me as if he didn't realize he was the source of my discomfort.

I felt his rough polyester clothing against my skin. His hands started to venture down my body, moving back up and down again in a petting motion. The petting continued. I braced for what came next. His one hand dropped to my groin. He wouldn't stop the back-and-forth motion on my loins until I was erect. Reluctant desire crept into my shame, and my cock achieved the desired effect.

"You feelin' better, I see," Jack said, caressing my cock.

I didn't know what to say, so I said nothing.

"I'll get some blankets. Get up."

I heaved a sigh of relief. Hoping the ordeal was over, I stood up, ashamed of my erection. Jack walked into another room. I shivered, imagining he would return with a gun or a knife. Instead, he came back with two blankets.

He stopped and stared at me with an evil-looking leer. Then he laughed. "It's not often I get sexy boys coming here. I've waited for this moment for a looonng time; you'll have to excuse me if I enjoy your company."

He made a bed for me on the couch.

He stared again, suddenly looking shy. I was beginning to feel things would be okay.

"I'll go easy on you if you come into my bed." He waited a moment in silence. "Come on in if you feel lonely, boy. Don't worry about waking me; I sleep deeper than a tortoise." And then he quickly walked away to his room.

Thanks to the beer at dinner, I had to pee but figured I could hold it until morning. I put my underwear back on and crawled under the blankets on the couch. Shifting on the lumpy piece of furniture, exhausted from discomfort, worry, and fear, I fell asleep.

Chapter 11: Decline and Disappear

I was sleeping restlessly on the lumpy couch. At once I felt a presence.

I opened my eyes. Jack was standing over me. He was in his underwear but clearly sexually aroused. A terrible sense of deja vu overcame me when I saw him. This had happened before, and I knew what I had to do even though the thought of it repulsed me. He took my hand. Again, at first very gently but then with force, he got me up.

"You want it, don't you?" he asked softly.

I was afraid. "No, please, I don't. I like you, but I don't—"

He placed his hand on my cock, and with the other found a firm grip on my ass.

"That's more like it. I thought you'd come around." Then his Southern drawl turned almost childlike. "Sorry, little slut, you ain't gettin' away that easy. Doin' Rags in the toilets, I thought better of you. But now you don't worry, here is someone who appreciates you."

"It's not what you think. I wasn't ... What are you going to—"

"You want it, boy. Yes, you need it. Look how he's just twitchin' between your legs. Come on."

He walked me into his room. I hated myself so much, I wanted him to kill me when he closed the doors. I started to cry.

"It's okay to cry. I used to cry, too. But I'll be gentle, gentler than they were with me, I guarantee that. You'll see." His hand sank to my buttocks and squeezed. He grabbed each cheek and let his fingers go deep in between them so his fingernails painfully scratched my anus. "You need me. I need this. Just lie down on your belly."

Lying face down on his bed, I wondered why I didn't fight back. I felt something slimy and cold on my ass.

"Just a little lube boy."

Why did I feel I deserved this degradation? He moved a wet finger down my back into my ass, violating me. Why did I lie there? I could not think. The shame and humiliation crowded all other thoughts out of my brain. I should have run; instead, I just lay there letting it all happen.

In the deepest humiliation, as he moved his finger back and forth in me, my only protest was a bizarre statement: "The ring, my mother's ring." I buried my head deep into the mattress so I could barely breathe. I braced myself for the worst, wondering how much deeper I had to go until I suffocated myself.

"I won't take no ring, honey boy; you're all I need." He slid in another finger. I tightened. "That won't do. Fuck!"

Filled with dread, I braced myself. I closed my eyes. Behind me, he started shaking very forcefully and moaning to himself: "Oh dammit, oh dammit, fuck, not now!" The suddenly he yelled, "Get hard!" More violent shaking, while his finger jerked inside of me, painfully jabbing and stretching my sphincter. I was sure the next thing was going to be jabbing his cock in there.

"Please stop, please," I begged, unsure if I said it out loud.

He was going to do something horrible. I knew it. I wasn't ready. I shut my eyes tighter as if the darkness could make him go away. I squirmed as he started moving his fingers slid easily inside of me. Then some horrible thing inside of me kicked in.

My once sacred desire for love melted into an impossible desire for being raped. I muttered intensely, "Please!" And I thought of a name: Gary. I suddenly wanted it. I became silent. I waited. I began to hate myself again, just like when I was in the closet as if all the therapy I had did not matter.

He bent over me, the shaking still continuing, I braced for him to enter my asshole, but I felt nothing except his breath on my back. As Jack got excited, I realized he really was just masturbating behind me.

"You love it, you fucking sick bitch! You fucking bitch!" he yelled.

"Fuck me," I whispered intensely. I was horrified to hear those word escape from my lips.

I don't know how, but at that moment, a stabbing pain from inside my rectum made me have an orgasm. I felt my own penis pulsating under me, making me wet. Then Jack forced his large penis up my ass cheeks and instantly came on me. I felt like I was scum—the worst, the lowest, the nothing.

"I am a whore," I moaned.

Quickly, coarsely, Jack's cock withdrew. I looked back. Jack gazed in disgust at his dirty fingers. Then his ecstasy turned on a dime … into anger.

"Get out of my bedroom! Get out! Now!—Please!" he shouted.

I ran out of his bedroom. I wiped myself with the blanket. I got dressed as fast as I could.

"Go to sleep! I'll take you back in the morning! I won't harm you … anymore," Jack shouted from behind his now closed door.

As soon as I was dressed, I ran out the front door.

I could still hear his voice crying and screaming, "I'm sorry! God forgive me! Please come back. What have I …"

Running, I cursed myself for not leaving earlier. I ran for my life and tried to block out everything that happened. In the freezing cold, I broke out into a sweat.

Soon I realized 'the middle of nowhere' was just east of Woodward Avenue. Crossing over and rushing back to the campus took little more than an hour, albeit in the miserable cold. Nevertheless, back on campus, I was not eager to go back to my dorm room. I stank of cheap cigar smoke and Jack Devlin. Tim would smell it on me and know all about me. Suddenly, I was also exhausted and numb. The cold began to slow me down. It was an odd feeling as if I were dispassionately witnessing myself freezing to death. A witness yet not a participant in my own agony, I walked over to the Theater Arts building.

I plopped down on the green bench where I used to wait for Casper. It had started to snow lightly. The snow was calming. I did not know what to do, where to go. I started to fall asleep. Pain shot through my ass, awakening me. It subsided, and I returned to the odd detached state of mind, witnessing myself in the moment. Observing myself. Not feeling myself. The more the cold bored into me, the less involved I felt in it. I saw someone walking toward me.

All at once, I felt scared.

The man came closer. I did what seemed like the logical thing to do. I tried to scream. But I couldn't. I started shivering. The man came closer. A big hulk of a black man, coming to rob me, I was sure. He took slow threatening steps. I didn't dare speak. If I played dead, maybe he would walk right by me.

"Buddy? Hey, buddy!" he whispered. I saw clearly he was homeless, ugly, poorly dressed, violent. He grabbed my body, to beat me, I thought. "Keep movin'; come on, keep movin'. You'll freeze. I am serious. You're shiverin', man. Ain't good. Come on. Come on." I found it difficult to walk. He put his arm around me and held me up. He smelled a wretched body odor.

"Hold it, buddy. Which way? Which way? Just point."

I pointed toward my dorm. He started walking me over there. The first steps my feet dragged—tingling, burning, and yet numb. A few steps and I got my balance. Then, the man disappeared.

"Thanks, good night!" I yelled after he was long gone. I walked up to the back entrance of the dorm. I rang the bell. The student keeping the night watch let me in.

"What the hell happened to you?"

"I am cold."

"Wow come on in, Jamie. Warm up." I recognized him but didn't remember his name. "Want a cup of coffee?"

"Yes. Thanks." He went to the break room. I didn't want Tim to see me like this. I wouldn't know how to explain the smell, the frostbite, or the emotional state I was in.

"Can I sleep on the couch in the lobby? I don't want to wake my roommate."

"Sure, go ahead. You're not supposed to, but I don't care."

I drank the warm coffee. The pain in my ass would not let me forget what I had done. I had said it … I said, "Fuck me." And I let it happen. The self-hatred burned my face, sucking all the energy to carry on out of my body.

The coffee's warmth, stronger than its caffeine, granted me the calmness to be drowsy. I sunk down on the couch, setting the coffee cup on the floor. Winter jacket still on, I closed my eyes. I could hear the faint sound of a television.

Sometime later, I woke. The television was off. In the disquieting silence, I felt my face burning. I felt the stabbing pain in my ass. The world seemed like a lonely poisonous place. I knew of only one antidote to this problem. Curled up on the empty lobby couch, my mind went to sleep creating its own safe loving world. Music wafted into my brain accompanied by lyrics I faintly knew; but recognized their rhythm enough to take me away, out of my body, into another realm where comforted by Casper everything was all right:

> *O sink hernieder,*
> *Nacht der Liebe,*
> > *O Descend over me,*
> > *Night of love,*
> *gib Vergessen,*
> *dass ich lebe;*
> > *grant oblivion,*
> > *that I am living;*
> *nimm mich auf*
> *in deinen Schoss,*
> > *take me up*
> > *into your bosom,*
> *löse von*
> *der Welt mich los!*
> > *make the world*
> > *let go of me!*

Variation: Hammerblow I, The Summons

Early December 1980

II Scherzo: Wuchtig
(Musical Joke: Powerful)

Chapter 12: Thank God It's Monday

My face turned red. Temples pulsating, I was ready for a fight.

"What do you know about this mendacity thing?" I snarled stepping closer to Ben. "Huh? Hell! I could write a book on it! Don't you know that? I could write a goddamn book on it and still not cover the subject anywhere near enough!"

I am right in his face. It looks like Ben could hit me, the bully, but I feel ready to stand up to him regardless. The pent-up anger from Jack and from Ben's bullying had reached a boiling point I could scarcely contain—in a play. "Think of all the lies I got to put up with!—Pretenses! Ain't that mendacity? Having to pretend stuff you don't think or feel or have any idea of? Having, for instance, to act like I care about—"

"Whoa!" yelled Ben, "Stop it!"

I was caught up in the anger but conscious enough about the class that I could copy Mr. Nathan and just step out of character and smile: "Scared? It's only a play." For once, I got the class laughing at Ben.

Ben furiously turned to Mr. Nathan. Mr. Nathan, our playwriting professor, was small in stature and bespectacled, his short salt-and-pepper hair and mustache gave him a staid professorial look, which was just what he liked in order to keep people off-guard. When reading from a play he had the spellbinding energy of an Arthur Ashe. Even though he had a doctorate from Yale, he despised being called 'doctor' or 'professor.'

Mr. Nathan liked my reading. "Jesus, Ben, don't break the tension. Jamie's just building to the great convulsion; that's the most important point here. Big Daddy's cancer, which is itself mendacity. Remember, no one has told him yet."

"But is it necessary for this fag to spit in my face?" brayed Ben. Students guffawed. I turned red, I wasn't expecting that.

"Don't think I have not noticed, Mr. Geln," Mr. Nathan said. "Ben, you have been teasing this kid all semester long. Now he's just playing a character with the upper hand in a play, and you cry foul? Bah! Outstanding job, Jamie. You, on the other hand, Ben, cannot let someone upstage you like that. A character doesn't roll over and play dead like you just did. If you wanted your real revenge, all you had to do was turn the page and read your lines."

Ben glared at me, his flawless athletic body hyperventilating under the stress of the scene; he got the mental beating I could never pull off physically. What started out as a simple class reading from *Cat on a Hot Tin Roof* had turned into a chess-like confrontation between Ben and me. In character, I could get out all my hostilities that were otherwise bottled up inside.

I enjoyed the chance to attack Ben, even if it was just a role in a play. Ben enjoyed intimidating me, getting people to laugh at me, and deride my shyness. Now he was getting it. I was reading Big Daddy's role from *Cat on a Hot Tin Roof* and really lit into Ben, who was reading the role of Brick. Luckily, Tennessee Williams was on my side and gave me the juiciest monologue.

"Jamie, you did well," said Mr. Nathan.

"He's spitting in my face," Ben complained. "I don't want that mug in my face."

Mr. Nathan comically threw the handkerchief from his jacket to Ben. "Ben, you're in the wrong class if you want things nice and neat," he switched to a far more ferocious voice, spitting in every direction, including Ben's—"'Ain't that *mendacity?* Having to *pretend* stuff you don't think or feel or have any idea of? Having, for instance, to act like I care for Big Mama—I haven't been able to stand the sight, sound, or *smell* of that woman for forty years now!— even when I *laid* her!'—Do you all get that? You see what he wrote! Of course, he's yelling and spitting; he is admitting, 'I have to lie to myself just to keep it up when I am *fucking* her!'" Mr. Nathan's emotional outburst stunned every-one into silence. "There, now that I've sprayed the whole room, can we go further with the play?"

"I think Brick is a stupid name," said Cindy Prite. Everyone looked at her. "Well, it is, like as dumb as a brick."

A nervous laugh echoed in the small classroom. The class had started out with twenty students but dwindled to fifteen as some students did not care for Mr. Nathan's confrontational and dramatic style of teaching theater. Most of the other students were his groupies except Cindy's who was a clueless detractor.

"Okay, Cindy, thank you for that," said Mr. Nathan. Then he turned to Ben, "As for why Jamie is yelling at you, Ben, if you turn the page, you'll see why Big Daddy is so upset with Brick. He is about to challenge him to commit suicide. Why is that, Ben?"

"Because Brick wants to confront the lie that Big Daddy's going to live. He's dying of cancer, and the lying makes him sick."

"Bullshit," Mr. Nathan sneered.

"Bullshit?" asked Ben.

"Come on, people, who here knows what I am talking about?" The class was entranced by Mr. Nathan's energy. "Eula, is that bullshit? Of course it is; tell me why."

"Because it's not the only lie?"

"What other lies?"

"Well, the competition for the inheritance. People pretending to like each other?"

"Pretending to honor Big Daddy," said Mr. Nathan before switching to an outraged Southern belle voice: *"The concert is still going on! Bravo, no-necks, bravo!"* That's not the voice of anyone pretending to be nice. Is it, Jamie?"

"Well, I am just noticing it now, but there are layers of lying—lying to each other, lying to themselves. The play is built on lies—lies meant to help people fit in, lies meant to get along with the family—"

"And lies to write the goddamn play! Tennessee Williams himself is a liar here. He isn't even ready to deal truthfully with his own subject. Everything starting from that point will be a lie; even the so-called reconciliation at the end is a lie. Don't write on a subject you aren't ready to deal with. Williams was not ready to deal with his homosexuality, and so the play just prances about the subject like the very characters do to each other in the play. Of course, it is a tribute to a great playwright that he can lie and still write a great play, but don't think you can get away with it. Do you all get that?"

"But Brick's buddy—Skipper—is gay and commits suicide, right?" Eula asked.

"But that is not handling the issue. Williams has Brick hint for so long that he is gay, and then there is this clean neat little out. Williams was not ready to write about a real gay hero. So he builds us up and lets us down." Mr. Nathan stopped and sighed. He looked around the room. "Does anyone know what I am talking about? Williams never did write the great gay apotheosis he should have been capable of writing. He really never accepted his homosexuality." My mouth had dropped open. I had never heard a professor—or anyone—talk so openly and positively about the 'gay' subject before. And apparently, neither had any of the other students, even with their experience with Mr. Nathan. He stunned his audience.

"Tennessee Williams wasn't a homosexual. How do

you know that?" asked Cindy. "For crying out loud, you think everyone is a weirdo." Some kids in the class snickered, which offended Cindy to no end, though she must have been used to it. Her tenacious inability to understand anything discussed in class impressed everyone.

"Well, it is true that I believe being *different* is normal—certainly it is in the theater," Mr. Nathan said, the class bursting with laughter. "But Cindy you make a good point which we should take very seriously. In fact, your comment gets you a little extracurricular assignment. I want you to read and give us a report on two of Williams' short stories. I think you'd like that it will prove your point just to your satisfaction. One is entitled *Hard Candy* and the other *The Mysteries of the Joy Rio*. Write up a report on those short works, and I will opt you out of having to take the final." It wasn't the generous offer it sounded like. First, Mr. Nathan opted almost everyone out of the final. Second, he picked two outrageously overt gay themed stories. "Lucky for you, Cindy, I have the short stories back in my office. See me during tomorrow's office hours and pick them up if you accept the challenge."

"No final if I read two short stories?"

"And report to us about them."

"Deal!" Cindy said triumphantly.

"Good. Anyone who wants the same deal as Cindy, come by my office hours and I'll make copies. Just remember you need to deliver the report before the final. In the meantime, everyone—even you, Cindy—should be able to write intelligently on the levels of lying in *Cat on a Hot Tin Roof* and include examples. Mr. Benjamin Geln and Mr. James Goldberg may stay behind for a moment and have *the pleasure of my mendacity*. The rest of you may … go!" That was Mr. Nathan's way of dismissing class and clueing his groupies that he was not available after class.

Ben and I were hardly friends, so it was with reluctance that we did anything together. He hated me because I was gay—though how Ben had found out, I still had no idea. He seemed to have known before I did.

I hated Ben, actually because he hated me. I thought he was disturbingly attractive, which made me all the more mystified of his hatred.

"Come, sit here in the front seats. Come on, be quick, I have places to meet and people to see." Ben and I sat next to each other. He refused to look at me. Part of me wondered what stroking his muscled arm would feel like, and I even peevishly wondered what he would do to me if I kissed him. "Hey, you two may not know this, but you each have something in common."

"We do?" we both asked.

"Yes, you both were going to try out for *The Caretaker*."

"But we're not in competition or anything; we're trying out for separate parts," said Ben defensively, who clearly knew more about this than I did.

"I know I asked you to try out for the role of Davies, and you, Jamie, for Aston. But there is a bit of a change. You can drop your little Pinter plays. I got a budget for a larger work. We're doing Shakespeare."

"We are?" asked Ben.

"Yes, Ben, you're going to try out for Hamlet and Jamie for Horatio. I want you both to study these roles very carefully. I want you to be at the top of your game. We won't do the auditions until next term. That will give you the break to learn and research your roles. You boys up to it? Of course, I can't guarantee you the roles. We really can't tell how these things go until we hear a reading, know what I mean? Anything can happen. And I hope it does, too. That's why I wanted to talk to you two. I want you both to … spice things up. Try something out of the ordinary, play around with the roles, have some fun. See what you can do to flesh them out more. You two are both pimply-faced Detroiters, so you really have to reach beyond yourselves."

"Is that all you wanted to tell us?" asked Ben as he stood up. He wasn't nearly as thrilled as I was for being asked to try out for a role.

Mr. Nathan walked up to Ben, right into his face. "I am expecting no mendacity, from either of you boys, understood? There, I got an 's' and a 't' in there so I could spit." Mr. Nathan stepped back to address us both. "I am trying to tell both of you that I have higher expectations for you. I don't want to see the clichés that I will get from the other students, no, not from either one of you. So, I hope you spend the winter break with Shakespeare close by your side. I expect you to shine somehow during the auditions."

"Shine? How are we supposed to do that?" I asked.

"Figure it out, Jamie" Mr. Nathan used his most theatrical and contemptuous voice, which oddly conveyed how much confidence he had in us. "You've got time to prepare. But to get back to your first question, Ben, actually it is a competition. The play, just like life, is a fucking competition. Don't let yourselves down. Now get out of here."

I looked at Ben with a new sense of respect because he'd been asked to take on the lead role of Hamlet. Ben glanced at me with a new sense of contempt. I knew right then and there, I was going to read for Hamlet anyway.

Chapter 13: Magic Island

O sink hernieder,
Nacht der Liebe,
*   O Descend over me,*
*   Night of love,*
gib Vergessen,
dass ich lebe;
*   grant oblivion*
*   that I am living;*
nimm mich auf
in deinen Schoss,
*   take me up*
*   into your bosom,*
löse von
der Welt mich los!
*   make the world*
*   let go of me!*

The door suddenly opened.

"Oh my God! It's not what you think—" I let out a scream. My roommate, Tim, had walked in while I was singing the love duet from *Tristan und Isolde*. When I thought I was alone, I had this terrible habit of not just singing opera but singing all the parts—in this case, both Tristan *and* Isolde. I was singing her role in an admittedly unpleasant falsetto.

Tim chuckled. "You need to get that vibrato out of your voice."

"Sorry, you surprised me, Tim. I wasn't expecting you."

"No, apparently not," he said smiling, "Don't sweat it; I sing to records too when you aren't around."

As usual, Tim was cradling a stack of books in his arms. Sometimes the stack was so high you could only see his dark mop of hair and soft brown eyes. His books were mostly musical scores and science history, his favorite subjects, which he deposited on the already mountainous collection on his desk.

He offered a meek yet friendly smile. A music major, he usually frowned upon my amateurish wailings. "You know, if you take a couple classes you can get rid of that vibrato in your voice. It's good to see you singing. I emphasize see. You've been kind of down lately."

"Anything you want to talk about?" he asked. I wasn't sure how to respond to this seemingly innocent yet dangerous question.

"Nothing." I looked into his dark dreamy eyes holding guard over his prominent nose. Those eyes seemed so warm and welcoming. His concern for me, which made only rare appearances, was touching, but I didn't dare to tell him what had happened with Jack or my parents.

Earlier in the morning, I awoke on the sofa in the lobby. I waited there until Tim left for classes before I snuck back into the room and showered off the dirt and cigar stench from the previous night. Then I stuffed the cigar-reeking clothes in my laundry bag. I was surprised how redemptive a shower could be; one thorough wash and that wretched smell was gone, the slimy feeling vanished. I emerged from the shower almost as if the whole wretched night had never happened.

Tim sat down next to me on the couch. Lazily, or on purpose, our bodies slid together. How I wished he kept his thigh next to mine. I needed the nice touch. Though I was not convinced, as Jack Devlin was, that Tim was gay, I did find Tim more affectionate than the average male.

"Sure you can't talk about it?" Tim asked.

It would mean spilling the beans about being gay, and I wasn't sure I could handle another freak-out. I had no idea whether Tim was homophobic, having been thrown out by my parents, jilted by Casper, and now what? Raped by Jack? Anyway—I was alone and unloved. Tim seemed like my last friend. I had no desire to explore his position on homosexuality.

Did I want to talk about it? No. I did what most homosexuals have to do; I lied. I took a deep practiced sigh. "It's my parents' health," I fabricated.

To my relief, he put his hand on my shoulder. I felt like a thief stealing a treasure, the warm touch intended to comfort me for the fictionally ailing parents.

"Oh, I am sorry, Jamie. No wonder you've been down. Is it serious?" His soothing tone encouraged me, so I leaned closer to him. We didn't cuddle, but he didn't move back.

"My father had a heart attack. He'll be okay ... but

he … has to stop working." Under false pretenses, I got to soak up the warmth of the soft cotton clothes covering his thin vulnerable frame.

"Wow, that sucks. He's in the hospital?" Tim put the weight of his arm on my shoulder, and for the first time, I thought Jack could be right. Maybe we did love each other.

"He's not out yet—of the hospital. He'll be okay, but they can't support me anymore," I said, internally marveling at this stroke of genius to explain my parents no longer supporting me.

"So you'll go and see them this weekend?" He withdrew his arm and slid apart from me on the couch.

"No, actually, I am starting a job this weekend."

"What will you be doing?"

I didn't want to answer him. He'd never worked a day in his life, and I felt uncomfortable admitting my blue-collar background.

"What is it?" he asked again.

"I'll be baking bagels at the Brooklyn Bagel Factory."

"Oh, the place on Amsterdam Street?"

"Yes," I confessed, looking away.

"Oh. I bet it's not a good-paying job."

"I don't have much choice."

"No, I mean. … do you think you'll be able to stay in the dorms next term?"

"Not very likely, I'm afraid."

Now it was Tim's turn to look away.

"Shoot. I need to look for a new roommate then. I don't know what I am going to do."

"You could live off campus with me," I offered, but he did not seem to warm to the idea.

"You mean in Detroit?" His was the typical reaction of a suburbanite who thought the DSU campus was an enclave unto its own, separate from the Motor City beyond. "My mom would have a hemorrhage. Oh, but if you don't go home this weekend, then you'll be here?"

"I don't see where else I can go."

"Then you'll also be in town for Nina's graduation concert. Want to go with me?" My heart pounded. I could scarcely contain my joy. This was exactly what I needed. "Nina and your friend Dorothy are giving their graduation recitals on the same program."

"She's hardly my friend, I said. "I just like her dramatic voice." Nina and Dorothy were two singers whose careers Tim and I followed by attending all the student recitals. Dorothy had a rough raspy voice, which Tim found unmusical, but I thought was dramatic. Nina, the department's reigning diva, had become a particularly nice acquaintance. "I'd love to attend the concert. Do I need tickets?"

"You do. They're making a big deal about it for some reason. They are having it at the Theater Arts building, your neck of the woods. I guess they expect a crowd for Nina. But I'll try and score you a free ticket."

"When is it?" I asked eagerly.

"Friday night at eight."

"Far out. Know what's on the program?"

"Schubert songs—that's Dorothy, something up your alley, but Nina is doing an opera of some kind."

"Really? What's it called?'

"I forget. I think it's *The Magic Island* or *The Magic* something or other."

"You mean *The Magic Flute?*"

"No, it's nothing I ever heard of before. Something short that requires a big orchestra. That's what I heard anyway. Gotta go. I'll see if I can score you a ticket."

The Magic Island. The title did not sound like any opera I'd ever heard of. But of course, I said "yes." I desperately needed some magic in my life.

Chapter 14: Crossed Wires

But I am pigeon-liver'd sissy
To make oppression bitter, or ere this
I should have fatted all the region kites
With this slave's offal: bloody, bawdy villain!
Remorseless, treacherous, lecherous, piece of shit!
O, vengeance!
Why, what an asshole am I! This is most brave,
That I, the son of a dear mother murder'd,
Prompted to my revenge by heaven and hell,
Must, like a whore, unpack my heart with words,
And fall a-cursing, like a very drab asshole!
Shit upon't! shit!

"I don't think Shakespeare would approve," said an entering voice.

"Oh, fuck!" I jumped. My head shot up; I knew that voice. It was Casper standing in the doorway. He had walked into the empty classroom where I was practicing my lines for *Hamlet*, trying to see what "shine" I could put into it. I put the script down.

"How's it goin'?" Casper asked.

How's it goin'? A kind tone from Casper. Maybe he really did love me. My heart beat like a drum. I tried to grasp for words, but they eluded me. Casper in this room.

Saying friendly words to me. It was overwhelming.

"I guess I was taking my frustrations out on Hamlet."

"I'd say so, I could hear you down the hall."

"I–I–was j–just studying my lines, I mean Shakespeare's lines, ha ha. You sur–prised–surprised me." I desperately wanted to show him I was a decent nice person. But I couldn't just blurt it out; I had to show him. "Casper, I am really a decent nice person," I declared.

"Huh?"

"I mean, I am not the whore you think I am—I mean, I am not who you think I am."

"Okay." He stood in the doorway. Then, after a pause, he stepped in. "It's cool. Anyway, I am glad I found you."

He's glad he found me. Oh, rapture! You love me! Yes, I know you love me! O Descend over us, Night of love, grant us oblivion …

"Jamie, did you hear what I was saying?"

"Yes! Of course! … Ah, no, actually—sorry, heh heh, could you repeat it?"

"I was just talking with Arthur." Arthur is what the cool kids called Mr. Nathan. "He told me I might find you here and thought we should talk."

"He did?" I began to feel the power of his presence. "What did he want?"

"This is your first audition, and you've only been a theater major for scarcely a term. Arthur thought you might need a mentor. Someone to help you."

All is forgiven, Casper; really, all is forgiven. We were

getting a second chance. It was so obvious to me. There really was a God, and my prayers were answered, even if I had forgotten to pray. "Casper, thank you; really, I can't tell you how much this means to me ... to have you help me."

"Good. I am glad to hear that, Jamie. Arthur mentioned how you and Ben seem to be a good tag team." My mouth had dropped open at Ben's name. "Yes, you are. So anyway, Arthur asked me to get you two together to help each other."

"What? Ben and me? But with you, of course."

"No, he thought it would be better for me to introduce you two and get you both together on your own."

"Me and Ben?"

"Look, Arthur asked me to do this, so he thinks it's in both your interests. Understand? I know you and Ben do not always get along, but—"

"Don't get along? He's a homophobic bully," I snapped, disappointed to that Casper was only here at Mr. Nathan's insistence. Casper was not going to mentor me.

"Jamie, we have to get along with all sorts of assholes. Ben has a lot to offer. He needs to open up, and so do you. You're both talented—"

"Really? Mr. Nathan said that?"

"I say it too; I heard about your little showdown with Ben in Mr. Nathan's playwriting class."

"Me? Thank you, Casper." I tried a weak flirt.

"Arthur said you almost clobbered Ben in front of

his playwriting class."

"It was just acting—hardly clobbering," I replied.

"Anyway, next term, you and Ben will work together on the *Hamlet* auditions. I'll get you both started, but then you'll be on your own."

"Okay." I sighed. Casper turned to leave. "Wait, Casper, can I ask you something?" He sighed and turned around again. "You know when we were … together … didn't that mean anything?"

"I'd hardly call what we did as being 'together,' Jamie."

"I know, but you must know—" I couldn't look at him, but I had to say it. "You're special to me. I thought or hoped I was special to you."

"Special?"

"Well, do you think I … you're the only one … how could—"

"Jamie, you'll have to finish your sentences if you want to talk to me." Sarcasm was better than anger. I relaxed. Still, Casper seemed to be getting angry, though why I could not fathom.

"This past school year, Casper, you must have noticed me, didn't you?"

"What do you mean?"

"I used to watch for you—you know—before we met."

"What? You were cruising me or something, Jamie?"

"Cruising?" I had to mull that one over. I had never heard the word before. "So, you do know? You know you are special to me?"

"I think you mean Dwight."

"Who's Dwight?"

"Oh, come on—Dwight, the director of the play you're trying out for."

"You can't be serious," I said. He laughed. "*That* Dwight I know, but I am certain I never cruised him, whatever that means." The very thought that Casper thought I was interested in Dwight was distasteful. He was a fat creep, but I didn't want to say that to Casper; they might be friends. I often saw them together when I was 'cruising' Casper. "You're the only person I ever did …"

"Oh, come on, Jamie, don't give me that. There's no way I can be the only one you ever cruised before."

"Of course. Who else could there be?"

"Really?" he countered angrily.

What had I said now? "Really! Look, Casper, don't you see what I am trying to say to you?"

"Jamie let's clear something up. You're friends with Dwight, right?"

"Friends? Dwight?" How could I say politely that I despised him? "He made a … pass at me at the Student Union one day—I was there studying, just studying. That's all."

"Oh, the Student Union building. Right."

"It's not what you think."

"What was I thinking, mister green boy?"

"I was there studying. Really, I was. I study there sometimes. Casper, when I first saw you, you really—"

"You and Dwight have nothing to do with each

other?" he cross-examined. I could not imagine why he had this fixation on Dwight.

"No, of course not. Can we forget Dwight? Casper, can't you just let me tell you how I feel about you?" I tried to get closer, but he backed away.

"I don't want to hear about this ridiculous fantasy life of yours. Look, you sucked me off, and now I am sorry for it for the rest of my life. Jesus, back off will you?"

"What did I do that was so wrong, Casper? You're the last one I wanted to offend. I just did what I thought you wanted me to do."

"Now you're gonna tell me that you never sucked anyone before. Give it up, Jamie." He put out his hand to stop me from another approach.

"Give it up?"

"No one sucks like that unless they are a real pro, get me? I am on to you."

That felt like a dagger. As if he knew something about me, which I didn't know myself. But how could he know about this? It had to be my past catching up with me. But what past? Why else was Casper getting so angry? Just because I didn't like Dwight?

"Okay, just tell me, apart from falling off the planet, what can I do?"

"Stop talking to other people about me and what we did for starters."

"Stop talking? I didn't tell anyone about you." Frustration was getting the better of me. I was pretty sure he was talking to others about me.

"You didn't tell anyone about us?" Casper walked closer to me. Far from intimate, his approach was intimidating.

"I swear I didn't. I never did. I certainly wouldn't," I shot back. Then I tried to lighten up. I forced a smile. "Please, maybe we can just get together and talk? I am sure if we could go to some private place where we could just talk, we can clear the air. Look, can't we do that? Really, the last thing I want to do is hurt you. Can't we talk—you know, somewhere private?"

"Private like where?" he challenged.

I didn't know. I thought what could be safer than the gay bars Eula mentioned. "Somewhere where we don't have to worry about being overheard by who knows who. How about one of those gay bars, like Dreamland?"

"You want to talk there?" He was upset again. I wished I knew what made him tick.

"Sure, or Menjo's?"

"You know you can't have a decent conversation in those bars. The music is too loud."

"I—I don't know. I've never been there before—but I've heard about them."

"Oh, really? You've never been there before?"

"No. And now that I think about it, I can't go there, at least not until next month. I'll turn twenty-one in January. Maybe we can go to your place—"

"Come on, you can't be serious about never being there. You're a real pro."

His bitter sarcasm hurt, and it was the exact

expression Eula had used! Someone else must have spoken to both of them somehow. Someone from my dark past, I knew instinctively, was the only one who could be involved in this. I wished I knew how, and suddenly I realized Casper was right, I did know how to suck his cock—I even remembered the feeling I had then of a disconnected deja vu. Maybe Dr. Wire was wrong; I was some kind of a disease after all. "A real pro? How do you know?" I asked.

"Finally, you admit it. Jamie, look, let's just be honest about this, okay? You never knew about Dreamland or Menjo's or Palmer Park?" I found Casper's closer presence more and more irresistible.

"I heard about them. I fed ducks in Palmer Park when I was a kid."

"Ha ha ha. But you've never been there?"

"Well, Casper, please, I really just came out of the closet ... Do you know someone named Gary by any chance?" Casper looked at me quizzically.

"Gary? Who's that?"

"I don't know—no one. Look, I haven't been to Palmer Park since I was a kid."

"Oh, stop it; you've been out. You've been cruising me for over a year."

"You do remember, Casper, I was *cruising* you a long time before I ever admitted I was ... who I am—gay."

Casper seemed to calm down. "I find this very hard to believe."

"It's true!" Now was the moment; I had to give it my all. Drop all pretense. I wanted to be as open as I could be. I would just suffer the consequences for what really had to be said, even if it was apparently hopeless. "It is true. I … I fell in love with you," I confessed. "It's really what started me on this path to admitting I was … gay. For that, I am very grateful to you. There. I said it. I love you, and I am grateful to you. I wanted to show my gratitude before, and I am sorry I didn't do it the right way, but I didn't know better."

To my surprise, Casper seemed genuinely touched. "Really? And before me?"

I had to think about the past, my childhood. I no longer knew how to answer that question.

"There was no one before you," I said tentatively.

"You mean it?"

My heart beat faster. There was a nagging feeling there was someone before him.

"Oh God, I don't know anymore, but it's the truth. I don't know what you heard about me—it seems Eula did too—but you must know G-G-Gary? That must have been so long ago, and it doesn't count. There isn't anyone else but you." Then, I remembered a different incident, when I was fifteen going to a dilapidated house with this guy I met in Detroit. But who? It must have been a long time ago, certainly long before Casper knew me. And why did I mention Gary? He was my brother's best friend.

"Jamie, I really don't know what to make of you. You fell in love with … with me?" I was getting through, I was winning. Then why was I beginning to feel panic? Everything that was simple seemed to get complicated all at once.

"That's what I've been trying to say to you all this time."

Casper stepped back away from me.

"Really?" he challenged. I nodded my head.

"Can we go to Dreamland?"

"I thought you said you're underage." And just like that, he slipped away, back to being suspicious of me.

"Yes I know, I don't know why I said it, Eula suggested it once. I mean let's just go somewhere we can be alone; someone could walk in here."

"Jamie, this is a charade. I feel sorry for you, I do, but that doesn't mean I am going to swallow all this bullshit."

"Bullshit?"

"Come on."

"What bullshit?" I braced myself for some unknown horrible truth about me.

"Jamie, why make it so dramatic? You know your reputation."

I wanted to cry, scream, yell, but the frustration got the better of me.

"Reputation? One, okay, a couple of screwups—and I get a reputation? How can I have a reputation? I just came ..." Before I could finish the sentence, I came to some realizations. First, he's good friends with Dara and probably knows all about our sleeping together. Second, the gay world must be very small, in which everyone probably knows everyone. Third, he must know Jack. I had intimate knowledge of how Jack talked about people. Jack had insisted I was trying to have sex with that guy Rags in the toilet, and then there was that horrible night when I asked him to fuck me. I sighed. I was defeated. Casper might even know this Rags guy. If it's three strikes and you're out, I was out. "Okay. I give up. If that is all it takes, I am dead meat."

"Can you deny the facts?"

"No. But can't you cut me some slack?"

"Slack? You had me going. I was swallowing that love crap."

"I do love you! Okay, I admit some of what I had done was pretty terrible; it wasn't my fault. And I know what you must have heard from Dara must sound awkward—"

"Dara? Who said anything about Dara?"

My face felt as if it was on fire. "Oh, you didn't know."

Casper turned a frightful shade of red.

"You didn't … look me in the eyes and tell me you didn't …" I looked down instead. I wanted to crawl away. "Oh, shit, you're … what, you waited until he was drunk and sucked him off? Or did you get Dara's boyfriend Ahmed to screw you?"

"Ahmed? So, you didn't know at all," I said too softly because I was choked up. Something so innocent at the time was now hopelessly confused.

"You did it with Ahmed! Getting some innocent straight guy caught up with—"

"No. No, I didn't."

"No?"

"No! I didn't do it with Ahmed."

"You didn't?" Casper looked at me with initial disbelief, followed by a curious look, until the quarter dropped, and he figured it out. Powerless, I could see the killing hatred in his eyes. "Oh, great. Perfect. Beautiful, just beautiful. You fucked my best friend's girl."

My heart broke.

"Ahmed knows," I babbled. "He was … okay with it … eventually … it was just one of those … spur-of-the-moment things. You know, I was playing opera for her—well, that was the—"

"That makes it perfectly fine. Tell me, is there anything you don't screw?"

"What? Wait a second, it's not like I am Don Giovanni. I can count my sins on one hand." I looked at him. I don't think that helped the defense of my case. The power of Casper's pain and outrage undid me. And it was aimed at me, the person who was trying to love him.

"Look, I don't want to debate this, Jamie. I don't really care, but will you just drop this love for me; it's pissing me off." He said "love" like it was a dirty word. "Look, believe it or not, I do like you. Let's just be friends. I want to help you and Ben; that's all I came here to do, okay?"

"But … it's not the way it seems."

"Right, you just said you never did it before and now on top of admitting everything else, you say you did it with Dara." Casper, exasperated, heaved a deep sigh and then forced a smile. "Look, Jamie, let's just leave our personal lives out of it. Can you just do that for me? If you love me, do that for me, okay?"

"Yes, Casper I will do that. But you do know Gary, don't you?"

"Jamie, listen to me good here: Never tell anyone what we did. I want to help you, and we need to trust each other. Okay, can we at least just settle on that?"

"You want to help?" I moaned.

"Yes—acting."

"No Dreamland?"

"Dreamland? Honestly. If you have never been there before, tell me, Jamie, how did you hear about it?"

"Well, people talk—" I realized I should just stick to the truth. I stood upright and looked him straight in the eye. "Dara—I mean Eula! She told me—and oh, oh sh … shit. I think I accidentally told Eula about us."

"Eula?" he howled.

"It was an accident. I thought you had told her. She seemed to know, but now I can see you didn't tell her. Right? It was something else entirely. You didn't tell her; she knew … someone … I thought … Well, she acted like she knew, but when I mentioned it, she said she didn't." I flinched; I thought Casper was about to hit me.

"Jesus, Jamie, you're fucking with my graduation, dammit. You can't talk to other people in the department about this. Do you understand me? Do you? Fucking tell me 'yes' right now, you understand that?"

"Yes, Casper." I was truly contrite. "I understand that. Never talk about it or about you to anyone. Never. I swear. Promise. Hope to die."

"Feeling's mutual! Don't you have any fucking sense? Jesus fucking Christ, Jamie, how stupid can you be?"

"I am sorry. You never spoke with Eula about that night in the small theater?"

"Oh shit, you didn't give any details—"

"No! Nothing. I swear! But ... you never told her either? She seemed to know something from someone."

"I never talk about my personal life with anyone at school. You talked with Dwight too?"

"Dwight? I won't talk to him about anything, I swear."

"Jamie, you're infuriating. Oh God." He stared at me and again forced himself to calm down and smile. "Look, I am helping you; we agree on that?"

"Yes."

"Then let's just agree to stop this, okay?"

"Of course, absolutely, of course. It is the end. I just want to say—" I wanted to at least explain the misunderstanding there must have been.

"We don't have to. Just forget it."

"Please, if we can only talk in a place where we don't have to watch our every word. I'd still like to go with you to one of these gay places to talk. Would that be okay?" This was the wrong thing to say. Casper turned red, and I could see the fury burning in his face.

"Drop it. Jamie, you are impossible. You think I don't know what you have been up to? Jesus, how stupid do you think I am? Look, I am willing to overlook what you've done, but you've got to face up to your own shit. Why did I bother? I am telling Arthur that you're meeting with Ben yourself next term."

"I can't do that!"

"Deal with it. I will be really pissed off if you don't. But I won't be surprised either." Casper stormed out in disgust.

I felt a horrible pain in my gut. I buckled onto the floor. I had no idea what was happening to me. I laid there for a while dazed feeling like I couldn't get up. But then I stood up, it was easier than I thought. I saw the script. I opened it randomly to when Horatio was spotting a ghost. In a halting shaky voice that sounded remarkably like Horatio should sound like:

As harbingers preceding still our destiny
And prologue to the omen coming on,
Have heaven and earth together demonstrated
Unto our country and countrymen.
But soft, behold! lo, where it comes again!

Chapter 15: Matched Set

Dreamworld was blindingly dark in this dungeon passing as a bar, but it didn't matter as all of my senses were overwhelmed by the stench of smoke, industrial waste, and humanity. The floor creaked and my soles stuck to the floor as I walked in. This was a creepy dive bar. I looked around, squinting as my eyes tried to adjust. I could make out shadows of drunken old men; seeing their faces leering at me made me queasy. I didn't dare walk any farther, but I was pushed from behind.

"Come on, Jamie, you're getting your butt in here," insisted Casper. He stepped around me, grabbed my shirt, and dragged me in. I bumped into something slimy. What? I had no idea; it let out a growling sound. My eyes adjusting, I could make out pitbull-like predatory eyes staring at me from the shadows.

"Now you know the place, don't you?" Casper demanded.

"I've never been here before—honest."

"Liar. Get me a drink, Jamie, something expensive," Casper ordered petulantly. I looked around and realized the room was narrow. My arm struck the bar that was just to my right. I felt something touch my leg, then I jerked as I felt something crawling. I bent over to shoo the thing away.

"Hello, Jamie, the usual?" asked the bartender.

"The usual?" Casper looked angry.

"What? I have never been here before. You don't know me!"

"You filthy liar!" Casper screamed.

"You sure are," laughed the bartender while mixing a drink. "They're waiting for you back there, as usual."

"Figures," said Casper. "You heard him, go on Jamie. They're waiting for you in the back."

"Here, take your drink," said the bartender, handing me a tall glass filled with some kind of green slime.

"I don't have any money," I pleaded. Casper and the bartender guffawed. "I can't pay for the drinks, honest." The entire bar erupted in laughter.

"That's funny, really funny. You're a regular riot tonight. Right, Jamie buddy, get back there for crying out loud," said the bartender. Then turning to Casper, he said, "The nerve of this guy, pretending he's Peter Pan."

I turned to Casper. I wanted to say, "I have no idea what he's talking about." But I got the shivers, and before I could recover, Casper was gone. Then I instinctively knew there was some kind of slasher, a serial killer, in the bar. Whoever it was, he was looking for me. And I knew, intuitively, I should go to the dark back end of the bar. I walked back and lizard-men slithered around me, tails wrapping around my ankles so I couldn't move. They shoved me into a reeking room.

At once, more lizard-men slithered around me,

wrapping their tails around my legs, then my thighs. I slipped, but their grip kept me standing. The rest of the people crowded around me, then they made way for someone. I knew it was the killer. He was a young guy in a dirty green shirt and tight blue jeans. I couldn't move, but I had to. I wanted to scream, but I couldn't.

The killer grabbed me, I tried to twist free, but the lizard-men held my legs, so I fell back, and Jack grabbed me from behind. He jammed my arms into my lower back.

"You asshole, you slut!" Jack yelled at me as the killer brandished a familiar-looking knife. "Sleeping with everybody, you bitch!"

"I wasn't sleeping with anyone!"

"What about me, you bitch?" said the killer.

"And me," said Jack.

"Yeah, and me!" said a lizard-man named Rags.

"And me, too," several lizard-men hissed in a chorus.

The young guy in the green shirt walked up to me holding the knife. I recognized it as the one my mother used in the kitchen for carving the Thanksgiving turkey.

"Stop, I don't want this!" I yelled.

"Of course you do," said the killer to general laughter. I could hear my mother and father laughing.

"Goodbye, Jamie," said my mother, laughing merrily. "That's what you get for doing it with everyone just like Dr. Reuben's book said you would."

"No! It was only Casper!" Loud laughter erupted. "I swear!" I screamed, but the laughter grew. "He's the only one I wanted!" I knelt to pray, but the lizards crawled all over me.

"Jamie, you're having a nightmare."

I lay on the couch; Tim was shaking me. I panicked—did I really yell that last line? "Oh, I am sorry—" I gasped.

"Calm down, you were screaming in your sleep."

"Did I just say anything out loud?"

"Nothing intelligible."

I was never so happy to see Tim. "Thank God it's you, oh—I was screaming—" I flushed with shame, remembering the nightmare.

I sat up on the couch, my schoolbooks on the floor. I shook myself, hoping to shake the nightmare and all its lurid characters out of my mind.

"You're fine now. Come on, Jamie; we should get ready."

"I guess I fell asleep. I missed dinner? What time is it?"

"It's almost seven. We better get dressed. We don't want to miss Dorothy and Nina's recital."

"Oh, right." I was still a little groggy and still guiltily wondering what exactly Tim had heard me scream.

"It's a special night. Maybe we should get dressed up for it, Jamie."

"A special night? Sure, let's do it. I'll get my dress jacket on." The idea of dressing up appealed to me like I was rejecting the filth that was surrounding my dream.

"I'll get my jacket, too," said Tim.

Standing in front of me and not bothering to move out of my sight, Tim began to undress. Unbuttoning his shirt, it seemed like he was doing this strip show for my benefit. I tried to be discrete, remembering Jack's vile leering. Still, I could not help glancing at his sweet, vulnerable body.

"Do you remember what they are singing?" I asked, just to hear his kind voice as we changed clothes.

"Let's see if I remember ... First Dorothy's doing the Schubert songs." He took off his shirt, revealing that smooth skinny chest, cute except for a disturbing concave rib cage that made me wonder how he could breathe. I wondered how soft his flesh was. It seemed to barely cover his rib cage. "Let's see, then Nina's doing that opera ... Oh, it's an excerpt from something ... with other singers ..." He took off his pants and leisurely walked over to his desk, showing off a small bubble butt. I wondered why I had not noticed that before. He stood in his white briefs. He bent over and picked up the program from his desk. "I don't see a composer. It's called—I was right the first time—*The Magic Garden.*"

"*The Magic Garden?* There isn't any opera called *The Magic Garden.*"

"Oh, well, maybe it's a modern piece, or maybe it was written by a student here. It's a graduation project, after all."

"I've really never heard of anything like that." I was encouraging Tim to see more opera, but I also wanted to protect him from premature exposure to anything that might be off-putting. No Alban Berg, Arnold Schoenberg, or George Frideric Handel.

"That's all it says, Jamie. *The Magic Garden.*"

"Who are the other singers?"

"In *The Magic Garden* thing? Brian Crowley ..."

"Oh, the tenor." I perked up. "The muscular one, remember? He did that recital almost without a shirt on—I mean, he has a really memorable voice."

"Oh, that was *him*. Not very tasteful. Let's see who else is there ... there's Sheila Watkins, Berta Bremer—I know her, Hannah Feinstein—she's not graduating, yuck and that conductor, Eric—the one I told you about, the one Nina was breaking up with, oh, and our beloved D-State Orchestra—ah, with some volunteers from the Detroit Symphony. That might not be bad."

"Sounds like a big production."

As we got dressed, I fumbled knotting my tie. I saw Tim did it perfectly.

"Hey, Tim, can you help me with my tie? You do it so well, and I am just making a mess of it."

"Sure, it's easy. Let me help you."

He stood directly in front of me and made eye contact. He moved quickly to the tie. He suddenly fumbled around with it and could not tie it. I suddenly felt a throbbing between my legs. I hoped Tim didn't look any further down than the tie knot.

After trying a few more times to tie my necktie, he looked at me shyly. "I don't really know how to do it except from the way I usually do it."

"What do you mean?" I asked.

"Just turn around."

Unbelievably, he grabbed my shoulders and turned my body so that my backside was pressing against his frontside. He put his arms over me, pressed against my back in what could only be described as a compromising position. He reached over my shoulders and effortlessly tied the knot. My heart nearly burst, as did another organ. I finally started to suspect that maybe we were more than just friends.

"Thank you," I sighed, realizing that life could be surprisingly merciful. I was feeling happier than I had ever felt since coming out. I was going to the opera with Tim. Something I could never do with Casper or Jack. It amazed me how one person could make such a difference. I could even think of Casper without feeling the pain because I didn't feel so alone anymore. Maybe Tim was his replacement.

Sneaking a peek at Tim's lanky body, I realized he was attractive but in different ways. Casper was strong, so I could be vulnerable. With Tim, it was he who was vulnerable. And somehow that made me feel good.

Tim had put on a blazer. We were both wearing blue jackets. They were different shades of blue, but still we sort of matched.

"Ready to hit the town?" I asked.

"We're ready."

Chapter 16: Gretchen at the Spinning Wheel

We walked close together to the concert. It was in the Theater Arts Building's main hall. That meant we had to walk past the smaller theater where Casper and I had done it. My heart pounded as we neared the small theater's gray door. My thoughts were storming—about Casper, and of Tim possibly hearing rumors about me from someone backstage. Then thoughts of Jack, Rags, mysterious men, all my sexual fears. I had to put them all out of my mind. I would concentrate on pure and innocent Tim.

We gave our tickets to a very cute student usher. He took Tim's ticket, tore it, and handed it back to him. He took mine and then looked up at me.

"Hey, don't I know you. Are you a music major?" asked the usher in a very effeminate voice.

"No!" I snapped belligerently, surprising Tim and the usher. "I mean no we haven't met, haha."

"Come on," said Tim. Tim smiled at me. "This is going to be fantastic."

Tim and I entered the auditorium. We sat in the middle seat of the middle row. I looked at the program guide: "Graduate Music Program," and in small print, "in cooperation with the Theater Department."

My gaze darted to the stage. I could have sworn I'd just seen someone I knew out of the corner of my eye. I shot a worried glance at Tim. He was bright and cheerful and seemed quite comfortable, his right elbow touching my arm as we sat together. The lights dimmed. Stage lights went up. There sat the school's prized Steinway concert grand and a lone music stand.

The mountainous Dorothy took the stage with her pencil-thin accompanist. Dorothy's commanding stage presence easily upstaging the imposing piano. She scanned the audience diabolically, almost defiantly. The first notes sounded. She heaved a sigh big enough to suck all the air out of the theater. Then, off she sang with amazing force, bellowing Schubert. Her voice was amazing, even profound. Such a powerful sound layered with complexity, because her seeming lack of musicality nevertheless boomed with emotional drama. Her grunts and moans seemed more compelling than her grating trills or gravelly crescendos. Her voice suggested she had been through hell, and now she was there to comfort the audience. Sometimes I broke out into a sweat in embarrassment for her; at other times I was moved to tears. Either way, her singing was dampness-inducing. Despite the vocal gymnastics, the audience responded coolly. I overcompensated with my more enthusiastic vocal encouragement after every song. Tim glanced disapprovingly at me, whispering that my response was 'a bit over the top.'

Dorothy gave her emotions and her saliva unfettered reign in her last song, *"Gretchen am der Spinrade,"* about a lonely girl at a spinning wheel, pining for her lost lover.

The penetrating music started out simply yet so woefully. First, the piano wove a repetitive spinning melodic line, a circular theme with a detached staccato rhythm meant to mimic the whirring of a spinning wheel. It went on incessantly like a repetitive chore carried on through life's worst tragedies. This introduction, in a sad minor key was the deep wonderful world of musical heartbreak. She opened that final song with a disarming lushness she had almost hidden the entire night.

My peace is gone,
My heart weighs heavy;
I'll never find peace,
No, *never again.*

Dorothy seemed to sing to me as if her parents had thrown her out too … and her own Casper had rejected her … and all she wanted was to get him back.

When he is gone, my life is a grave,
The whole world has become bitter.

Dorothy's singing told me how I was feeling about Casper. She sang how desperately I felt the loss of Casper and how much I wanted Tim to substitute for him.

My poor head has gone mad,
My poor brain is broken.

I squirmed in my chair as more guilty flashes about

Casper arose. I'd had a chance at love when we spoke, and I had lost it.

I look only for him as I gaze out the window,
I look only for him as I walk through town.

Dorothy threw herself into the song's deepening pain. Her voice trembled, and I felt exposed. I wanted to grab Tim's hand for security. From the stage, her eyes met mine as if she knew what I was feeling.

Suddenly, remembering her lover, the music changed to the major key. At this point, I could not help gazing longingly at Tim.

His noble bearing, his intimidating presence,
The smile on his lips, the power of his eyes,
And his voice's magical flow,

Tim looked back at me, as if he understood my torment. Then my eyes darted away.

Just squeezing his hand,
but, God, his kiss!

The music came to a standstill to let me contemplate that aborted gaze and longed-for kiss. It seemed Dorothy lost her will to continue, but the weaving spinning-wheel piano theme returned and forced the song forward, back to the minor key. Reluctantly, she sang again:

My peace is gone,
My heart is heavy ...

When we thought she was completely exhausted, the piano accompaniment reminded us that it must all go on. I broke out in a sweat. Dorothy was singing my desperation, and I felt it in my forehead, hands, and underarms.

As she sang, her agony mounted:

My heart yearns after him.
Ah, if I could only grab him and hold him

She belted out the words, louder and more desperately, the room filling with the crescendoing force for which Dorothy was famous.

And kiss him all I wanted,
And in his kisses I could disappear!

It sounded as if her hope would triumph. But the accompanying spinning-wheel theme brought back the resigned, disarming, and lush voice which started the song.

My peace is gone,
My heart is heavy ...

The song ended in a tense silence. Dorothy, instead of just taking a bow, held her large frame stiff as if to stave off any applause. The pause allowed the emotions of the music to sink in. It seemed like an hour passed before anyone dared to clap. Then, finally, the audience's rain of cheers and applause came. She had triumphed after all.

"You have to admit that was amazing, Tim," I said breathlessly to my companion.

"Quite nice," said Tim. "Especially that end. Quite

unique—and right on score, I believe."

Dorothy took a victorious bow. To my surprise, Tim yelled, "Bravo!"

I, too, shouted "Bravo!" which made Dorothy blush.

After Dorothy walked off the stage, a student came out and wheeled the piano away. The house lights came back on.

"Where are they going with the piano, Tim? It's not over."

"I don't know—oh, yeah, it's the opera. They have an orchestra for that."

I loved opera, but for some reason, this one was filling me with dread.

Chapter 17: Parsifal

During the preparations for the opera, I could have sworn I saw Casper on stage. Then center stage a couple of students piled flimsy red fabric. Maybe I had started imagining Casper everywhere.

Other stagehands pushed a beat-up old couch toward the pile of fabric. My disorientation grew. I could swear one of the girls pushing the couch was Eula. Then the other familiar looking students started draping long lengths of red velvet over the stage. I was almost certain I saw Mr. Nathan backstage, but could not imagine what he would be doing there. Then I saw him.

"Casper!"

"What?" asked Tim.

"Oh—just someone I know from school—the Theater Department."

I grabbed my program. It confirmed my suspicions.

Excerpts from the "Magic Garden" scene, Act II from Parsifal, *by Richard Wagner (1878). A co-production with the DSU Music Dept. and Theater Dept.*

Graduation project for Nina Hudson, Kundry; Brian Crowley, Parsifal. With Sheila Watkins,

Berta Bremer, Hannah Feinstein, flower maidens.

The performers thank members of the Detroit Symphony Orchestra, and Prof. Richard Saxon who will sing the role of Klingsor.
Eric Turner — Music direction
Stage direction — Eula Meyer
Sets — Casper Tyres.

There they were: Casper and Eula the ones who knew the most humiliating details of my life. My heart pounded. At once it sunk in what I had done. I had knelt on the floor of a tech room and sucked some-one's cock. Even if Tim loved me, wouldn't he find that as compromising as I now did. Why did I do it? I was just like any other faggot "caring about the penis over the person," to quote that sex-ed book I had read as a child.

I knew Tim. Afterwards, he'd want to go backstage and talk to Nina. I panicked. I couldn't go backstage. There was no telling what could happen. Eula, or even Casper, with all they knew could really embarrass me. I was too terrified to even think of the consequences.

At that moment on stage, Casper stood still, looked into the audience, and I swear he made eye contact with me. Then he walked over to the couch on stage and moved it slightly this way and that, his muscled legs and muscular arms laboring against it. Then Eula walked on stage. I sank in my chair. She started talking to Casper. She pointed out into the audience. Then he laughed. My face burned. I buried my face in the program.

"You know, I never heard Parsifal before," I said, nose deep in the program, feeling suffocated and afraid. "Let's go; I don't think you'll like it."

"What?" Tim asked, astonished.

"You won't. It's really very Christian-oriented religious music, not actually an opera; that's what I heard anyway."

"I don't mind that. And Jamie, you love Wagner." Tim said. "Let's read the libretto. You taught me that: Read the libretto first before listening to the music so you know the story when the music starts."

"Yeah, Tim, of course, but there isn't a libretto here, you see?" I quickly flipped through the program pages without looking at them.

"Nonsense, it's probably in the back of the program." He flipped to the back of the mimeographed program. "See here?" He pointed to the text and translation. "There, that must make you happy, Jamie. Right?"

"Yes, I know. Let's read." I glanced at the text as if it were poison. I pouted. I didn't want to look up, but I didn't want to look down either. I was afraid this religious opera would preach a secret and subversive gospel.

However, as I started to read the text, the words did not strike me as particularly Christian. In fact, this scene seemed more like a bizarre sexual seduction.

The scene begins with young flower maidens mourning their dead lovers who then, at once, gleefully turn to seducing a young man who is clearly not interested in them. Parsifal does not mind playing at a distance, but when they get intimate, he pushes them away. The maidens' flirtations become nasty. They grab at Parsifal, who clearly is not into these seductive girls.

"A gay opera character?" I murmured.

"What?" asked Tim.

"Oh, nothing, just reading. Funny opera, eh?"

"It's a bit thick."

"This is different from any opera I've ever seen."

I read on, and the impression that Parsifal was gay was only confirmed. After he definitively pushes away these maidens, yet another woman, Kundry, arrives to try to seduce him. She tries to flirt, but that clearly is not going to work on this guy, so she reverts to laying on a bizarre motherly guilt trip.

Finally, this Kundry forces herself on Parsifal, and they kiss. He gives in for a moment and then is repulsed and yells out the name of a friend he promised to help, "Amfortas!"

After the kiss, Parsifal guiltily remembers a male friend's torment, perhaps a lover he must have abandoned:

Amfortas! Your wound! Your wound!
It now burns in my heart!
O lament! Lament! Fearful lament!
From deep in my heart it cries out
Oh! Misery! Deepest despair!
I saw his wound bleed; now it bleeds inside me.

I remembered my own betrayals. Parsifal merely kissed, but I knelt in a dark room, and I let Jack do it, and I slept with a woman I wasn't even attracted to. Parsifal and I both felt this deeper guilt. His words rang true in my own soul:

> *The terrible longing*
> *which seizes and grips all my senses!*
> *O torment of love!*
> *How everything trembles,*
> *quakes and quivers in sinful desire!*

I was no longer reading Parsifal but my own torment, and begging for the only way I could see out of it—through some savior, a redeemer. But Kundry was not giving up on seducing him. Giving up any pretense of love, she turns into a predator to have him 'for just an hour.' Jack had me for barely a few minutes. Parsifal has the presence of mind to repulse the predator for a loftier love.

Finishing the story, I was shaken. That was me: Parsifal's searing search for a solution to purge his soul of his sins. Could I, like Parsifal, do something that could redeem me? And if so, what did that mean? I thought about Casper. I looked at Tim. I was confused.

"Tim, we ha—have ta …" I could barely talk, as if there was a softball in my throat I could not swallow, "have to talk after the performance."

"What is the matter?" he asked.

"I don't know." I tried to look away and forced a smile. "Oh, look at the stage!" I rasped.

The stage had been transformed into a garish-looking brothel. There were streams of blood red velvet cloth draped like a wall spilling over onto the floor. The velvet cloth hung at the front of the stage and slanted steeply back behind a now grotesque pink-and-black lace-covered couch. The set looked lurid and claustrophobic. As a final touch, the stage was strewn with roses.

Just then I saw Casper again, my eyes unable to look away. Casper or Tim? Whose name would I call out if Kundry kissed me?

My heart pounding as I watched Casper bend gracefully to reposition the lace on the couch, I felt a terrible pressure in my chest as if any breath would be impossible.

The stage darkened. Casper walked off stage right. The crowd went quiet. The house lights started to dim. What would happen when Tim and I walked backstage? What would Casper do? What would Eula say? Tim's presence. Casper's body heat. My former escape, opera, now seemed to have me cornered. For a second I thought of darting out of the auditorium. Too late. The lights dimmed. The orchestra droned a chorus of A-notes as they tuned their instruments for the performance.

Tall pencil-thin Eric Turner, bouncing big afro, baton in hand, waded through the musicians in the orchestra pit. Applause erupted again. He stepped up on the conductor's stand. He magically silenced us as he turned with a flourish to face the orchestra.

Eric raised his baton, swung it downward.

I sat upright and stiffened to face the music.

Chapter 18: Compassioned Enlightenment

The music starts mournful yet childlike, with an un-Wagnerian simplicity. I wonder whether this is Wagner or a Gilbert and Sullivan.

Scantily clad young maidens fill the claustrophobic stage. I can see the outlines of skin and hair through the thin cloth, not always such a welcome sight with all the chorus members. But the frolicsome music helps suspend disbelief and pretend that these are, indeed, alluring young girls.

> *ALL MAIDENS (outraged)*
> *Here was the uproar!*
> *Where is the offender?*
> *Who is the scoundrel?*
> *Let's get our revenge!*
>
> *ALL MAIDENS*
> *(PARSIFAL wanders on stage.)*
> *There he is!*

Brian Crowley, playing Parsifal, shows off his physique, appearing on stage wearing a tight white shirt and white pants. His shirt is open in front, showing a brawny muscular hairy chest. He looks around at the maidens curiously as if he'd never seen a woman before.

MAIDENS
Why did you harm our lovers?

PARSIFAL
They barred me from seeing you.
Never before have I seen
such a graceful gender.
If I call you beautiful,
don't you think I am right?

MAIDEN GROUP II
So, you don't want to harm us?

PARSIFAL
No, of course not.

MAIDEN GROUP I
But you have done us so much harm!

MAIDEN GROUP II
You struck down our playmates.

ALL MAIDENS (abruptly happy):
Who will play with us now?

PARSIFAL
I will, gladly!

The maidens, whose anger has changed to gaiety, break into hearty laughter. Adoringly they encircle him. The music becomes even more frivolous and bouncy, almost like a Broadway tune. The girls break their circle to grab flowers from around the center-stage couch. The tempters tease Parsifal who somehow turns into me on stage.

They stroke my face with the flowers. Looking closer,

their genders were unclear; some look female, some male, yet others in between. They were still very attractive, but I wanted to stay away. For me, they represent those who care more about 'the penis over the person.'

I look at them. I am repulsed but yet attracted. The man-maidens form a half circle around me. I don't know what to do. The music grows soft and lush. Sweet fragrant scents rise from the ground; intoxicating. The orchestra's operetta-like perkiness gets a dash of Wagnerian sensuality. The man-girls' singing changes into cooing around me.

THE MAIDENS
Come, draw near, pretty boy! Come!
Our loving care
is for your delight and bliss!

JAMIE (entranced)
How lovely you smell!
Are you boy-flowers?

THE MAIDENS
We are all male, beauty
and alluring essence—

I feel a poke on my shoulder.

"Wow. Did you hear that?" whispers Tim. "If they can't sing the note, they shouldn't try." Tim jolted me out of the opera.

"That was pretty bad," I whisper back. Clearly, some singers are more successful navigating around the high notes than others.

The maidens on stage are still trying to seduce the uninterested Parsifal. They entwine him in a sea of limbs not unlike my nightmare.

The maidens tighten their grasp, and Parsifal snaps out of his stupor. He is uninterested—don't they understand?—but the maidens try harder to seduce him.

Malevolent intent combines with the erotic rhythms, turning the music into an opera on drugs. One by one, they pull, tug, and hug me, each maiden trying to outdo the other in luring me toward them.

FIRST MAIDEN
Take me to your bosom!

SECOND MAIDEN
Let me touch your cheek!

THIRD MAIDEN
Let me kiss your mouth!

PARSIFAL:
(trying to shake free)
You lovely throng,
if I am to play with you,
leave me some space

MAIDEN GROUP I:
What are you complaining for?

JAMIE:
Because you are bickering.

MAIDEN GROUP II:
We're only quarreling over you.

JAMIE:
Then stop it!

The man-maidens lunge after me, not caring about me as a person but only as some kind of receptacle. Still, it is alluring. What do they want to do? What would it feel like? What harm would it cause to give in? Do they want to love me, or hurt me or devour me? How would I know? The maidens stroke their roses over my cheeks—the flowers burn my skin. These creatures are repulsively sweet, yet I feel such a compelling attraction. Their beauty is disgusting, yet I am also sure I could forget all about Casper and Tim if I let them.

Slowly, they encircle me. The darlings continue teasing, touching and caressing. I feel my willpower weakening as if I don't want to fight them off, but I am.

CUTE MALE GROUP I:
You resist us?

MUSCLE MALE GROUP II:
(Crowding tighter around JAMIE)
Are you afraid of kisses?

SOME MEN
Just kneel before me.
Come to me, we need you!

OTHER MEN
(pulling JAMIE)
You can kneel in front of us!

YET OTHER MEN
Come on, forget them,
Undo our jogging pants!

OTHER MEN
(grabbing JAMIE)
No! Come to us!

FIRST MAN
(beginning to pull at JAMIE's clothes)
Loosen your shirt!

SECOND MAN
Undo your pants!

THIRD MAN
First, suck me!

FIRST MAN
Do me!

SECOND MAN
No, me!

JAMIE
(tearing himself away)
Leave me alone,
I don't want any of you!
(JAMIE is about to rush off stage, but he is
blocked by KUNDRY. She is dressed in what looks
like a gown of blood.)

KUNDRY:
Jimmy, stay here!

JAMIE *(stunned)*
No one's ever called me
That name except my mother

"Nina looks, great doesn't she?" whispers Tim.

"Amazing," I say, once again taken out of my revery.

I look on stage. Nina is stunningly beautiful. She places an arm caressingly on Parsifal's shoulder.

> *KUNDRY*
> *(KUNDRY gently guides PARSIFAL to the center*
> *stage near the couch.)*
> *I am bringing you*
> *the bliss and salvation*
> *you need.*
> *(KUNDRY glances contemptuously at the chorus.)*
> *You childish seducers, go away;*
> *he is not meant for your games.*
> *(The chorus droop in sadness.)*
> *Go home and tend to*
> *Your wounded men.*
>
> *MAIDEN I:*
> *Must I leave you?*
>
> *MAIDEN II:*
> *Must I shun you?*
>
> *CHORUS:*
> *Oh, woe is me!*
> *(Then suddenly happy)*
> *We'd gladly give up our lovers ...*
> *Just to be alone with you.*
> *(Venomously)*
> *Just you, you handsome tainted fool!*

The music becomes dark and threatening. Operetta-like frivolity leaves with the chorus. Alone with Kundry, the music turns dangerous, using the same erotic maiden themes but with lush orchestration and a lurid tonality.

Instead of being bouncy, it throbs with sensuality and forbiddance. I start to edge my way off the stage. But as I slowly move, Kundry circles around me like an animal sizing up its prey. Her movement stops me hypnotically.

KUNDRY
I'm calling to you, foolish naif—
you tainted fool, Jimmy.
(Moves closer to JAMIE, who stiffly tolerates the
approach.)
When you were still safe
in your mother's home,
you broke her heart.
(JAMIE lowers his head in shame.)
You lost her and
are now blind to her pain
and abandonment.
You're alone and unprotected.
You need someone to save you.
What brought you here,
if not for my protection?
You want me. You need me.

JAMIE (shaking his head)
I have never seen, nor dreamt, of anyone like you.
You who fills me with dread.
Do you also grow here like those flowery men?

KUNDRY
No, Jimmy, you tainted fool!
I am not like them,
I waited here just for you.

Kundry, transformed into a man, has this seductive

but sneering smile. He puts his hand on my shoulder to comfort me. At first, it is gross, the blood from his clothes staining my white short. As I draw away, he softly pulls me back smearing more blood on my shirt. Against my will, I come even closer as if pulled by a magnet. The disgust from the blood does not repel me enough to allow an escape.

> *KUNDRY (sneering)*
> *As your mother sang you to sleep*
> *her hot tears*
> *Were symbols of her fear and worries.*
> *Protecting you from your perverse world*
> *was her highest duty.*

The dark sensuous music seems to throw me in league with Kundry against Tim, against Casper, against any hope for love. Kundry continues her bizarre maternal guilt trip.

> *KUNDRY*
> *(now circling JAMIE, ready to go in for the kill)*
> *Your mother was all concern and love.*
> *But you abandoned her.*
> *Couldn't you imagine her*
> *wailing grief when you ran away?*
> *(sarcastic sympathy)*
> *Fearing her disapproval*
> *you did not consider*
> *her desperate grief.*

> *JAMIE (to himself)*
> *No, did not.*

KUNDRY
You recklessly loved man,
You violated her sacred laws

JAMIE *(to himself)*
Yes, I did.

KUNDRY
She waited for you for nights and for days.
Only your distance silenced her cries.
But her heart broke
And she found her only solace and peace
When your own mother vanished.

JAMIE
What did I do?
Where was I? Mother!
Your son, your own son killed you!

"Are you okay?" Tim whispers.

I didn't realize tears were streaming down my cheeks. Embarrassed, I quickly wipe the tears away.

"I am okay—fine—beautiful music," I whisper back. On stage, Kundry continues her emotional chess-like seduction. But Parsifal begins to recall what he has been trying so hard to hide from himself.

PARSIFAL
What else have I forgotten?
Have I been so heartless?
I haven't thought of anyone
Except myself!

KUNDRY
(moving uncomfortably close to him)

If pain was unknown to you,
Then I could never console you!
I'll make it all go away.

The compelling alluring music pushes me closer to Kundry. She holds out her soft hands. I want to approach her, but something tells me not to. With a sly grin and quiet confidence, Kundry crowds me. But I step back. With a grimace, Kundry turns into a delicate and mean man, someone I vaguely knew. He backs me toward the couch. The energy alternates between repulsion and obsession. As he draws near, I still back away in excitement and fear.

KUNDRY
(backing JAMIE ever closer to the couch)
Give into me.
Your love will create repentance,
Tainted fool, let me cleanse you,
I will give you the salvation you yearn.
Come, know the passion and love that
Once created you,
Your mother's last gift—
This first kiss of love!

I step back until I fall back onto the hideous couch. The flowers and fluff surround me like a sexy plague. I lean back trying to sink away from him into the cushions. Lying on the couch, I look up as Kundry bends over me and folds sinewy arms around me like a spider over its prey. The repulsive bloody cloth drapes over my body, staining my clothes with his hot damp blood.

Kundry mounts my body, lowering his face to my mouth. I feel myself giving in to this madness. Kundry's heavy breathing floods my senses. I can't breathe. I choke. The past I have so loathed to remember confronts me at once. As Kundry kisses me, I remember clearly the first time when I violated myself when I was once—untainted—so innocent. And I recognize who Kundry really is. I push him off the couch. He falls to the floor. I jump off the couch and address the confessor audience.

JAMIE (wailing like a wounded animal)
Gary! Yes, Gary!
The wound!
The wound burns my heart!
Fearful grief!
From the depths of my heart it cries out.
I can't believe what I did to myself!
I was just a child!
I saw the wound bleeding;
now it bleeds in me!
(JAMIE touches the bloodstains on his shirt and
gets blood on his hands, which he regards with
awe and disgust.)
No! It is not this wound.
Here in my heart is the burning!
I loved him. I loved him!
(JAMIE falls to his knees, grasping his heart.)
The longing, the desperate yearning,
which seizes and grips me!
O torment of love!
How everything jolts, trembles, and quivers

with desire!
(KUNDRY stares at JAMIE in terror and
amazement; JAMIE falls into a trance.)
Finally, my dull brain focuses on a higher love;
Something above myself, outside of me,
where holier blood flows:
love's redemptive bliss, divinely mild,
which quivers through every soul.
(Jamie suddenly finds the enlightment he craved.)
Only here, in my heart, the pain cries out.
Tim's lament I hear,
the pleading—the painful pleading:
"Someone, help me, come out of the closet!
Save me, I don't want to
commit suicide in this isolation!"
Thus rang his terrible plea clearly in my soul.
And I—a fool, a coward,
Giving into senseless regrets!

What a fool and coward I have been fixating on my own worries. I have been so self-centered when all this time Tim might need me. When I was closeted, I had tried to commit suicide. This pain could be plaguing Tim, sitting right next to me. How blind can I be?

But now it's Casper in Kundry's blood-soaked clothes. He ignores my torment for my newfound pure love. Casper comes toward me again, but I back away.

CASPER
Don't be frightened of me;
I forgive you for pushing me away.
Forget Tim.

He's young and pure.
You're just a tainted
damaged fool.

JAMIE (Meditatively)
(CASPER guides JAMIE to his knees. CASPER
caresses JAMIE but he is lost in thought.)
Yes, your voice.
It was a voice just like yours.
Your smiles, your caresses, your lips.
Laughing flittering lips,
Then you lowered your pants,
Quivering and erect
Before my very eyes
And I opened my mouth—
Ha! This kiss!
But I didn't know better, I was too stupid!
(JAMIE, abruptly aware of CASPER's touch,
jumps up.)
Corrupter! Get away.
Get away from me forever
Both you and Gary!

CASPER (hurt, begging for sympathy)
Don't give me that,
You loved it.
We didn't point a gun to your head.
We did nothing,
You did everything yourself!
You even let a stranger fuck
your once-virgin asshole.
We are willing to forgive you,
But you need to come to us,

Make us feel better, help the ones who
Really need what you have to offer!
Look at yourself!
(JAMIE looks ashamedly at the blood smears on
his clothes.)
You are stained so deep in sin.
Leave Tim; he can still save himself from you
Otherwise, he's better off dead
than tainted by you.
You sucked off Gary,
more times than we can count;
you even went up to a male prostitute,
By then you were already a pro.
But we forgive all that; no one else will.
We can give it to each other.
Even if it violates God's holiest commandments,
We can have at least an hour of salvation's bliss,
Just give me an hour and we can be damned
forever.

I feel a hand on my shoulder. The orchestra blares
an alarm. A trembling hand takes my arm. I look. Tim
lets go. What is he going through? I look at his face; it
seems as moved as mine. Has he similar nightmares? Is
he going through a similar hell? How could I have missed
it: he needs me. Me? No one ever needed me before. But
now I can help someone in need, someone I love.

JAMIE
(pushing CASPER away)
No, if I were to betray him now,
You and I would both be damned forever,

Even for just an hour.
(CASPER tries to bear-hug JAMIE. JAMIE
wriggles away. CASPER draws nearer.)
There is a different salvation I seek,
One that I now see:
To help someone in need,
To truly love someone
For themselves.
But to save them I must be lovable
(JAMIE pushes CASPER back.)
Go away, Casper, don't you see
what you are doing?
What a mistake?
(CASPER gropes JAMIE, who turns away.)
What misery is there
in this world that
we seek salvation
at the very source
of our own damnation.

Hot tears, again, stream down my face. Something is changing in me. Something profound, and I am going to be called to action. To discard a protective naiveté. Yet removing that protective layer of a fool is perhaps the most dangerous act I can ever perform. I fear leaving its protection but not as much as the fear of cowardice.

CASPER
(Getting up, CASPER grabs JAMIE tightly. His
face is incredibly close to JAMIE's.)
My cock revealed the world to you;
I brought you out of the closet!
(CASPER sprays spittle on JAMIE.)

While you were humiliating yourself
in a basement,
I let you love me.
You owe your enlightenment to me.
(CASPER unzips his pants. Forces JAMIE on his
knees. CASPER smiles triumphantly as he towers
over him. JAMIE looks up plaintively to
CASPER's glowering eyes.)
If I awakened your spirit then
Redeem me now! (CASPER shoves his erect penis
threateningly in the face of JAMIE, who seems
repulsed yet immobile.)
Save the world.
If that's your calling
Just save me, too.
Now I can make you a god for an hour!
And you will save me,
Heal my wounds,
And for that ecstasy, let us both be damaged forever.

JAMIE
(repulsing CASPER, JAMIE gets up)
Save you?
That's exactly what I am trying to offer you!

CASPER
(angrily grabbing JAMIE from behind and trying
to undo JAMIE's belt)
Just do me!
for one hour in deathly longing.

The orchestra triumphantly blares my defiance and
gives me new strength. A resolute horn call sounds my

new determination. The final decision has been made.

JAMIE
(tearing myself away)
My love and redemption are yours!
Just guide me back to Tim!

CASPER
No, never!
You'll never go back to him.
I'll stop you, no matter what it takes!

I feel a squeeze; I shudder in my seat. It's Tim, squeezing my hand. Somehow, we are holding hands. When? I wonder. How and when did he grab my hand? And isn't this exactly the proof I need? Quickly, Tim releases my hand. I look at him; his face quickly turns rigid. Slowly, he notices that I am still looking at him. Tim gazes back at me. I look into his eyes. I am not going back. I expose myself. I take the risk. I am going to help him.

Suddenly, the orchestral music takes on a violent marching rhythm driving Kundry's anger. Nina is now standing on the couch. She stretches out her arms in a grotesque sign of a cross. She realizes Parsifal's rejection is final. Furiously, she calls out. Her voice rings out clear as glass. Nina has been saving up her vocal reserves for this moment.

KUNDRY (calling out)
Stop him! Block him!
(glaring at PARSIFAL)
You will never find him!

Or any road
that leads you away
from being a degenerate.
(shouting)
Stray! Be lost!
I call to the one I trust
To destroy you!
(Onstage lights flash. She jumps off the couch. A
garish green light glares from the back of the stage.
PARSIFAL stands up defiantly center stage.)

KLINGSOR (an unseen vengeful voice)
Stop there! I'll strike you
with just the right weapon!
This fool falls to me by his own master's spear!
(A huge spear appears above the stage. It soars
dangerously toward PARSIFAL. He raises his arms
in the air, and the spear floats harmlessly into his
hands. The cheesy staging provokes unintended
laughter, but the music overpowers it.)

PARSIFAL
(holding the spear aloft, forcefully mimicking
KUNDRY's cross-like stance)
With this sign, I destroy your power.
Just as it shall heal the wound
You inflicted with it.
Now, into misery and rubble
It will destroy your lies and magic!
(PARSIFAL smashes the spear against the floor.)

The red velvet on stage flies off into the wings and
with it any pretense of hiding the miserably ugly set. The
orchestra wails a pathetic crescendo. The music echoes

a mutilated version of the erotic maidens theme.

*(The magic garden disappears. The naked stage is
bare and dark; only Parsifal's spear glows.)
(A dim spotlight upstage reveals flower maidens in
ragged street clothes lying in a heap as if dead.
Kundry sits on the floor, insecurely wrapping her
arms around her legs. Parsifal stares directly at
Kundry. He seems veiled in blood.)*

One last time, the erotic maiden's theme returns with
vehemence.

*PARSIFAL
(looking down at KUNDRY in bitter compassion)
If you truly need me, you know
where you can find me!
(Parsifal walks resolutely off stage. Kundry is left
rocking in a fetal position.)*

The music ends with a horn braying like a wounded
animal and then a dissonant drum roll. Kundry
collapses.

Everything is ephemeral.
Stage lights black out.

Chapter 19: Release

Thunderous student applause rained down on the stage, complete with screaming and whistling.

I covered my face with my hands to mask my silent crying. Tears were still streaming down my face. I felt delivered from some unfathomable phantom. I realized I had to be honest to finally realize my integrity, to try and save Tim. If he was suffering, I had to help him. As Parsifal was saving Amfortas from destruction, so I would be Tim's redeemer—redeeming him from a closeted hell or worse, a possible suicide. I felt an urgency I had never known before. But I first had to get him back to our room to talk intimately.

Joining the crowd, I applauded wildly, not just for the performance but for the opera. Parsifal was a redeeming gay character who seemed to have redeemed me and shown me how to redeem others. Parsifal's last words still echoing in my ears:

> *If you truly need me, you know*
> *where you can find me again!*

To me, it sounded like, "For the first time, I know who I am and what people should expect of me."

House lights back on, Nina took a bow, her fan club

in the audience yelling and whistling. I jumped to my feet clapping my hands raw.

I was in a post-performance euphoria. I looked with loving eyes at Tim. I beheld the one with whom I had to speak. I could redeem my past by doing this one decent thing. Our relationship had been transfigured. Tim holding my hand—however it happened—had sealed it. And he smiled back at me. I felt this moment of grace, the grace Parsifal longed for. Tim would forgive my sins. Finally, I had someone who I could tell about Casper, about Jack, about the guy in the burned-out house, even about Gary—and he would understand. More than understand, he would help me figure this all out. I felt a strange courage to delve even deeper into my childhood and confront whatever demons lingered there. This one would not hate me for whatever I did.

"Want to go back and talk with Nina?" Tim asked, snapping me out of my reverie. "We have to congratulate her, Jamie, that was fantastic,'" Tim insisted. Too late to protest—Tim was already pushing through the crowd— I followed along backstage.

There is something breathtaking about going back-stage after a performance. In front, you see the magic of the stage; in the back, you feel the magic of the per-formers' relief as if it were raining excitement. In addition, you see all the smoke and mirrors responsible for that sorcery: the simple wires and pulleys that made the magic garden disappear, the rolled red construction paper that formed the roses ... and Casper. Our eyes met for a second. I smiled. He flashed a half smile, winked, and walked away. I heaved a sigh of relief, wondering what I was afraid of in the first place.

Backstage the performers' adrenaline is sky-high, and people are overjoyed. I joined Tim in the receiving line to congratulate Nina. Nina was beaming, though drenched in sweat. She hugged and kissed Tim. Then she hugged me tightly and kissed me, giving my butt a Kundry-like squeeze.

"You were fantastic, Nina," I gushed. "That was dramatic and beautiful. And that was amazing music. It suited your voice perfectly. I never heard this opera before, but you really made a fan of me."

"You don't know *Parsifal*, Jamie?"

"Never before tonight."

"Really, you disappoint me; you're the school Wagnerian."

"I noticed ..." I said, having remembered one of her few vocal gaffes.

"You noticed what?"

"Toward the end, I am sure you're not supposed to declaim 'Irre! Irre!' like Maria Callas."

"Okay, you restored my faith in you." She looked over my shoulder, then impetuously kissed me again. "You are such a darling."

"You were ahead of me!" cried Eric from behind me.

"It's not my fault; you did it much faster in rehearsal," Nina quipped without taking her eyes off me.

"Really? That's your excuse for your early entrances?" snapped Eric.

"She was fantastic!" yelled Tim defensively.

"Thank you, dear boy. Now tell me, Jamie, did you think I was ahead of the orchestra?"

"Let me see, how can I answer this and still keep my future comp tickets to the Metropolitan Opera?"

"Wise answer, kid," barked Eric.

"Don't pick on my cutie, Eric; you've had yours."

Then I saw Casper and Eula approaching.

"Nina, we're holding up your line," I said, anxious to go.

"Okay, but not before a kiss."

I went to give her a peck on the cheek, but Tim beat me to it. I followed suit. She grabbed my face and French-kissed me the way she had just kissed Brian on stage. Embarrassed, I muttered, "It was amazing, Nina; it was. I loved your performance."

Then I turned to Tim. "Wanna go back to the dorm?"

Tim flashed a beet-red blush. "No, I wanna go out for coffee."

"Coffee?" I asked.

"We have to talk about something. I would feel better doing it away from the dorms, if that's okay."

"Okay? That's fine," I agreed with my new boyfriend. Oh, just the thought of that made my heart pound. "Tonight is her night; we can see her tomorrow."

"I think she likes you," he said defensively.

"Don't be ridiculous." I was tempted to grab his hand again, but discretion won the day. "Where should we go? Harmony Café? It's open all night."

"Okay."

Outside, it was cold and snowing. There was an awkward silence as we walked. I was very happy. I had a feeling this talk over coffee would be trouble-free in contrast to what I'd anticipated. His shy smile gave this away as we headed over to the Harmony Café.

Chapter 20: Pure Fool

The Harmony Café was a run-down Formica-countered coffee shop. Since it was open all night, students often frequented the place when they needed to pull an all-nighter study session. The night manager, Harmon, was an acerbic old man with a lack of concern that allowed us to hang out on a single cup of coffee as long as the real head of the place—the waitress, Melody—was willing to put up with us.

Melody waddled over toward us as if every step was a world-wearying pain. She looked haggard and wise, with a very tough exterior—the kind that developed to protect a soft soul in a harsh life. Melody was very kind when she was in a good mood, but she felt obliged to masquerade it in a cloak of futility. Melody always let me stay and study as long as I never made any demands. This meant waiting patiently for the next refill when a nearby paying customer asked for a cup.

Melody looked in a bad mood this evening, but when she saw me, she smiled sharply. That could mean sweetness or bitter sarcasm. "Oh, Jamie. Great," she greeted me sarcastically, "you and your *friend* can just sit at any *small table* you want."

I looked around, hoping for privacy. But people were

spread out everywhere. I led Tim to a small half-booth in the back.

We took our seats, and our eyes wandered the room until they finally found each other.

"I don't want no faggots in here!" bellowed Harmon's crotchety voice.

I looked over and saw a very drunken woman say in a man's voice, "That's Mr. Faggot to you."

Tim turned and looked on in disgust as a drunken drag queen demanded service and the manager clearly refused to serve her.

Melody rushed from the back of the kitchen to the front of the café.

"Harmon get back in the kitchen. I'll handle this. You gonna ruin the whole place; go on, git."

"I don't want him here!" Harmon cried.

"He's leaving right now," snapped Melody, who turned to the drunken drag queen and said, "Sugar Lee, wait till the old pill goes back to his cage."

"No, I'm going, I know when I'm not wanted."

"Will you sit down? I'll bring your tea. Don't pay him no mind."

The drag queen rolled her eyes, "Tell that old man to chill out. Say, can you bring me a doughnut, honey? I need some comfort food."

"We got cherry pie tonight."

"Girl, what can I do with cherry pie? Them been popped long ago."

"Faggot!" Harmon cried from the kitchen. Melody and the drag queen laughed.

Tim's face burned dark red. And I knew I was exactly correct: He was in the closet.

"Does that bother you?" I asked.

"Not a very dignified spectacle, is it? No wonder they're hated."

"Drag queens? They're not harming us, Tim. They don't do anything to you, do they?"

"No, but ... strange, they're just strange."

"Colorful's more like it ... it just takes getting used to. Come on."

I tried to gaze into his eyes, but he avoided mine. He looked nauseous.

We nursed our coffees. We traded stiff smiles. An awkward silence fell.

The café quieted down. The couple next to us left, leaving us with relative privacy. The time was right. I was confident. Tim had held my hand in the theater. He freaked out over the drag queen, but he was closeted and hypersensitive. I had been there, too. We exchanged glances; we enjoyed our silent intimacy. The time for the Parsifal-inspired courage was now. With measured words I put my integrity on the line.

"You can be honest with me. Is anything on your mind—concerning us?" I asked. I was determined to be truthful, but I would prefer if he made the first move.

"The Magic Garden was great, wasn't it? What did you think of the performance?" asked Tim.

"It was beautiful. Nina was great; Brian was better—but Eric was wrong. She didn't race ahead of the orchestra. He's just jealous. You said they were breaking up, right? But the music was great, the story. ... Did you know The Magic Garden was actually an excerpt from Wagner's *Parsifal*? I didn't know *Parsifal* at all. After how he treated those flower maidens, Parsifal certainly wasn't interested in girls, was he?" We shared a laugh, and we both relaxed.

"No, he sure wasn't, at least not the way Brian played him," Tim said.

"It's in the libretto. He's ... like us."

"I suppose."

Tim blushed. Finally, I had the inroad I needed. I felt compelled to kiss him right there, but we were in a café, so I restrained myself.

"Brian sang okay," said Tim, "but that sword floating into Brian's arms was really cheesy. And the way the magic garden was supposed to—I don't know, what was that—collapse?"

"They did their best with a nonexistent budget," I replied defensively. "I thought it was clever from a theatrical standpoint. The spear was awkward, but the music made up for it, don't you think?"

"The music is the whole point."

"What do you mean? This whole production wouldn't have been possible without the Theater Department."

"They just provided the hall."

"No, Tim, they provided a lot more than that. The director and the set designers, I know some of them. Eula, the director and ... Casper, the ... whatever are in my ... class." I looked at Tim. I imagined him cutting his wrists or worse. The thought made me shiver. "Tim, I am just very glad we got to go tonight, together—"

"Oh, I know. This is a really special day." Tim perked up. My heart pounded for joy. This was going to be easier than I thought.

"Special?" I asked.

"Yes, that's why I wanted to talk. About love. I need your advice," Tim beamed. He stole my line! He put his elbow on the table and propped his chin in his hand. He had a relaxed, silly smile. I was relieved. It looked like I didn't need to worry about his committing suicide, after all. This would be effortless.

Melody came by with her coffeepot. "My coffee boys. Having anything else?" We shook our heads no. "Well, just holler if you hustle some money off of someone. We got cherry pie tonight." She walked away. I turned back to Tim.

"Love? You were saying? You mean, we're both in love," I said. "I have to be completely honest, Tim, I really learned tonight that in loving someone, you can really actually save yourself, redeem yourself. Through our love, we are able to redeem agonies in our past."

"Exactly," said Tim with an odd kind of sigh.

I started feeling a tremor as if the room were vibrating. I snuck a discreet look under the table. It was Tim's leg shaking like a mini-earthquake.

"It's true. Might as well admit it," said Tim in a moment of resolution. He smiled again and seemed confident. I thought he was about to kiss me. *Oh, when we get back to our room!* I thought.

"You'll think this is crazy, but I was actually a little worried about you," I said as sensitively as I could.

"Believe me, I know; you weren't alone. But still, love, like you said, redeems us all."

"Who would have thought … for us two, right?" I said, barely able to put the sentence together.

"Too true," said Tim. Then, in a suddenly shaky voice, he added, "Say, tell me who you're in love with, and I will tell you who I am."

Of course, he was shyer than me. I looked at his sweet smile. He looked at me. He waited for me to say something.

It is obvious who we love, isn't it? I thought.

Awkwardly, he waited for me to say something. I was trying to think of what to say as it suddenly seemed more complicated than I imagined. The jumbled communications with Eula and Casper still fresh in my mind told me not to lay down my cards just yet.

"You first," I said a little too quickly.

Tim looked down at my hands. I thought he would hold them, to set my mind at ease. He continued to look down. He did not move. I felt my hands shaking. He glanced at me as I spilled coffee, trying to lift the cup with my trembling hand.

"Oh, this is just a nervous twinge." I forced a laugh. "It runs in the family … you were … saying who … you love?" We were quite pair with shaking limbs.

"Who do I love?" he asked. Tim's face went crimson; and he seemed about to cry. His emotional turmoil subsided, and a strange smile came to his face. I knew I would be safe.

"Nina," came the bombshell.

Did he change his mind? How could I have been so wrong? He didn't love me. And, oh God, what had I committed myself to?

Then I realized he was still talking, saying something I needed to hear. Panic set in; I could not think straight.

"She's seeing Eric," he hastily babbled. "You know, that conductor. But she asked me if I wanted to go to the Art Institute with her next weekend. She did. She really did. That means something, doesn't it?"

No, it doesn't, you fool.

Which was more clueless of Tim: not noticing Nina was flirting with me or not noticing that I was flirting with him? Tim thinks Nina loves him. I thought Tim loved me. We were both pure fools.

Tim misinterpreted my distress.

"I know, you must be friends with Eric," he continued.

I didn't even know Eric. I felt my stomach tighten, and then realized he had stopped talking and was waiting for a reaction of some kind. I wasn't even sure what he had said.

"I am happy for you. That's great. I am just ... surprised."

"Yeah, I know," he added.

"You have been alone for so long. This is just ... what you need. But are you sure it's a date? I mean, like a *date* date?"

"What else could it be?" Tim replied, oddly relieved

and sighing. "I have never even been on a date before. I am so excited. It's so important for me to hear you ... approve."

Tim smiled and shot that sweet longing look into my eyes again. I guess it hadn't been love in his eyes after all. But there they were; his deep brown welcoming eyes. Those eyes were apparently open to misinterpretation. But hadn't we held hands? I almost kissed him. He must have noticed how physically close we had been. We smiled into each other's eyes. The incongruity of it all had my brain swirling. What to do seemed murky now.

Tim looked at me with a happy smile.

"Wow. It's really getting late. Classes tomorrow. We better get the check." I flailed around, looking for Melody. She was arguing with Harmon behind the counter. I looked at Tim; his nervousness came back, as did our personal earthquake. Unsure what to do, I babbled, "Nina, good choice. She was great tonight. She really made Brian look good. Eric was great, but he rushed it. Don't you think? Yes, it felt rushed. That's why Nina sounded a little bit out of sync, just a little bit. Didn't you think? The performance. It was a bit, you know, rushed ... Melody!"

Melody was still too involved in her discussion with Harmon to notice my plea for attention.

Tim looked at me and laughed. "Don't worry. I promise I won't disapprove, no matter who *she* is. Come on, tell me ... Tell me who's the lucky one? ... Who do you love?"

LET ME OFF THE HOOK, DAMMIT! I need a

break, Tim. I lost my parents. I lost everything already. Don't do this to me!

"It is getting late," I said looking at my wrist. "We should get back to the dorm. I am relieved I told you. We can cuddle up tonight. It will be cold; I don't mind." I no longer knew what he was talking about. Two men don't cuddle. He was very confused. I could not let myself off the hook. I had a responsibility.

"I need to tell you, Tim." I stared coldly at him, trying to center myself. I felt sick thinking of the appalling idiocy of believing I could save him. Still, what if he needed to hear it? Hadn't I slept with Dara before I really knew myself? I still felt obliged to try and save him; but who would save me? I wondered. I cast about for words.

He smiled encouragingly.

I relaxed. Maybe it wouldn't be so bad. He'd be understanding. I took a big gulp of coffee but breathed in a deep sigh at the same time. The coffee caught in my throat. "I don't think I should tell you." I spit out coffee between coughs. Coffee even spurted out of my nose.

"Of course you can." Tim seemed to be almost pleading as if he needed to hear it.

The coffee-induced gagging continued. Tears formed in my eyes but did not leak out. The coughing stopped. *Improvise something, anything*, I urged myself. I had one more chance. Was there a way out of this with honor? Cold calculation. Could I make up someone? Stage phone calls and write letters to myself? That's probably what he was going to do. I wished I had given in to Nina backstage or stayed with Casper again.

Anything but face this.

What price integrity? I was about to find out. I could not lie anymore. That was the whole point of all this struggle, of *Parsifal*, of this pain, this coming out. Wagner inspired me to a new level of responsibility to be myself because more was at stake than just me. It was also the people around me. I'd lied too much to myself, to my mom, to too many people. And to Tim, it could really be a sin if he were really struggling.

"I need to tell you," I deadpanned.

"It's okay, Jamie. Hey, I was nervous telling you. Just relax. We're friends. How bad could it be?" he asked with a laugh.

His smile started to falter. He no doubt had begun to wonder why I was hesitating.

"It's nobody the way you're thinking, Tim ... it's different ...you know ... I love him very platonically. Intellectually, know what I mean?"

He didn't. Plus, I had just used the male pronoun. Tim's smile began to fade, and the earthquake suddenly stopped. Honesty would exact a high price tonight.

"Parsifal and Amfortas, you know ..." *Give it up, Jamie,* I thought, *just say it and be done with it.*

I stopped myself. I smiled a bitter, hopeless smile. I was so ashamed, but I didn't want that. I straightened myself up, cleared my throat, and tried again with all the dignity I could muster.

"I love you, I do. I love you," I stated clearly and loudly and—to me—unconvincingly.

When the L-word fell the second time, Tim's smile

disappeared. The couple two tables over stared at us. We both blushed. I forced myself to look at him, pleadingly, right in the eyes. Instead of that joyful meeting of eyes for which I had longed, I saw a face that betrayed that he was grossed out. He looked at his hands.

"You held my hand," he said bitterly. Then, worst of all, he started to laugh, not at me, but a defensive kind of laugh. The laughter was unbearable. I wanted to dive into my cup of coffee and hide beneath the rim. His face had flashed shock and disgust, though he did his best to hide it.

"F-Faggot," he spat. "Oh shit," he barely whispered. Then, looking at me, he muttered, "It's okay. You said it was an intellectual thing. I better get on home." He looked at the table, then he said something I didn't quite hear. He was gone.

I'd thought I was going to help him; instead, it felt like I had betrayed him and our friendship. Like I was putting the moves on him. As if all I wanted was sex. How did something so noble so quickly devolve? Why and for what? I thought I had a duty to a friend. *I thought!* How could I have been so completely wrong? Instead of saving Tim, I embarrassed us both.

Oh well, at least I had told the truth again. The truth had a pretty good track record: no parents, no friends, no love, no money. Coming out of the closet clearly was not for the faint of heart or the financially distressed.

I looked around the café. It was as if everyone had magically disappeared. Everything was ephemeral.

I passed out.

Variation: Eject, Reject, and a Haven

December 1980

III Andante moderato
(Moderately slow)

Chapter 21: A Coffee for Your Troubles

The sound of a cup landing on the table awakened me. I had fallen asleep. Across from me, where Tim once was, I saw Melody sitting with her own cup of coffee.

I stared at my coffee cup.

"You going home anytime soon?" Melody wiped away some coffee I seemed to have spilled. I guiltily noticed my cup on its side and set it straight.

"Melody can I stay for a bit? I just had a fight with my roommate. I need some space. I have nowhere else to go."

"Suit yourself; we're not gonna be busy no more. Just don't go spilling my coffee." She poured me another cup of coffee. She picked up the empty creamer. "And I suppose the next thing you want is more of this cream."

"No, I'm fine without it, I'll drink it—" I suddenly felt so sorry for myself a lump formed in my throat.

"It's cool," she said, getting up and taking her cup of coffee and coffeepot with her. She turned back. "Take that bigger booth and stretch out. Harmon's asleep in the back; he won't bother you none."

Moving to the booth she indicated, I felt myself collapsing. I lay down and, despite the multiple cups of coffee I had downed, I fell asleep. Later, I woke up with a shock, remembering I had to go to the bagel factory that morning. It was my first day on the job.

"Oh, shit! What time is it?" I yelled.

Melody ran over to my booth. "Jamie, calm down. You wanna give me a heart attack? Jesus, I don't want no fuckin' swearin' in my place, especially at five-thirty."

"Five-thirty? I have to go to work, Melody." I rubbed my eyes.

"Wash up in the men's room and splash some water on that face. Go on; get your butt in gear."

"The bill?"

"The bill? For your coffee six hours ago? Your friend paid the check. Go on; get ready for your work." Melody marched away.

"My friend?" I had to wonder who she meant until I remembered Tim. Tim, who might not be my friend for long unless I could find a good excuse for my behavior. The good news was that I had all day to think of one.

After washing up, I took one step out the door of the coffee shop, and there was the memory of last night's utter humiliation waiting to greet me. Earlier last night, I'd wanted to stand tall but ended up with Melody needing to mop me off the floor.

Groggy and miserable, I trudged through the darkness to Amsterdam Street, the location of my new job. Adding to my Tim-induced misery, the music of *Parsifal* was haunting me, as was my ridiculous fantasy of being his savior, which brought back the memory of my mid-afternoon nightmare of Jack and the serial killer. It was at once preposterous and bone-chilling. Usually I forget a dream—even a nightmare—before I get out of bed, but this one stuck. The images of slithering half-humans haunted my trek through the desolate streets.

My route led me through the deserted campus. At this early hour, even that island of civilization felt lonely and unsafe. Reaching Woodward Avenue, the empty street looked relatively calm as I walked by closed stores with thick iron gates shielding them from the Detroit night. The street was unusually silent except for the occasional long-haul truck rumbling by.

Eventually, I arrived at the bizarre storefront of Brooklyn Bagel. The weird, gaily-painted building on the corner of Woodward and Amsterdam was a grim reminder of what Detroit had become. The blue paint had long since faded and chipped, in contrast to the monster-sized bagel, bright dingy-yellow and smiling, painted on the front. At the base of the bagel was a door and huge picture windows clad from top to bottom in an ugly retractable steel grate. The bagel factory looked more like a high-security prison than a bakery, making a mockery of the building's smiling bagel.

A black button next to the door like a pimple on the bagel. A loud bell rang out when I pressed it. A low buzz came from the dirty yellow door. A second or two later, the steel gate and the door popped open slightly. The stench of starchy overdone spaghetti billowed from the opening. I pushed the door and walked in.

Chapter 22: Brooklyn Bagel Oasis

The Brooklyn Bagel store was a relic. The beat-up counter where they sold the bagels. The counter was made of old maple wood and scratched clear plastic. Plastic dividers partitioned the counter into large sections marked "Plain," "Egg," "Onion," and "Salted;" as well as small sections marked "Raisin," "Pumpernickel," "Cheese," and "Garlic."

I heard sounds of a struggle going on. I ran to the back of the store. An older man—Sheldon Kaufman, who gave me the job—stood with a young dark-haired woman locked in an embrace with a gigantic steel kettle.

"Get over here!" yelled a female voice with a Brooklyn accent. A twinge of internalized anti-Semitism coursing through my nervous system, I ran to the struggling pair.

They were wrestling with the kettle, trying to keep it from tipping over. At the same time, water was still pouring into the vessel from a pipe above and overflowing onto the floor.

"Don't just stand there; turn the fuckin' water off. What are you, a moron?" yelled Sheldon, a tall, potbellied bald man with a thick mustache.

"How?" I yelled back.

"The fuckin' knob right there!" he said. He couldn't point and I had no idea where he meant. I looked at the wall behind me.

"Not there, over here!" He nodded his head to some pipes just behind him.

I walked toward the odd couple. The closer I approached, the stronger the scent of a stale, cumin-like body odor became. I walked right up to the man, and the smell made me flinch. Above him was a knob on a pipe leading to the kettle. I grabbed it, turned it. But I'd turned the knob the wrong way, and water sprayed all over.

"Hey! Asshole!" yelled the man.

I quickly turned it the other way, and the water stopped.

The kettle made a 'plop' sound as it settled back onto its base.

"Oh, fucking-Jesus-Christ-motherfucker, look at that! The boil's dead; it'll take forever to get this fucker to boil now," said the man, using his apron to wipe off the water I had sprayed on his face. He decisively turned to the petite, freckle-faced girl. "Connie don't be a fuckin' moron next time. Just leave it alone."

"Jesus, I was tryin' to help ya." Connie must have been fifteen or sixteen years old.

"Stalin should have such help. Now we're so far behind I ain't gettin' outta here until noon." He suddenly turned to me. "Hey, who the hell are you anyway?"

"I am J—Jimmy Goldberg? Remember?" I thought 'Jimmy' would hold up better here than 'Jamie' would.

"Goldberg? You? Oh, yeah, it's Monday. You're gonna work here dressed like that?" I was still wearing my nice but crumpled clothes from the concert.

"Er … uh … I had a long night, Mr. Kaufman."

"You did? Yeah, well great, just save that partying for after the Saturday night shift. Connie, we got any of those T-shirts left?"

"I think so; they're all extra large though," she said. She turned to me. "Hi, I'm Connie."

"Hi, I'm Ja—Jimmy Goldberg."

"Go get what's-his-name a T-shirt. You can change in the back."

"Thank you, Mr.—"

"And just call me 'Shel' and we'll be copasetic." Shel stuck out his hand and sadistically squeezed all the life out of mine. "C'mon back here when you're done; I'll show you what to do." Then he shot a glance at Connie. "Take your time; this is gonna take for-evah ta boil."

"Fuck you, Shel, I was trying ta help! Jesus, last time I do that!" Connie and Shel's caustic words did not match their lighthearted voices.

"Dat's exactly the point!"

"Ha, ha, ha, *hilarious*."

"It wasn't supposed to be *hilarious*."

When he turned his back, Connie gave him the finger. Then she flashed an exaggerated smile at me and motioned me to follow her to the back of the store. I felt relieved that this fight between Connie and Shel was diverting him from me. This looked like it was going to be hard work, much harder than I had imagined.

In my oversized "I got a hole!" bagel T-shirt, I walked back to Shel. I had covered it with a white apron. Shel sized me up and down.

"That ain't gonna work. Do me a favor," he said, grabbing another apron off a rack and rolling it up, "don't be a fuckin' moron, okay? Don't come to work in these clothes again." He wrapped the rolled-up apron around my waist. His sensitivity to my clothes caught me off guard and instantly endeared him to me. "This way you won't ruin your pants; they'll get dirty and wet on the boards. Your mother evuh teach you aboutta good night's sleep?"

"Yes."

"Well, get one the next time before you come in to work, get me? I am fucking teaching a zombie here. You're smiling, terrific. You think this is funny? You gonna remember anything I tell you?"

"I promise."

He grunted in contempt. He looked at me with blanket disappointment, shaking his head. Yet, I knew this was half-hearted.

"Okay, this is the bagel factory. While we are waiting *for the water to boil*, young man, I'll go over this very carefully. And remember our slogan, rule number one: Don't be a fuckin' moron." He sighed. But I almost wanted to laugh. "Oh brother, you're the pip. Bagels. First thing you do is take the rack of bagels out of the cooler in the back. Rule number two: If you are not going to bake a whole rack of bagels, don't be a fuckin' moron and take it out and over-proof my bagels. Go grab an empty rack and fill it up with the bagels you need from the cooler. Rule number two:"—apparently everything else was rule number two—"Wait twenty minutes before you go from cooler to kettle. That is what we call proofing the bagels, letting them rise. Don't be a fucking moron and put unproofed bagels in the kettle."

"Proof—" I tried to interject, as the mysterious terminology piled up.

"Proofed! Raised—you know, yeast, young man. Fuck, you're half asleep."

"I am not," I objected as my eyes drooped. He went on as if I had said nothing.

"Rule number two: Never get caught short with no bagels up front and no proofed bagels because you were a fuckin' moron. Then you have to put *unproofed* bagels in the water. And that's bad. They balloon up and taste like crap. Not the sort of thing we're proud of. Get it, *Jimmy?*"

"Yes, I do, sir."

"Rule number two: Do not fuckin' 'sir' anybody in this fuckin' place, hear me? Not me, not Sid, no one. Except Lola." He laughed hysterically to himself. I was delighted in a strange way. It was the first time since I left the café that I had forgotten all about my roommate, Casper, and everything else.

"Once you learn the pattern, you'll get how many bagels to bake. Don't worry for now how much to bake. You'll get the hang of it. Just do as I say in the meantime. Right? And no moronic behavior, capeesh?"

"Understood," I said.

"We'll see. You'll be a moron the first coupla days; don't sweat it. And I'll scream and call you names …"

"He sure will," Connie brayed.

"Thanks, Connie."

"Pleasure is all mine, Shel."

"As long as I am not screaming at you in a week from today, you're doing great."

"Ha!" blurted Connie.

Shel looked over at her. "And no comedians either, because Connie has that job already."

Shel taught me the glamour of baking bagels. The first step: The bagels needed to be boiled.

"Now, once they're in the kettle, in a minute you pinch them. They should be firm and a little soft. If they are mushy or spongy, then you were being moronic and over-proofed the goddamn bagels. Don't overproof my goddamn bagels, get me? Now, pinch them. The water is boiling. The bagel is gonna be hot—fucking hot. It's boiling water, capeesh? So don't be a fuckin' moron and go 'oh ew, they're hot.' You start out with pussy fingers and they're gonna hurt. See, look at me. Look at these hands." They were heavy and calloused. "When you're lucky, they get like this, and you don't feel nuttin'. Until then, just deal with it."

Then the bagels had to be put on cloth boards.

"Be sure to water down the boards and scrape 'em with the squeegee—squeegee? I hate that word. Anyway, these boards are lined with asbestos, but don't worry; it's the good kind. Then put the bagels on the boards."

After that step they went onto a conveyer belt and

into a long metal dryer to dry the tops of the bagels. Then Shel would walk around to the other end of the dryer, take the boards off the conveyor belt, and flip the bagels into the oven, so they landed dry side up in the oven. The oven had a series of ten stone shelves that rotated.

"If the bagels aren't dry, someone has been a moron and set the gas jets too low. But you can set it too high and burn my fuckin' bagels. Moronic. So test the bagels first as they come out of the dryer to see if they're wet. If they are, just stop the conveyer belt for a second until they are dry. If you don't do that, your bagels will wind up like Connie, with a flat bottom."

"Fucking moron!" yelled Connie.

They both laughed heartily. I even managed a smile.

Finally, when the bagels were browned in the oven, we slid a large thin wood sheet under the bagels and slid them into a huge wicker basket to cool.

"In the morning we bake about seven-hundred dozen bagels and then fill up the front. That's about two-hundred-and-fifty dozen. I leave around ten to make deliveries—but today I'll be late and get my customers angry at me and then—"

"Fucking drop it, Shel," yelled Connie. "Enough."

"Touchy broad," Shel sighed under his breath.

"I heard that, too, moron."

"Fuck you, I ain't no moron. Anyway, like I was saying before I was interrupted, while I am on my late deliveries, Connie does the front—"

"Asshole," Connie fumed.

"—and you bake until noon. I see the kettle is boiling, my non-moronic friend, so throw in three boards of egg bagels—the yellow ones over there—and let's get busy. We'll make the whole rack. Remember to sprinkle on the poppy seeds before they go in the dryer."

I boiled my first bagels. "Ow!" The water was boiling hot. With a large wire disk, I scooped the bagels from the boiling water and poured them out on the boards. They were still hot as I positioned ten bagels to a board and shook poppy seeds on them. In the dryer they went. Then I heard it.

"Moron! Fucking moron!" I wilted at the scream. "Too soft. Have to give these to that stupid United Dairies Store that always pays late. Don't do it again!"

I boiled the bagels and moved rapidly, quickly tossing the bagels out of the kettle and throwing the next batch into the kettle. Then, as fast as possible, I put the bagels uniformly on the boards, shaking poppy seeds or sesame seeds or salt over them. By the time the boards were in the dryer, I'd set up new boards, tossed the next batch of boiled bagels onto the boards. What was Shel doing all this time? Patiently waiting for the bagels to come out of the dryer to put them in the oven, and then taking the bagels out of the oven.

Shel was amazed I was a fast learner, and I was amazed that he was amazed because it was pretty simple and routine. He stopped yelling at me around the three-hundredth dozen. I just got into the groove of concentrating on just bagels, counting bagels, boiling bagels, pinching bagels, racking them, drying them, then boiling again. Occasionally I over-boiled them; I knew that because every time I did, Shel would bellow, "They're bloated, moron!"

Baking hundreds of bagels was thankfully mind-numbing and rhythmic. We worked together so fast that the bulk of the bagel baking was finished around 10:30 a.m. The store was scarcely open, even though customers had been trickling in before the opening time of 9:00.

Connie's job was watching the front, taking care of customers, and after the bagels were baked and cooled, stuffing them into bags of half a dozen. These bags were tossed into huge metal crates, each with the brand name of different stores on them. When I finished making the bagels, I helped Connie. Six bagels in a bag and you had to match the brand name on the bag with the store name on the metal crate. Farmer Jacks, for example, would get the Maiden brand bagels. The A&P got Ann Page brand bagels. In all there were some twenty stores and a dozen delis who sold our bagels as their own.

So that we wouldn't bag more bagels than a store had ordered, Connie counted out the bags needed per brand and put them in the crates. When all the bagging was finished, Shel loaded the crates into a truck outside and drove off to make the deliveries.

Before Shel left, Connie yelled after him, "Hey, Shel, just curious, what time is it?"

"Fuck you."

"Fuck me? It's eleven a.m., about the time you always leave, so fuck you."

After a short rush of some early shoppers, mostly

secretaries picking up bagels for their offices or schools, the shop calmed down. It was almost noon, my quitting time.

I put one last batch of bagels in the oven and sat down. Across from the oven, there were two white wooden folding chairs and between them a little makeshift white-painted wood cabinet-table, on top of which sat a radio. It droned the same Top-40 songs all morning, but back at the kettles, I hadn't noticed it much.

"Hey, Jimmy!" Connie was seated, lighting a cigarette.

"What?"

"I was talkin' to ya. What do I have to do to get your attention?"

"Sorry, I was thinking about … school."

"Are you in high school?"

"What? Me?"

"Yeah, you. You in high school?"

"No, I go to Detroit State," I bragged.

"Oh, one of those."

Just when I thought she was impressed, she added, "Everyone in my family is going to U of M. Shel went to MSU—couldn't you tell?"

I couldn't. "Detroit State's … not a bad school," I added defensively. "Well, it's cheap anyway."

"Whatever. What's your major?" she asked, more a test question than genuine interest. I wanted to lie, but I didn't.

"Theater."

"Really? I knew it." She smiled, almost a sneer. I knew I should have lied. "I had you pegged for that sort of thing," she said, looking me up and down, then turning her attention back to the front. "You look awful. Your eyes have dark circles under them."

"I had a bad night," I said self-consciously, unsure how I could explain it.

"I could tell the way you came in this morning. And the way you were dressed … Say, what happened to you?"

"I couldn't sleep." I wanted her line of questioning to just stop. I looked vainly for a customer to come in. But she was clearly losing her patience with me.

"Oh, come on; you gotta be a little more specific than that … What was it? Boyfriend dumpin' on ya?"

"Oh, come on! Boyfriend? … How could you tell?" I braced for another attack, yet another place to get thrown out. I felt like screaming and it must have showed.

"Relax. I don't bite. But believe me, you have it written all over you."

"I do not!"

"I can tell. Besides, those clothes."

"Why? It was the same thing Tim—never mind … You can't tell Shel." I said a little too sharply.

"Your secret's safe with me. *Faygela's* don't bother me none." Somehow, faygela out of her mouth sounded much less threatening than it did from my mother.

"I need this job, Connie. If anything should happen … I wouldn't be able to afford school or a place to live."

"That bad. Like I said, your secret is safe. But don't worry, no one here is gonna do anything."

"Not even Shel?"

"Shel? I don't think he cares about anything. You're all right. Hey, calm down you're not the only fag I know."

"Great, I'll be fine." I stiffened up.

"Yeah? Well, I want to ask you something. Can I?"

"Sure."

"It's personal."

"Go ahead."

"That's what I love about you fags, I can say anything and it don't upset you none. You're all alike and I love that. Anyway, get this, my boyfriend—he's a senior, see, and I'm a sophomore, you know."

"High school?"

"Of course. How old do you think I am anyway? ... You're not going to answer that, are you? ... You're gonna take good care of yourself, Jamie. Which by the way is a fag name if ever I heard—"

"You had a question?"

"My boyfriend, he says he wants to ... you know, do it."

"Have you done it before—"

"I ain't finished. He wants to do it, you know the way you do, know what I mean—of course you do: up the *tuckus*."

"He does?" How could she talk about this so freely? She paused, then looked at me like I was an idiot.

"Don't be retarded; you know all about it. Anyway,

like I was sayin'? Oh yeah, you know, it's not clean up there, and what happens if he fucks me in the *tuckus* and then wants me to suck him off? You know that sort of thing has to happen, doesn't it?"

"The bagels!" I yelled as I saw a shelf of dark-brown bagels rotating in the oven. I leaped to the oven, reached for the wood sheet, stopped the oven, scooped out the bagels, and put them in a basket.

I was staring at the dark-brown bagels.

She stared at the bagels and laughed. "Shel's gonna think you're a moron."

"Great."

"Relax. He's just glad you learn so fast. Jeez, you have no idea the bimbos we've had in here. Anyway, like I was saying, if you let him go all the way inside, you know, up there, and he comes inside your ass, what do you do when he wants you to suck him off? Would you do it?"

"Me?" *You're really asking me this question?*

"What do you do? He comes inside your ass, and you just suck him off or what?" Connie demanded.

"I get it, but if you let him cum in your ass, and— but wait, if he cums in your ass he won't need his cock sucked; he came already."

"Your boyfriend must be older than mine," she said, not knowing how painful it was to just hear the word boyfriend as if I had one—because my only reference was Tim or Casper, both personal disasters.

"I don't have a ... he wasn't my boyfriend."

"Whatever. José can come three times a night if I let

him. Jeesh, what a pig. Come on, you must, too. You probably jerk off at least three times a night, don't you? I know guys do it in the toilet in the back during their break; I can tell. They come back all red and huffy-puffy. Get real."

Lord have mercy.

"Why don't you suck him off first and get it out of the way—or, I got it—just tell him: 'Uh-uh, no way, José, you wipe that thing first!'"

Connie laughed hysterically. "Shel's right," she said. "You ain't no moron."

Chapter 23: The Curse of Homosexual Panic

Homosexual panic, a disease often used as a valid legal defense for the persons thought to be violently protecting themselves from homosexuality. Homosexual panic is described as a state of sudden feverish panic or agitated furor amounting to temporary manic insanity, which breaks out when a repressed homosexual finds himself in a situation in which he can no longer pretend to be unaware of the threat of homosexual temptation. This disease explains why young men commit crimes of violence and often batter their victims to death for no other apparent material gain.

In the university library, I read this paragraph from an old book on homosexuality over and over again. Yet the idea, a curse really, seemed pretty real to me. The reaction from Tim could still mean he's gay. Still, I wished I had read this book before coming out of the closet. Certainly before talking to my roommate.

There had to be some way I could salvage my relationship with Tim. There had to be some justification we could use to put this behind us. Our friendship was too important. Platonic love? Romantic friendship? I ultimately decided I would toss it off as a misunderstanding. I would pretend it never happened. That was my specialty, after all. I would walk in, punch him on the arm, and say, "All I really meant was that you're my best friend. You crazy dawg, you."

After dinner, I was finally ready to go back to the dorm and face the music. I opened the door to the room and walked in. The curse's power proved even more mighty than I had anticipated: Tim's stuff was gone.

I'd expected a lot of things, but not this. There would be no explanations. No tortured apologies. No making up. No renewal. No friendly parting. Nothing. He was gone.

Homosexual panic became a very real and powerful curse. A curse that attacked me inside and out. I shuddered at the thought of what Tim had told the other students on the floor, and what that would portend. I could not stop myself from wondering yet again what evil price I would have to pay for being gay.

I wrote Tim a supplicating letter. I left the dorm to mail it. Coming back, I smelled the odor of urine at my dorm room entrance. I opened the door, and there was a puddle of urine on the floor. I no sooner had cleaned up the mess when I heard a loud bang on my door and the sound of people laughing and then running away. I opened the door to see what it was.

Someone had leaned a huge garbage container full of water against the door. I watched when, as if in slow motion, the thing fell toward me. I was too frozen in horror to move. Filthy water came pouring into the room, splashing all over my feet. Guffaws rippled down the hall, the word "faggot" clearly audible.

I felt sick with humiliation.

I grabbed my backpack, filled it with random stuff, and left. Just as I suspected, Tim must have told them something on his way out, leaving me to deal with this new level of public humiliation and rejection.

With my overstuffed backpack, I ran away from the flooded room amid further catcalls from my unseen tormentors. In the stairwell, I suddenly realized I had nowhere to run to. My home was not an option. My room was not an option. My parents had thrown me out of the house, just like my dorm mates a moment ago. In a flash, I was homeless. I walked, zombie-like, to the third floor, where a small political science college held classes. There, I found an empty classroom.

I sat down. I stared straight ahead. I could not stop the thoughts: *Faggot. Traitor. Greedy pervert. Scum. Piece of shit.* On and on, the judgments played in my mind, blaming me for the mess. I tried to distract myself with a book, but that did not last long.

"Jim?" I didn't recognize the voice or even my name. "Hey, Jim!"

I looked up. It was the resident assistant of the floor. These RAs, as we called them, were students in charge of keeping order in the dorms. The curse was not through with me yet.

"You okay?" my RA asked.

"No, I'm not okay."

"Don't blame ya. Mind if I talk to ya?" he asked.

"No, go right ahead," I said numbly.

He took a chair next to mine.

"Sorry about this. You don't deserve it, man, I mean it … Hey, hey, Jim, chin up. It ain't so bad. I wanna talk with you. Not officially, but the real deal."

I was silent. I didn't think I was going to like the 'real deal.'

"What I mean is I won't bullshit you. Look, guy, you gotta get out of here. I can't vouch for your … safety. Know what I mean, man? That's not a threat. I am not threatening you. I don't have anything against you, but let's face it: You ain't so popular. You know that. You never were, but I looked out for you—yes, I did. But this stunt you pulled with your roommate. Man, that was just sick, man, real sick. Hilarious, just like you … but sick. He was your only friend on this floor." He shook his head in barely concealed contempt.

Great, I am a sicko too, I must add that to the catalogue, I thought. But the RA wasn't finished.

"Look, man, you're being … you're being disruptive. You know what I mean? You're really creatin' a … unstable atmosphere. Why don't you go where you're wanted? Okay?" I looked at him hard and bitterly: He was bovine and muscular with a cancerous tan and greasy blond hair. No one's mental giant, but the boss over me and my future.

"Are you kicking me out? Isn't that illegal?"

"Don't take that attitude, man. Shit, that ain't what

this is about. It's about what's right. Do you think it's right to stay here with half my floor wanting to kick the shit out of you? Even if I get why they want to, I don't approve of it. You hear me? Oh, don't get me wrong, buster, you can stay. Hell, yeah, you can stay. That's housing policy. But being disruptive is against housing policy, and you will probably end up out on your ass anyway. Yeah, you got rights; you can stay here. Understand? But if you think your life is miserable now, wait a week. That ain't a threat, man, not from me. You can't hang that shit on me. I don't care what kind of fruitcake you are. I mean, so what if you love weird. My girlfriend goes, 'Hey, that's better than not loving at all'—right? So don't look at me like that, because I don't care. But all those other guys do. And I am just statin' facts here. Can I watch them for you all day, all night, every day of the week? Can I do that just for you? I got a life. I can't protect you. Give you a for instance: I heard someone pissed in your room, but I can't prove anything. Can you?"

"I did smell it," I whispered, more to myself, I was so numb with shock that the outrageousness of this conversation didn't register.

"Look, make life easier for all of us just … beat it. I'll get your housing waiver. I looked into it. If I give the okay, they'll refund your unused portion. They don't refund food-service meals, but you can keep eating at the cafeteria till the end of the term if you want. Don't be worried about the rents here; it's not like this is New York City or Chicago. You'll get enough to move almost anywhere outside.

"Look, I know it sucks—oh, I didn't mean nothing personal, dude." He laughed, laughed for a while. "Come on, you gotta admit that's funny. Anyway, you see I don't wish this to happen to anyone. But is the entire floor wrong or you? If you are right, it still don't matter. You're gonna be in a living hell here." He got up to leave, stopped and looked at me—me, the sniveling miserable little runt who after one brief moment of courage now can't stand up for himself. Even this RA had started to pity me. "Look, I'll help you move out. I can make sure no one harms your stuff, the least I can do. I don't hate ya. Just get outta here; that's my advice anyway. Chill out, man; think about it. Make it easy on yourself. Give me your answer tomorrow. Gotta go, dude."

I didn't have to think it over.

After a couple of hours, I walked back to my room.

A baseball whirred by my head. When I turned around, I couldn't see anything but open doors down the hall. I turned back to unlock the room. A golf ball hit my backpack.

I didn't know where to turn or where to go. I plopped into Tim's stripped-down lower bunk. I sat there, catatonic. I must have fallen asleep because around midnight I awoke to my next-door neighbor blasting his stereo, just for me.

Without thinking, as if under attack, I got up, grabbed the stuffed backpack, and walked out.

As I walked out, I heard cheers.

Where does all this hatred come from? I wondered

as I stopped in the lobby of the dorm. I also wondered why I was so angry at myself. Why not be angry at these jerks, at Tim, at the RA. Why wasn't I pissed at Casper's over-reaction? Why wasn't I furious at my parents for throwing me out? Why did I think I deserved being bullied by Ben? Something inside me felt very wrong and I didn't know what it was but, for the first time, I became aware this anger at myself was not right. There was a cancer inside of me, inside my head, inside my heart, inside my soul. And then, I felt I did deserve this after all. Then I remembered the curse: homosexual panic. That had to be it.

But I had a bigger problem now. I needed somewhere to go. I went to the only place I could think of, the Harmony Café.

Chapter 24: Brother, Can You Spare a Dime?

I left my dorm room and headed through campus to Woodward Avenue, supposedly not the wisest place to be. Unfortunately, tonight there was no danger. There was barely a soul on the streets. The people I did see had neither the motive nor the means to kill me. Even my stuffed backpack was an uninteresting bounty.

With little to no money and nowhere else to go. I walked into the Harmony Café. Last night, there'd been a crowd. This evening, the place was deserted. The waitress, Melody, showed me to a booth near the door. Numbly, I plopped onto the seat, a puff of air going up with the blue vinyl.

"Hey, you look even worse than you did yesterday, Jamie."

"Thanks."

"What's the problem, sugah?"

"No problem … Just feeling down."

"You're lookin' pretty sad, babe. Wait a sec."

Among the stuff in my backpack was a copy of *Hamlet.* I took it out and started to read.

Melody returned with my coffee and a doughnut.

"I can't pay for the doughnut."

"It's on the house, sugah."

The kind gesture from a relative stranger just overwhelmed me. She slid next to me. Put her coffeepot down. Put her hand over my shoulder.

"Okay, now you're tellin' me what's wrong."

I didn't want to risk the curse again, and I wasn't sure she really wanted to know.

"I need help. I got nothin', nobody."

"What happened to you?"

Her concern—was it real, was she assuming I was straight? I did not want to find out. She was not getting the truth.

"I got thrown out."

"Thrown out?"

"I got thrown out of the dorms," I said stiffly.

"I'm impressed, ya have to work hard at that. What in Christ's name did you do?"

I hesitated. Despite my resolve to say nothing further, I was tired and fed up. I decided to risk getting kicked out of my last refuge. "They don't like my kind."

"Fuckin' dorms, hell, been there, shug, tell me about it. Think they like people like me? Just look at me. I get it from all sides. Mixed race and a punker to boot. Bastards. Hey, they did you a favor."

I looked at Melody again, and maybe for the first time I really looked at her. Her hair was short and looked like something was carved in it. How did I miss that before? "Melody, you're awesome."

"Forget it."

"I wish I could. But you're too polite to be a punker." She laughed.

"Yeah, just get me out of here, I'll show you rude."

"What's carved in your hair? Is that a tree?"

"A tree? You got to be kidding me. A tree?" Then she laughed loudly. "It's supposed to be a fist. I guess it's a little overgrown." She looked straight into my eyes as if she knew everything. "You need a place to crash?"

"Yeah."

"Well, you can't stay here again."

"I don't know what to do. I haven't got any money either. My RA said he would get me a housing refund— I suppose this week sometime."

"Hey, my ex-boyfriend is looking for a roommate. You're not queer or anything, are you? That would scare the shit out of him." I heaved an internal sigh of relief that I'd had the forethought not to tell her the truth.

"No, of course not," I lied, but I could feel the blush.

"He's okay but he hogs the place to himself. He wants to rent out a small room for half the rent. But it's still cheap. Also, he's a stoner, so he's pretty mellow."

"It's a nice place?"

"Four walls, roof is included for free." I think it's like seventy-five a month."

"I can get that. But I don't have anything with me now."

"Let me call him; hang on a bit."

All she asked was that I not be a fag. That's all anyone wanted from me—my mother, my father, Tim and now her friend. Lying about it at least gave me a place to sleep. In fact, what did the truth get me? Self-esteem? At least I would not need to sleep on the street.

I looked down at the copy of *Hamlet* in my hand. I thought intensely, *Will you save me?* At that moment a quote came to mind, from *Hamlet,* "There is nothing either good or bad but thinking make it so."

The thought made me peaceful. I wondered if something greater drew me into theater. I cracked open the book as if it were giving me magical guidance:

O, that this too too solid flesh would melt,
Thaw and resolve itself into a dew!
Or that the Everlasting had not fix'd
His canon 'gainst self-slaughter! O God! God!
How weary, stale, flat and unprofitable,
Seem to me all the uses of this world!
Fie on't! ah fie! 'tis an unweeded garden
That grows to seed; things rank and gross in nature
Possess it merely. That it should come to this!

How ironic. I worried Tim would commit suicide, now I was thinking about it. If only I could be as lucky as Hamlet and at least have a Horatio to comfort me.

Melody came back with news.

"You're in luck. He'll let you crash there tonight and ask you about moving in later. Dave's cool—or cool enough anyway, if you catch my drift." She handed me a napkin. "Here's the address. It's out on St. Antoine Street. It's a big building, a real student ghetto. Be careful, he's a psych student. He'll try and analyze you."

"Thanks, Melody, thanks. I can't thank—"

"Save it. Just remember when I come knocking on your door."

Chapter 25: Home Off-Campus

Piles of junk lined the freezing cold steps to the house: stacks of old papers, newspapers, and magazines all bundled together. Old rusted scraps of metal, car parts, hubcaps, and on the top stairs, bags of glass bottles. Loud music booming from the various apartments announced this was an off-campus building. The wooden door to apartment 18 was chipped. The door's broken wood revealed where locks had once secured them. I looked for a bell on the door and could not find one. I knocked timidly; it barely made a sound. No one answered. I tried a knuckle-busting knock.

The door opened and there stood a stoner with a big afro, a thick mustache, and a tie-dyed T-shirt. I shivered with a prejudicial fear. Then the friendly sound of jazz and the smoky-sweet smell of pot wafted out through the door. The smoke's association with my brother and this man's mild countenance mixed with Melody's kindness triggered that flash of shame my mother had taught me when I was thinking like an idiot.

"Hey man, you James?" he asked.

"Jamie Goldberg."

"Far out. Come on in; it's freezin' out there. Dave's the name," he said, as he extended an arm toward me.

He squeezed my hand with incongruous strength. "Come on in. I hear you need a place to crash. Total bummer from what Gina told me."

"Not Gina, it was Melody."

"Oh yeah, right, her." He giggled.

The living-room walls were covered with a bizarre pattern of ever-larger bulging squares converging into smaller ball-like shapes. If you stared at it for too long it gave the illusion that the walls were spinning. The only relief from this dizzying pattern was the stacked milk-crate bookshelves lining the lower sections of the wall. A lamp above was muted by red tissue paper, giving the room a seedy glow to match the smoky interior.

"Have a seat … er …" We looked around. The only couch was covered with papers. Dave let out a half-embarrassed laugh. "I usually sit on the floor. Just put your shit down anywhere." This place was impossible. I needed a place to sleep that one night. Staying there any longer was out of the question. I sat on the grimy floor, back against the couch. "Let me get you some tea." Dave staggered into the kitchen, which was a model of student neglect. He was listening to bizarre jazz music. It sounded like Miles Davis met Arnold Schoenberg. The female vocal was impossibly alluring unlike the dissonant accompaniment.

Dave came back with a greenish brew that bore no resemblance to tea.

"Herbal tea, hope you like it."

The honey he'd added made the brew barely palatable. "This tastes great." It wasn't an absolute lie;

I was grateful for something warm.

"Glad you like it, man; it kinda cleans you out, purifies the soul, know what I mean?" His eyes went wide for emphasis.

An awkward silence.

"So, Gina tells me you got run out of the dorms by some fascist assholes. That really sucks weenie. You ... you must be dating uh ... Gina, I suppose?" he asked.

"You mean Melody."

"Right, right, you're her new guy?"

"No, she's awesome, really awesome ... but not ... my type."

"It's cool. She still pissed off at me?" I was trying to think of something to say until he took my silence as a legitimate answer. "I fucked that one up big-time. But I always do. Can't seem to settle down, know what I mean? Driftin' but, you know, checking it out, waiting for the right stuff to come along, know what I mean? ... Shit ... You're cool ... You can stay. Even if you are Gina's boyfriend; I don't care."

"Thanks," I said, glad for the one night but eager to look the next day for a permanent solution.

"Rent's seventy-five. Got that on ya?"

That took me by surprise.

"Uh ... no, I don't because—"

"It's cool, I am sure you're good for it." He dug something out of his pocket and threw it at me. "Here's the key, man; I am going to sleep. I think I did a little too much tonight. Glad you can stay."

And with that, he got up unsteadily, walked into the

other room, and shut the door behind him. I sat there until the Jazz album came to an end and the turntable switched off, in the silence I felt incredibly alone.

I sat there, stupidly, with my now cold green witches' brew, staring at the key on the floor, wondering if he was even going to remember what had happened the next day. I looked at the wall—away from the sickening wallpaper. I noticed the lower milk crates were filled with LPs. I thumbed through his music collection: Sticking out was Jeanne Lee and Blake Ran. I thumbed through the others, Grandmaster Flash & The Furious Five, The Cold Crush Four, the Beatles, a small section of jazz, no Motown. The collection with a large section he labeled "Experimental." They included Frank Zappa, the Art Ensemble of Chicago, Zulu Nation alongside a couple Vivaldi and Handel albums.

I thought I could not live here. However, what was not lost on me was the fact that I had a key. Suddenly, the Hamlet quote, "There is nothing either good or bad but thinking make it so" took on new meaning.

I walked into another room. It seemed like a stoner's study: a desk with walls of more milk-crate bookshelves behind which was aluminum foil masquerading as wallpaper. There was no sign of a bed. I peeked into another room, a small closet-like space. There was a bare mattress on the floor surrounded by milk crates ready for stuffing. A desk had been formed against the back wall by placing a board across more milk crates.

I went to the smaller room. I turned on the light. It was an empty room with torn floral wallpaper on three sides and obscene pencil drawings of female body parts on the fourth. On top of one of the milk-crate shelves was one blood-red and several pink-tinged sheets.

I made the bed, rolled up my pants for a pillow, and used my jacket for a blanket. I lay there awake, looking at the ceiling, then the floor. I heard clicking sounds and thought better of finding out what they were. Outside, I heard footsteps going by. Then, I felt protected by the four walls. I thought of Hamlet and then fell asleep.

The next morning, a dark cup of coffee and an English muffin were waiting for me at a kitchen table. I was incredibly happy, a kind gesture when all seemed so dark and miserable.

"Mornin' James—or is it Jimmy?" came a voice behind me.

"Jamie." I turned around. Dave looked significantly neater and well-dressed, more like the self-respecting grad student.

"Oh yeah. You know, I can lend you the sheets until you get another pair." He remembered last night all right. "Thanks for the rent advance, man."

"I hate to tell you this, but I didn't—"

"Cool, it's cool." I wasn't sure what was cool—or what he thought I was about to say.

"I didn't give you any money last night."

"Yeah, I know; it's cool. Get it to me when you can. I like helping out guys like you."

"Thanks," I wondered what 'like you' meant. "Well, I really appreciate it—"

"You know, some asshole thinks he's taking you

down, well, we just showed him; you don't need that fucking dorm crap." He flashed a friendly smile. "You're better off without those bastards ... Well, yet me show you the rest of the place."

I wondered what Melody had actually told Dave but thought it was better to return the favor by just taking it all for granted and accepting this house as my temporary shelter. Dave showed me the house: the ragtag student kitchen with no matching anything, an old gas stove, and a miserable-smelling refrigerator. He showed me the living room with its dirty couch and bare wood floor. I was oddly relieved to learn the clicking was a faulty electrical switch. Somehow, I felt better about the threat of the house burning down than the threat of cockroaches.

"I use the second room there as a study ... but you can use the study, too."

It was impossible to see where I would possibly study in that room. It was just filled with book-stuffed milk crates with additional stacks of books all over the floor and tables.

"I can clear a corner. That one near the window has a small desk you can use. I'll let you use my typewriter for your term papers. Are you fucking her?"

"I am sorry?"

"Melody said you're in a bad spot."

"I am."

"You are fucking her, right?"

"No, we're good friends. I know her from the diner. I study there a lot." Then added, "My girlfriend lives in an off-campus studio with a couple of friends."

"Cool." Even if he was homophobic, as Melody said, he seemed pretty mellow.

"I don't know what to say," I said gratefully. "I can't get you the seventy-five until next week."

"That's cool, man."

"Seventy-five dollars is all you want, right?"

"It's all it costs. We can just do it month-to-month. But don't sweat it; you can stay as long as you like."

"Are you sure? You don't even know me?" I asked feeling insecure.

"I am sure you'll be fine."

"I am not so sure," I blurted. To my surprise he smiled at this.

"Hey, don't be so hard on yourself. You've been through hell, well hell stops here. We're bros." He laughed. It was clear we weren't bros. "I am sure it's gonna be busy here between the two of us. Give me a little advance notice if you can, okay?"

"Oh, of course," I humored him.

"But if you can't—I mean, Jesus, don't let an opportunity go by. I have a signal; just put a rubber band on the door outside."

"Far out," I lied again. At least I was consistent: I lied about everything he asked. Lying, I had come to learn, 'is the bane of the homosexual' just like it said in one of those moralizing homophobic books I'd read in the library. But now I understood why.

Variation: Hammerblow II, Warning signs

January 1981

IV Scherzo. Schattenhaft.
(A Musical Joke. Shadowy)

Chapter 26: Sgt. Pepper Blues

At first, it appeared that it was better to be a liar than a fag. Dave was cool, but I didn't want to find out how cool. I also had to remember Melody's warning question, "You aren't queer, are you?" He seemed nice enough, though I used to think the same of Tim and Casper. Still, under the cover of a lie, the place seemed safe. Life had been boiled down to its essentials. Dave was just attractive enough to be okay to look at but not cute enough to be dangerous. Once I moved in, it was easy to lie to Dave. He was uncritical of my lies, and we rarely saw each other. If we bumped into one another in the kitchen, we would share the odd meal, debate the odd liberal political issue, or vilify Margaret Thatcher together. Dave had a penchant for left-wing rants against banks and for smoking pot and eating strange organic vegetables like alfalfa sprouts. I wanted to keep Dave at arm's length. If we became good friends, I could blow my cover at any moment for—as it turned out—I was not a particularly good liar.

The last thing I wanted was to blow my cover and have to look for another place to live.

"I thought you said her name was Coco?" Dave asked when I forgot the name of a girlfriend I invented.

"Oh, Connie is her name, but Coco is kind of a nickname I made up for her ever since we saw … *Fame*, you know, the movie; I loved the music," I said.

"Yeah, well that's cool."

"Thank you, I really appreciate being here—"

"Look, you can stop that."

"Stop what?" I asked suspiciously.

"Stop thanking me for this place, man. You're here, you pay rent, you've a right be here. Stop acting like a scared puppy."

"I am?"

"You know, I study psychology and — forget it. Just be easy on yourself. man."

I was afraid Dave was seeing right through me. I was a bad liar because lying was pragmatic and humiliating. While Dave appeared to buy it, I couldn't. I knew the truth and once you peeled the onion, there was no putting the layers back on. I was far more convincing when I was lying to myself.

I didn't want to risk losing my new home and it seemed that I was at risk whether I was telling the truth or lying. 'My new home' was cheap and dilapidated. As with most student housing, the landlord was happy to collect rent so long as his tenants didn't cost him a penny in upkeep. The place was terminally cold. The bare hardwood floors were cracked and dirty—they creaked as you walked on them. The living room reeked of stale books and marijuana.

Blotchy stains covered the blue cloth couch. So when I moved in, like Dave, I actually preferred to sit on the floor, though to ease my mind I'd purchased a sponge from the corner drugstore and a blue oval of shag carpet from Hudson's.

I tried to always be on my guard with Dave and keep the interactions to an absolute friendly minimum. But as time went by, it was hard to keep it up. His attempts to psychoanalyze me, which Melody had warned me about, were particularly threatening. I had to work around Tim, Casper, my parents, and all the other closely related psychological issues I was having, and all the while getting entangled in lies and cover-ups that I couldn't always remember precisely.

Still, after a while, making it even harder to lie, Dave seemed to take a genuine interest in me.

"Hey, Jamie, doin' anything?" Dave asked as he entered the apartment one day, shooting a bitter cold breeze through the house.

I was caught off guard and accidentally said, "No."

"Wanna smoke some dope?"

"Sure, why not?" I said "no" so often, I wanted to pepper a few "yes's" in there to prove I was cool and not judging him. Whether I actually wanted to smoke never entered the equation because the only thing pot ever did for me was make me feel stupid. My life was absurd enough without it.

Dave sat down beside me on the oval carpet. I positioned myself, as usual, with my back against the couch, while Dave preferred to smoke sitting in an impossible lotus position.

"So, you likin' the pad?" He swooshed through his

toke. He passed the joint to me.

"Oh, yeah, definitely." I took a small breath in; the smoke irritated my throat enough for me to cough.

"It's not the Ritz, but it's comfortable, man."

Much to my dismay, after that single toke a senseless stream of blabber issued from my mouth: "Well, it's cold—but that just takes getting used to. At least it's affordable. I like it. Ha ha. Did you hear Michigan National Bank is one of the bankrollers of the Moral Majority?"

"Yeah, that's fucked up. Fucking banks," Dave said, passing me the joint.

"I closed my account there." I took a quick drag and passed it back, hopefully for the last time.

"They're all fucked up if you ask me, man," said Dave. The joint returned to me like a bad penny.

"Yeah. I am moving my account to the student credit union. You know, we're studying the influence of banks in my political science class," I lied. I was no longer taking political science courses, but I had taken such a course in the past.

"Oh, yeah, credit unions all have ties to banks, too … scumbags." Dave took another toke and offered the joint back to me again. He then put on a Beatles album, *Sgt. Pepper's Lonely Hearts Club Band,* which gave me the creeps owing to memories best left alone from when I was a kid. The song, "A Day in the Life" even gave me nightmares. It brought out some disturbing associations. The song reminded me of my brother, his creepy friends, and other things I dreaded. Just the opening line about reading the news brought back vague painful memories.

"Earth to Jamie. You gonna pass that back?"

"Oh, yeah, sorry." I passed the joint.

"Did you hear what I said?" He paused. "I asked you if you smoked often."

"Oh. No. Not a lot. Actually, mostly with my brother, Steven—well, he smokes a lot. He taught me at a young age—to smoke."

"Steven? Yeah, I know your brother."

That was so stunning that for a moment I could imagine what it was like to be hit in the head by a pitched ball.

"Let me guess. You buy from him?"

"That's what we're smoking."

"You're close with him?" I asked.

"Not really."

"Oh, I thought he only sold to friends."

"We do have some … mutual acquaintances."

"Wow, small world. Well, good for him—I mean, this is good stuff." I took another small hit, and again some negative associations of the music and my brother came back to me. But I could have guessed what they were; I just didn't want to know. A feeling of anger came out of nowhere, which I forced to swallow back.

"You okay, Jamie?"

"Steven had me smoke marijuana when I was a kid. Often with this album playing in the background … I have some bad memories about that."

"Enough to make you cry?"

"I am not crying … man," I slurred.

"No, I see tears rolling down your face? That's real. What happened to you?"

An alarm sounded inside of me. I'd let my guard down. "It was … cool."

"Don't sound like it to me. You know ever since you've been here you've been acting like you think I'm gonna hit you. Did Steven do that?"

"No, it wasn't him—I mean no he didn't, it was … cool," I replied defensively. Ashamed, I felt Dave could look right through me—even know more about me than I knew myself.

"I'm gonna venture out on a limb here, cause you've been very distant. That's not necessary. You can trust me."

Danger, Will Robinson! kept screaming in my head. Out of nowhere I burst into tears.

"Jamie, it's cool whatever happened to you."

"Nothing …" As much as I wanted to, I felt I couldn't evade this. Whatever *this* was. "Why do you say that Dave?" I liked the sound of using his name.

Jamie, when you were a kid did … people hurt you?" I froze. "That's fucked up if they did, you're okay." Never in my life did I feel this combination of terror and love before.

"It wasn't cool." Was all I could muster until terror took over. "I can't talk about it, Dave. Not yet anyway."

"Talking about it might help."

"I can't even talk about it to myself."

"Bummer."

"But it was Steve's friends, not him. Please, don't

mention this to him."

"Chill … Your secret is safe with me, whatever it is." Dave offered me the joint, and I took a deep hit sending me into a coughing spasm, then the pot really took over.

"I am scared, frightened, afraid."

"Afraid of what man, it's cool were friends. You didn't say anything to be ashamed about, in fact you didn't say anything, except you were hurt."

"I did?"

"I told you that's fucked up if someone hurts you. I'm ready to talk when you are, okay? In the meantime, you tell me if anyone's hurting you. Especially those assholes in the dorm. Or your brother? … What did he do, like what? He'd get you high and watch you freak out or something?" Terror, love and now my worst nightmare: I've been seen right through. I was afraid of what else he knew. "These other … friends, they—"

The psychedelic "Lucy in the Sky with Diamonds" wafted past my ears. My mind wandered.

"This music still gets me." I said abruptly as the sounds took me back to a period when hanging out with Steven and one of his friends named Gary, which I couldn't admit to myself let alone to Dave, because I let it happen.

Dave watched me take another drag. He leaned over to me and took the joint. I was frightened by the intimacy. "You were young then?" He must have noticed my shocked reaction because he quickly added, "When you started smoking?"

"Yeah … I was." His questions, initially so innocuous,

turned into guided missiles I was helpless to deflect, but this feeling of love of friendship kept my mouth moving, "About five. I know it sounds like I am some drug fiend," I said, taking a deeper hit.

"It's cool man, it's cool. Don't be so hard on yourself. Just speak your truth. I ain't those assholes from the dormitory … Why is it they threw you out again?" He wasn't supposed to ask that question!

"I didn't fit in. I played opera and … read books."

"I guess students don't dig those *book readers*." He laughed. I bristled. "Dude, you need to seriously chill. You got some major low self-esteem goin' there, and it's a bad vibe."

"How could you know that?

"You know Dr. Farley?"

"Maybe not."

"Dr. Wire?"

"No! Not at all!"

"You know Dr. Wire?"

"No! … I mean not really … family friend."

"Well, Dr. Farley's my advisor, but he's also a great psychologist. He sees people, I am sure he'd see you."

"Oh."

"Farley, he'd really get your number."

"Okay." Getting my number was the last thing I needed at that moment. Dr. Wire didn't get me, so Farley probably wouldn't either.

The song, "She's Leaving Home" purred from the stereo. I felt the pain of being thrown out of my parents' house, out of my dorm. But yet at the same time, I felt the comfort of a friend I never knew I had nor what I had done to deserve him. A lump started to form in my throat. I cursed the marijuana for making my brain soft. "I hate this song."

"Far out; it's cool. I mean, it's a bummer, but it's cool. Know what I mean?" "Jamie, you can loosen up. No one's gonna hate you for being yourself."

My lips started to move softly, and I watched words come out of them, "I wish that was true."

"This is a great song," Dave said. He took another puff looked up as if contemplating the stars and passed the joint to me and the song on played on.

Chapter 27: A Ritual Returns

When Dave left the house, the weight of my mistakes and lies started to take its toll on me. It wasn't enough to hurt everyone around me; now my lying was pissing off the new people, new friends around me as well. Had I learned nothing? But what could I do? Tell the truth and risk losing another place to stay? Tell a lie? I still might lose it. I had nowhere to go and no idea how to get there. Frustration and agony mounted inside of me. I was overcome with the compelling urge to punish the only person I could bring myself to blame—myself.

Dave was gone barely five minutes when I felt *it* creeping back and then I knew exactly what this punishment would be. I thought *it* was gone forever. Coming out of the closet was supposed to be *the solution.* Why did I feel this self-hatred returning? But as a neighbor pumped up the volume of his stereo to impossible levels, there it was: my chance to do *it.* Helpless, I didn't know how to stop it. To compound matters, the nightmare-inducing song "A Day in the Life" played on the record player. I only knew one way to stop this festering self-hatred. I felt a trembling inside of me. Thoughts that had been dammed up inside breeched and flooded my brain with a fury I could not control.

You idiot, how could you do this? How could you let this sexual perversion destroy your family and your friends? I had friends, decent friends, and you lost them. Bitter and cruel, the thoughts were just starting. *And now again? Must you destroy everything wherever you go! Look at the list of people your filth has destroyed: Tim, Casper, Dara, my parents, my home, and now someone I barely know and have to live with. No way, faggot. First, it's my turn to destroy you!*

How I wanted to be rid of that voice. It was like some mean stranger's voice, but it was inside my head and undeniably my own. The voice repulsed me and gripped me in a stranglehold until the hatred intensified. It was irresistibly moving me to my bedroom. *No, I want this to stop. I have paid the price. I hated myself for being gay for too long. I came out, now go away!* As I argued with myself, I was undressing, my body doing one thing even as I seemed to beg myself for mercy. I unbuckled my belt, and as I lowered my pants to the ground, I took the belt out. I stung with the humiliation of the pants around my legs like a schoolboy about to be punished. Yet, the humiliation stimulated the drive to punish myself. I held the belt in my hand. I knew exactly what I was about to do, and I was horrified and excited.

"You can't be serious!" I cried aloud. My hand told me I was serious. My right hand moved up and back. Then it thrashed downward. *Crack!* That first time, the pain seemed so profound, so demeaning, and so necessary. More had to follow—*crack! crack!*—and once it started, it was unstoppable. I had to atone. I needed redemption, salvation, grace, but for that, I had to pay. I had to pay for it with torrents of lashes aimed against my back and buttocks that couldn't be stopped. The pain didn't make it stop; it made it worse. It made a mockery of trying to repent. *"Harder! Make it unbearable! Harder!"* I urged. The cracks against my body couldn't be loud enough. The mean angry voice inside told me how much I hated myself; what a sick pervert I was; how I was selling my soul for the sake of disgusting sex on the floor of a theater tech booth, letting Jack rape me; how I really must have wanted it. I even needed Jack to do it again and again to me because that would at least turn me into the faggot whore I knew I had become. The pain throbbing in my body was not enough. I grabbed the middle of the belt so it would double up, and now the metal belt buckle would hit hard against my flesh. I could not stop; I kept hitting myself like I had to, like there was a god ordering me to do so. Then, finally, I felt it.

Appeasement.

Appeasement in the form of a soft warm sensation on my butt telling me I had drawn blood. The gods were appeased, and I was sick to my stomach with pain. I felt disgusted with myself. I lay down on my bed. I couldn't stand myself anymore. I couldn't believe what I had just done. I sank my face into my pillow, and I cried. As I was crying, my body writhed in pain on the bed. The agony made it too hot to lie still. It was only after a while that I realized I was aggressively rubbing my cock against the bed, and that angry voice was still projecting its hatred on me: *Sick pervert!* The voice got louder and louder, meaner and meaner.

"Sick pervert how dare you live! You worthless scum!" On and on it went, saying the most hurtful disgusting things about me, and it didn't stop until I was mentally, spiritually, and physically depleted. At once feeling I was about to die, but instead I ejaculated into the bedsheets. My sexual climax triggered an impossible calmness. Exhausted, I lay on my bed feeling numb. And as if I had committed a ritual sacrifice, I felt cleansed.

I rose from my bed to wipe away any reminder of what had happened. Quickly, I threw my clothes back on. Impossibly, I felt it was all clean and right again until I sat on a chair. As I sat down, I felt the stinging in my buttocks. Not just the dull ache of being bruised but a sharper pain. Then I remembered. I stood up and lowered my pants and peeked at my underwear and there were small but telltale bloodstains, a thin red line across the back of my underwear. I grabbed tissues and put it on my ass and put my pants back on. Sitting back down, I felt humiliated as I felt the stab of pain again. I stood up. I wanted to run away, but I had nowhere to run. I didn't know what to do with this drive, this compulsion to run, so I stood up and screamed at the top of my lungs.

Someone outside yelled, "Shut the fuck up in there!"

I fell into a heap on my bed. Shame and humiliation rained down in a torrent. Afraid, I didn't know how much this person who'd yelled heard or saw even though

I knew he couldn't see through the blinds. I pressed my face as tightly into my pillow as I could. I heard myself singing lines from *Parsifal,* but not Parsifal's lines.

> *I cannot weep, I can only shout, rage,*
> *storm, rave in an ever-recurring nightmare.*
> *And even though I am repentant*
> *I can never awaken from this nightmare.*

Then, exhausted, I lay there in peace. I swore it would never happen again. I swore that every time the ritual took place. That was true, as each ritual was unique and never recurred. This one would be no different. It would never happen again, and my memory of it would fade and disappear along with my fleeting sense of grace. But for now, that grace gave me peace. I just stopped thinking. lying exhausted and drained on my bed. It felt magical, so magical. I felt an overwhelming gratitude.

And in this delusion of grace, I fell asleep.

Chapter 28: Sassy Cat

"Last rack," announced Shel as he wheeled out the final rack of bagels to be boiled. Saturday nights we worked late at the bagel factory. But I had to do the double work of boiling and baking the bagels, while Shel schmoozed with the customers up front. We never had a front counter person on Saturday night, partly because of the perceived danger, partly because of the minimal number of customers, but mostly because it was the "Saturday Night with Shel" Show at the Bagel Factory put on for the motley crew of regulars who came to receive his wit and wisdom. Shel never let the ovens interfere with his schmoozing. He could rely on my disinclination to hear him call me a moron to keep me running to the ovens to prevent the bagels from burning.

I had just put the last batch of salted bagels in the dryer to send them on their way to the oven when the timer went off. I ran around to get some baked bagels out of the oven because Shel was busy talking with a stocky, middle-aged customer dressed in a formal tuxedo. The man's pasty thick pear-shaped head looked all the more ridiculous because about ten strands of long, greasy hair were draped and drawn over his bald pate.

"Hey, Shel, gimme a dozen, will ya?"

"Gimme? A dozen? What? You're broke? You wanna cost my job? The kid here will turn me in and take my job. Pay for 'em yourself, you fucking cheapskate." He laughed, and then so did the customer.

"All right, all right. I'll take—*I'll buy*—two dozen but give me those the kid is taking out of the oven. I want 'em h-o-t and with hair on 'em. Get it?"

"Got it, chief," Shel said with an army salute as he took a bag and deftly filled it up with steaming hot bagels from the wicker basket.

"Aren't you afraid being open so late around here?" the greaseball customer asked.

"It's Saturday. We've always been open late, Merv."

"I know, but that was back when it was a kosher neighborhood, capeesh?"

"Okay, so we don't do good business at night like we used to, but we're here anyway baking for the stores, so why not sell? You know?"

"I know, but aren't you afraid of getting held up or something with all the *schvartzes*?"

"They don't bother me, Merv."

"You're consortin' with danger; that's all I'm saying. This isn't Farmington Hills if you know what I mean."

"I know what you mean, Merv."

"Okay, I gotta go. Here's two bucks."

"Merv, it's two-sixty."

"Okay, here; keep it." He handed Shel three crumpled dollar bills. "Take it easy, Shel."

"Okay, Merv, I will do that. Have a great night. Say 'hi' to everyone for me." Shel watched as Merv shut the door on his way out. "You pathetic racist bastard." Then he turned to me. "You have the easy job, Jimmy; you don't get these fuckin' morons I gotta schmooze with all the time."

"I thought you and Merv were friends," I said.

"With that asshole? Three fucking dollars and he says, 'Keep it'? Fuckin' moron. Look, I don't care much about anything, Jimmy, but don't be a fuckin' moron, okay? I'm gonna go to the bathroom and shit this guy out of me; watch the front. Don't forget the bagels in the oven." He walked away.

Every Saturday night, the bagel factory was open until two. We baked the bagels for grocery stores and restaurants. True, the neighborhood had changed. The mostly African-American community had limited use for bagels and lox. But we were close by the university, plus the smell of the freshly baked bagels could lure almost anyone in. We had our share of problem customers but nothing Shel couldn't handle. Behind the counter was a baseball bat, just in case. Shel rarely used it on anyone— except to bang on a chair to get me to bake faster.

After the bagels were baked and cooled, Shel and I would bag them for early pick up the next morning. Then I cleaned up the store, including mopping the floor, cleaning the bathroom and, last, sifting the poppy seed bin for mouse droppings.

"Scoop them bastards out of there!" Shel would growl if he ever saw signs of mice.

Finally, I was finished with the poppy seed detail. "We're done!" I cried.

"Okay, Jimmy, tonight is the night?"

"Oh, yes, it is," I chirped trying to hide my dread.

"The Sassy Cat," he said as he locked up the store.

"You're the boss," I said in faint agreement. As it was past midnight and officially my twenty-first birthday. I could drink legally—and go to the strip joint where Shel used to work the kitchen. Sensing I needed guidance in this area, he had made it his personal crusade to 'educate me' on my twenty-first birthday.

On the one hand, I was feeling insecure; on the other, it gave me the chance to reinforce my hetero-credibility. Not just for Shel but for Dave, as I would have a great story to tell about my exploits at a strip joint. I'd even brought some extra money in case I was 'lucky.'

"Hop in the car, my young man."

We got in Shel's old boat-like white Cadillac and drove to east Detroit. That late at night, Detroit resembled a demilitarized zone after curfew. Stores with thick metal bars; offices with tiny windows, protected by iron rails; and the occasional burned-out lot left as it was after the 1967 riots. The only stores still open were a smattering of convenience stores, but even they were protected by thick bulletproof glass covering the doorways. Patrons asking at the door what they wanted.

"Jimmy, you're in for an adventure. Don't be no fuckin' moron. We're there just to have a good time, so let the other lowlifes have a good time too … and respect the girls, capeesh?"

"Yeah, of course. Respect the girls."

"They got a tough job. Don't matter what you think

of them; compliment them on how sexy they are. You'll charm the pants off 'em—if you're lucky." He guffawed. "When we get to the entrance, Jimmy, let me do the talking. And … you should …" he let out a chuckle, "you should stay away from the men's room."

"Pretty dirty, I imagine," I said.

"Likely, but there's some," and now he switched to a pseudo-female voice, "interesting people that might want to meet you." He burst out laughing. Then, again switching to the female voice, he said, "Oh don't go in with him; he uses his teeth." He burst out laughing again, and I was shocked silent.

"Don't worry about them," he went on. "They are really harmless. People make such a fucking fuss about them; they don't hurt anybody—except when *they use their teeth*," he chuckled. Then, seriously looking at me instead of the traffic: "In other words, leave 'em alone, and don't cause a scene. Got it?"

"Got it, Shel," I said.

"I knew it; you're no fuckin'—"

"Moron," we said together.

The large parking lot stood out amid the desolate emptiness of late-night Detroit because it was packed.

I saw a sign, "The S ssy Cat," with the capital letter 'S' forming the neon outline of a cat. The letter 'a' had burned out.

"Here we go, kiddo," he said. A security guy sitting in a chair at the entrance of the parking lot was reading the *Detroit Free Press*. He looked up from his paper and waved to Shel. Shel nonchalantly waved back.

As we drove in, I noticed the lot wasn't as full as I thought. Most of the cars were parked at the far end of the lot away from the entrance to The Sassy Cat.

"Well, welcome to your birthday party. Come on, kiddo."

We walked up to the ticket booth. An older woman was in the booth reading a Harlequin romance. "Sheldon! You old crow, what ya doin' here?"

"Come to say 'hi' to the girls. Is Sissy here tonight?"

"Oh, you bet she is. Like clockwork."

"This is my buddy's twenty-first."

"Really? Well, happy birthday. Maybe we got a gift inside for ya." She cackled with Shel, and I forced a smile.

"He's never, you know, seen the ladies."

"Oh, I bet he hasn't! Look at this little mensch. We'll treat you right."

"I want to show him around. He just might get a special birthday present if he behaves." He winked at her. They both erupted in laughter. Her book fell to the ground inside the booth.

"Two tickets," she handed them to Shel. "So, when you coming by to visit me, you big palooka?"

"One of these days, sweetheart, one of these days," and they both laughed hysterically at what must have been some private joke.

Sheldon opened the door and we walked into a cloud of cigarette smoke and human stench.

"Lot of smoke for hardly anyone in here, Shel."

"It's late, I'll get you a beer."

He walked over to the bar. I stood immobilized at

the back. I thought it would look like a Las Vegas casino with women instead of slot machines. Instead of red plush and gangster molls, it was rancid and smoky, tables arranged helter-skelter in front of a bare stage with no curtain, no backdrop, just stark, bright lighting. The guys were working class—my dad's kind of working class. The fifteen or so small round tables were surprisingly sparsely populated. Some men with their hands under the table.

A few made it more obvious what they were doing than the others. At one table, a man was draped around an over made up middle-aged woman. I was expecting the women to be very young, sultry, and attractive, like a row of Marilyn Monroes. These women looked like over-made-up, middle-aged housewives. The one dancing, or rather slithering, on stage looked disassociated from her surroundings.

Shel came back with two plastic cups. "Drink up."

"Thanks, Shel."

"Happy birthday, kid." We clicked cups like it was champagne. I knew the taste would be awful, so I just gulped it.

"You surprise me, kid," said Shel.

"How's that?"

"You're drinking like a real pro," he said.

I bristled at the comment.

"Where are all the people?"

"This is a busy night for this place."

"But all those cars outside?"

"Oh, that. There's a fag bar in the shopping mall

across the street. Here they charge two bucks to park, and across the street, they charge three bucks. So, they get the cheap fags to park here." He chuckled. "We'll just stand here in the back. Just wait till Sissy or Sally come on," said Shel. 'Fag' was an ugly word, but it rolled off his tongue without contempt or disgust.

"If there's a f-fag bar there why do they hang out in the bathroom?" I asked, wondering if my curiosity was killing the cat.

Shel turned to me with a raised eyebrow. "There is a huge *sociological* difference between the old ones here and the fairies across the street, capeesh?" Then adding distantly, "If you don't, then talk to Connie, she knows all about it." He chuckled again.

We looked up at the stage, where a plump middle-aged striptease dancer was doing a poor imitation of a belly dance to a disco tune.

Curiosity killing this cat, I looked over at the men's room. I didn't see anyone.

"Over there, is that where they are?" I asked Shel in my best imitation of shock.

"It's none of our business, don't be a …"

"I am not a fuckin' moron," I snapped, defensively.

"This is the place you're free to be … whatever. I'll introduce you to some of the girls when they're finished dancing."

"Awesome!" I said mustering my enthusiasm.

Shel laughed. "Just don't fall in love, kiddo."

"What if I want to?"

"You let me know; I can handle it for ya. Get you a

good deal on falling in love." He chuckled. I shivered. I felt I was capable of this, for appearances' sake. Besides, a female prostitute was probably much safer than my experience four years earlier with a male one.

"Okay, but … I think I have to pee. Is it safe? I don't see anyone in there." I nodded to the men's room.

"Of course, it is. Just don't linger, kid," Shel said his eyes still glued to the stage.

Chapter 29: Men's Room

Unsure why I was going or why I was so terrified, I walked toward the bathroom, my heart pounding. This was it—where the other homosexuals hung out. Maybe this is where I was destined to meet my peculiar species. Could this be my future?

The bathroom had no door. It was dimly lit. I saw no one hanging out. So, I walked in. One step, and the smell was breath-arrestingly bad. I realized immediately, this men's room was not exciting, nor erotic, instead, it stank. It stank like, well, like a toilet: urine, feces, and ammonia. Thanks to the chipped brown paint, it looked even dirtier. The floor was painted a grotesque green. It was chipped too, revealing gray cement. I really did have to pee, but that was not going to be pleasant.

"Hey, handsome," announced an effeminate voice. My heart sank.

I turned my head. There was an obese boyish-looking man dressed in a prim tight-fitting suit.

"We know why you're here," said another singularly unattractive female-looking man. He seemed to emerge like a cockroach.

"You don't have to play shy. You been eyeing this place all night."

"Just relax and pull down your pants," said the fat man.

I shuddered.

"Yes, let's see what you got," the prickly woman-like man said.

"Just pull it down, and I can do you," said the fat guy.

"I had to pee," I protested.

Warily, I started to undo my belt.

I felt a hand on my butt. I turned around. It was the fat man. "That's not all, is it, sugar? Relax, you think we gonna hurt you or somethin'? I want you to feel good, get a silly-looking smile on that sweet face of yours. You can go sugar this one's mine."

I turned my back at the wall. Maybe I'd try to stay and undo my pants for whomever wanted to do whatever, but I felt sick.

"Don't touch me please, just leave me alone," I said.

Bracing myself, I stepped closer to the urinal, away from the hands and faces. If this was being gay, I could do without it.

"What's your problem, dear?" asked the Woman-like man. "Space? Are you afraid of us?"

"Yeah, what's the matter, kid?" said the fat one. "We're just fighting over you, hon."

"Well, stop it," I said. I was reattaching my belt and got ready to run. I could wait and pee tomorrow.

"Oh, sorry. We're not actually bothering you with all this attention, boy, are we?"

"Just get away from me!"

"Leave the kid alone," said the younger man. "Here,

let me help you—girl, go on out. You're not a bad kid; you're a good kid," he said. He got closer and began to whisper, "Real good. Real good." He began to undo his pants. His hands grabbed my shoulders. I felt faint. My hand went for the erect penis that suddenly emerged from his pants. I touched it. It was hard as a rock, while I was limp as wet toast. In a flash, I thought of Casper. Then I remembered there was a 'fag' bar nearby, an alternative to this. And there were more bars: Dreamworld and Menjo's.

"Well, go for it, kid," the guy whispered intensely.

I ran.

I raced back to Shel. I looked back, and to my surprise, no one from the men's room came after me. I had escaped. Shel looked at me. I could feel my face was red and my breath heavy.

"You don't know what these guys tried to do to me."

"Oh, yes I do. I thought you weren't going to stay there, and then I'd have to worry about you, kid." Shel smiled with a wink.

"It was awful, really."

"Okay, kid, don't be a moron. Besides, here comes Sissy; she's really good. Be careful when she dances that you don't fall in love."

Sissy came out on stage, and much to my surprise she looked just like Marilyn Monroe. I was so grateful.

"Thank you, God!" I said. Shel laughed.

At least her body looked clean. At least sex with her would not be as disgusting as sex in a toilet. I would have done anything Shel arranged for me to do with a woman just to wash away the awful memory.

"She's really hot, Shel."

"Right, kid."

I watched her as she began to take off her clothes. She was sexy and inviting. She was quite thin and boyish. I could stare at her and enjoy the sight. For Shel and my hetero-reputation, I made sure I added extra enthusiasm. Sissy revealed her beautiful thin legs. I thought I could easily do it with her and just imagine she was a man.

Still, I couldn't shake thoughts of the men's toilet. Those two scared me. Suddenly, I felt a tremendous urge to have sex with Sissy.

"Jamie, this is Sissy," said Shel, introducing me to Marilyn Monroe. A skimpy cloth robe now covered her semi-nude body. She had finished her dance and walked over to us.

"Hi Sissy, great ... performance," I said. "I'd love to ... know you more ..."

"Thank you, sweetie. He's a little sweetheart, Shel, ain't he?"

"He's all right; he's no moron, I'll tell you that, Sissy."

"I ... I ... Could we talk in private?" I couldn't believe I heard myself ask.

"Talk, dear? Is that what you want?" She looked at me. "I know what you really want." My body obeyed as she put her hand over my crotch, I could sport a miraculous boner.

"I'd like to know you."

Then Shel said, "Not tonight, Sissy."

"Huh?" asked Sissy.

"No? Well then how about you? Nice seeing you Shel, come back later if you can." Sissy walked away.

"Not tonight, Sissy, I'll see you around." Then he looked at me with a strange grin, "Okay, enough education for one night, kid. I'll get you home."

Sheldon and I walked outside.

"She is very beautiful, Shel. I was quite surprised; she looked much better than the other dancers. Can I just do it with her, I can pay for it. Honest, I can."

"But I can tell she's not your type, Jimmy. Let's go. This was fun, but it is gettin' late for both of us."

I didn't say it out loud, but I shouted it inside my head: "Thank you, Shel."

I escaped. Getting back in his car, I looked across the street for the gay bar. There were hardly any cars left, and no sign of anything but a warehouse across the street, but it still pointed to the fact that there were alternatives.

Chapter 30: The Abyss

The darkness challenged my eyes. I could barely focus on anything.

The smoky stale smell attacked my nostrils.

Disco music banged against my ears.

The booming pulse from the overtaxed woofers rippled through my body. A sea of bodies crowded in like sardines, billows of their cigarette smoke adding to the haze. The smell of the smoke mixed with a musty human and alcohol stench was bad enough then came the burnt-coconut smell issuing from the faux fog on the dance floor. Perspiring men armed with watered-down drinks and lit cigarettes moved recklessly about the dance floor. It seemed opulent and rapacious. I was ridiculously happy. Compared to the Sassy Cat, this hell was pure heaven.

There were young guys barely visible in the dark, pulsating disco lights orchestrating the appearance and disappearance of beautiful faces, prowling glances, and plenty of lost souls like me.

The men's room of the Sassy Cat had been out of the question, but this bar, Dreamland, wasn't. And this was even wholesome by comparison to the strip joint. I was most definitely going to do something I'd never dreamed of by the end of the evening: I was going to prove I cared more about the person than about sex.

I had dreaded going to my first night at a gay bar. Ironically, I might not have done it without the advice from Dave. Not that Dave had told me to go to a gay bar; he just said I needed to 'get laid.' That plain statement made everything seem so straightforward. I'd heard that the Palmer Park neighborhood was a gay area. Sure enough, walking around Six Mile Road, I found a bar with a line of men around it. I saw the sign, 'Dreamland,' the bar that Eula had mentioned.

A long line of mostly young men sprinkled with the occasional older man wrapped around Dreamland. Waiting in that line, I got my first introduction to the mostly white clientele. "If I see that kike prick in here, I am going to scream!" said the guy ahead of me.

"Well, scream away and scratch his eyes out, honey; he's gonna be here with that Miss Thing."

"Ugh, not El Creepo."

"Yeah, El Creepo has a thing for Jewboys."

"How do you know?"

"Evvverybody does, sugar."

"*Everybody?*"

"Don't you know nothin', girl? You know what they say about them, don't you? 'A big schnoz means a big dick.'"

They giggled. I tried my best not to listen as they went on, freely dishing their disdain for Jews, blacks, lesbians, and anyone else who wasn't them. Apparently, they were deluded into thinking that there is just something superior about being white and living in Hazel Park.

I finally arrived at the door.

'Two dollar cover. Have ID ready' read the sign.

I took two dollars out of my pocket and showed my ID. A middle-aged man took my two dollars and looked at my ID. "Ha, good for you, kid. Happy birthday."

"Thanks," I said, even though my birthday was yesterday.

"Here," he said, handing me a poker chip. "First drink is on us, boy. Give me your hand."

"Thanks, thank you very much."

I thought he wanted to shake my hand. Instead, he roughly turned it over, stamping it with a black ink star. "Next!"

I walked in. The loud pulse of the song "It's Raining Men" attacked my ears. I walked over to the bar and ordered my first drink. The guy ahead of me had ordered a Long Island Iced Tea. So, I ordered one, too. I paid with the chip.

"What's the occasion?" asked the bartender.

"I just turned twenty-one."

"Oh, you're legal. Well then, congrats. Here—one on me." The bartender poured us both a shot of tequila. He raised his glass to mine, and we swallowed down the shot. It tasted awful and burned my throat. I forced a smiled. The bartender winked back. The drink's effect was strong and immediate.

As I drank the Long Island Iced Tea, I noticed the drink made me looser, more relaxed, but also less focused and dizzy. Someone offered me a cigarette, which I actually took, imagining myself to be Humphrey Bogart. I took a puff to get it lighted, then coughed hysterically. As soon as the guy walked away, I threw it out.

In no time, my drink was gone, so I bought another. I then stood by the dance floor in the dark. Alone. No one to talk to, which was just as well given the volume of the music. I now understood how preposterous my suggestion to Casper that we go to Dreamland to talk had been.

I looked at people dancing mindlessly. One beautiful body after another. I felt echoes of Casper. I tried to tell myself it didn't matter. Like Jack said, a cock is a cock. But who was I kidding? Casper's image was still there. If I could only explain things or understand what was bothering him. Here were all these undulating mini-Caspers. Some were cuter than Casper but they were probably shallow like the guys ahead of me in the line. I felt the superficiality of their dance, their talk, and their gestures. I wanted what I could not have: Casper. Casper had become a kind of saint, in part due to his unreachability. Holding him up like that shielded me from wanting anyone else. So even though he wasn't there, he was keeping guard for me … for a little while.

For two-and-three quarter-hours to be precise. Because then I finally moved from my statue-like base to drunkenly standing in front of the dance floor. I decided I would dance alone. I was no sooner on the dance floor than I felt woozy. Was it the third, or fourth drink I just had? After a while, the room started to spin. I walked off the dance floor, abandoned my last drink on a random ledge, and decided to go home.

I turned and walked into a kind of hallway. It was quieter. I saw a soft bench. I plopped down and waited for the spinning to stop.

The room was almost empty. In a rare lucid moment, I realized I had missed my last bus home.

A man sat down next to me, holding two bottles of beer. He seemed to say something; the oddest things issued from my lips in reply. "Hello, man," I said, feeling a little merry and then profoundly embarrassed. I caressed his short afro.

"You like black guys?" he asked.

"Fuzzy hair," I slurred.

"Want a beer? I bought it for a friend, but he seems to have disappeared."

I did not want the beer. But he was smiling, and he had cute fuzzy hair. I felt obliged to accept.

"Thanks, sure," I said.

He handed me the beer.

"Thank you, my name is … I'll get it in a moment," I joked as I stalled for time. I was unsure if I was Jimmy, Jamie or James. "James," I said.

"You're sure? James?"

I nodded.

"James, nice name," he leered unambiguously.

"What's your name?" it suddenly occurred to me to ask.

"Jimmy." He extended a hand to me. I shook it.

"Jello, Jimmy," I slurred. The mistake, I thought, was the height of hilarity. I laughed embarrassingly. I expected that he would lose all interest after this display of drunkenness. The opposite seemed to be true.

"Glad to meet you, James ... You know, you're cute."

"Thank you." I felt obliged to return the compliment. "You're beautiful," I said perfunctorily.

The next thing I knew, he was kissing me. His tongue worked its way into my mouth, forcing me to taste alcohol and ashtray-flavored saliva. He started to grope my groin, slid his hand to my butt. Rather than fear, I felt an astonishing flood of self-worth. He desired me. He wanted me. I felt like I was finally worth something. I guess he knew I was really there for sexualization, not socialization. Casper would give way to an old thirst for ... for what ... being desired? intimidation? Humiliation? I wasn't enjoying myself, so why was I doing this? Or was this enjoyment? I didn't know.

We paused. Then I finished the beer. Things got blurry. I realized I had had too much to drink as I went to kiss him, and the strange thing is, he had mysteriously turned into an older guy named Adam. Adam looked like a mini-First World War had taken place on his face, with little micro-bomb craters littering his cheeks and forehead. He was old, at least thirty years old. Overall, he was ugly and care-worn, but his little almond eyes made me think of Casper. I found that thought disturbing enough that I knew I had to leave. "Okay, I just missed my last bus, I think I should be getting home," I mumbled. Adam looked at me appraisingly.

"I can give you a ride."

"Really? Thanks. I need to get home," I said.

"You live alone?" he asked, putting his arm around my shoulder.

"No, I have a straight roommate." He stroked my back reaching my buttocks which he squeezed. I felt warm and desired.

"You know, we can also go back to my place."

"You want me to?" His desire for me was overpowering. *But he's ugly,* I thought, feebly debating with myself what Adam had already decided. And what I had subconsciously already realized that it felt sexy to let myself be 'victimized' by him.

"You're hot, kiddo."

"I am?" I was horrified with myself as I agreed to go home with him, having no idea what this would mean or what would happen. At once I was sexually aroused; at least the organ between my legs was convinced something would happen. But I was scared, too. He could be a serial killer, a closeted homophobe, or even a Republican.

He hugged me. He helped himself to another assault on my mouth. The charge I got out of it was a frightening switch. I felt desired but then also felt worthless and being taken advantage of. But I was letting it happen and I seemed to be getting off on it.

Adam's face lit up, and I also felt good for making someone happy. "Great, my place it is!" he said with a blink of his eyes.

We got in his car. It stank of cigarettes. Butts overstuffed the ashtray. He turned on the ignition. Motown music blared. And off we went, not knowing exactly where or why. Maybe, I thought, at his house maybe I won't need to kneel on the floor. Perhaps we would do something more comfortable? I wondered. Like doing it sitting down.

Chapter 31: The Tree of Knowledge

Adam's place was an upper floor of a dingy old downtown apartment building. But opening the door to his apartment revealed another world. It looked very sharp. His taste in decor was sparkling white. Drunkenly, I wondered why a black guy would like so much white. I puzzled over this until I thought I arrived at the brilliant answer: their naked bodies would stick out better on white furniture. I was going to share this brilliance with Adam until I noticed the carpet was a thick white shag. *Maybe kneeling on the floor wouldn't be so bad,* I thought. A collage of Diana Ross pictures was plastered all over one wall. This compared favorably to Jack's wall of tortured saints. I began to relax. Another wall had nothing on it but a small portrait of Judy Garland, my mother's favorite singer. I thought this had to be a sign from God it would be okay.

"Just clear off a spot on the couch; I will be right there."

The couch was covered in a heap of clothes and a greasy pizza box. I had barely piled the stuff on a small coffee table when Adam, my black knight in pockmarked armor, returned with two beers. He turned on his stereo, playing Diana Ross's "Love Child." The music was a soft reminder of my childhood; however, accompanying the music was the sound of Adam opening the can for me, which incited a different kind of flashback to my childhood: What was about to occur had happened before.

Suddenly, it was too clear: the cold can, guzzling the beer ... I knew the routine. I was going to let him rape me.

"You want another beer, baby?" he asked. "You drank that fast."

"Yeah ... thanks for ..." *Whatever.*

"I am so glad you're here, honey. You're cute."

"Thank you ..."

Adam looked deep into my eyes. "Are you okay, kid? You seem distant?"

He looked even uglier than he'd looked in the bar. He was wearing clothes for a far younger guy: preppy knit shirt, designer jeans. I was tying my best not to freak out calming myself that he wouldn't rape me. He seemed nice and decent.

"Do you live alone?" I asked.

"Of course."

"Ever live with a ... another guy?" I asked.

"Sort of. But not really. It's not like we're breeders."

"Huh? Right." I laughed. I didn't know we had a disparaging term for normal people. "It's mostly about the penis, not the person, isn't it?"

"What?"

"That's what I heard."

"I care about you. You're not just a piece of meat,

kid. We're not animals. Fuck … Allow me to introduce myself. I am a person, a thirty-three-year-old librarian, Adam Washington."

"Thank you." I forced a laugh. "Jamie Goldberg, student at Detroit State."

"Student? Sweet. Hello, Jamie. Jewish?" he asked, surprised. Adding softly, "You don't look it." He put his arm around me. I could see desire getting the better of him, not caring if I was a yid as his inevitable arms enveloped me. He started to paw at me. I yearned for Casper to rescue me. It felt awkward, Adam felt at once like a total stranger and yet we were so intimate. He enjoyed squeezing me and groping me. He stroked my back. He slipped his hand into my pants and rubbed Casper away.

"Can I know something about you?" I asked.

"Okay, what?" He stopped rubbing.

"Do you have a boyfriend?"

"A *boyfriend?* No. Do you?"

"No," I replied meekly.

"You okay?" he asked, withdrawing from being so close to me.

"This is kind of my first time." I didn't know how to explain this was the first time I willingly—in the overt sense of the word—did this.

"Oh. I guess we both got more than we bargained for."

"Great, I'll go home."

"Jesus, chill." Then his voice went softer. "Are you ready for this?"

"I think so," I said unsure of what 'this' meant.

"Let's just have some fun. We'll go slow, okay? I promise not to hurt you. And stop means stop."

"Thank you, Adam." I looked him in the eye, at first grateful for his gentleness. Yet somehow, I had this perverse desire to be hurt somehow. I had no idea what we were going to do. His looks ceased to be an issue, something else made him attractive to me. I wanted to make him happy no matter what it cost me. I softly caressed his arm.

"What do you want, Jamie? It's okay to have sex … if you want it. I don't want to pressure you into anything."

I kissed Adam. Willfully disobeying myself, my right hand went to Adam's butt and squeezed it. "I need you," I said.

That was all the encouragement he needed. He became unstoppably aggressive. It horrified me to let a stranger do this to me. I was now convinced he was going to rape me. Yet, I let him, as a burning need for his desire outstripped anything else.

"You're so fucking hot. Take your clothes off!" Adam ordered.

A page was turned. I took off my shoes and socks. Inside, I felt something warm and needy, grateful and grotesque. What was this new thing? I didn't know. I did know I was officially betraying my feelings for Casper. Nevertheless, I continued. It wasn't love because love makes you feel noble, and this made me feel like shit, sexy shit. It wasn't enchantment because enchantment would last a long time. This would scarcely last an hour. It was a fling, I suppose. 'Just one of those things.'

Clothes off, Adam came in for the kill. I let him put an arm around me. I let him caress me. I let him breathe on me. I smelled his horrid alcohol and cigarette breath. I told myself I didn't care. He caressed my cheeks. He hugged me, sliding his hands up and down my ass. A storm of conflicting emotions was settled suddenly.

"Fuck me, please, I need it," I whispered.

"What?"

"Take me."

"Relax, honey; we have all night."

As if from the top of the ceiling, I saw myself slide down the couch until I was lying down. Part of me said, *"Don't do it, not with him."* But it was happening anyway. He looked down at me with his Casper eyes; I tried my best to imagine he was Casper. It seemed like an obscene fantasy and then it came. The saving grace of the evening, this evil voice in my head: *You bitch! You fucking dog! DOG! Rotting in hell! You're getting just what you deserve!* A vision of Jack, and the mysterious Gary, came back, and I knew just what I had to do. I felt an inner evil and relaxed and let it happen, my own uncontrollable self-hatred making me suddenly insatiable.

"Relax, honey, just relax; I'd love to do you." He kissed me and again sent his tongue deep into me. His desire again overwhelmed my disgust, my disgust turning into need. Coming up for air, he looked at me with a diabolical smile, which made him quite cute. Without taking his eyes off me for one second, he raised a finger to his mouth. He sucked his own finger. I closed my eyes. I did not want to see the world as this happened. But I smiled for the confirmation I needed.

The Confirmation of what? I felt the intrusion of his finger into my anus. A breathtaking wave of sadness came over me, *ah bitch,* and I relaxed. This had all happened before and would happen again and again.

"You're tight. Wanna relax, make it feel better? You'll enjoy it more."

"Yeah, I want to relax."

"Ever try poppers?"

I didn't reply.

He reached over the couch to a side table. I saw him unscrew a small brown bottle. He put it under my nose. It smelled like industrial waste.

The next moment, my heart was pounding, and I felt wild. Everything went dark and sexually psychedelic. *Sex was the world, and I became the primeval bitch, the desired satisfier!* I begged in an unrecognizable voice to be fucked and fucked hard. Adam leaped on top of me— my feet shot in the air, and we were off to the raunchy races. A desire to be fucked sang in a high Wagnerian voice inside me. Adam became the evil saint I urgently needed.

He inserted. Effortlessly! My ass had turned to butter. This was easy. I had wild thoughts of melting into him if only he could fuck me hard enough.

Ah, Parsifal, you don't know what you've been missing.

My brain was pounding. My heart was pounding.

My ass was being pounded. A compulsion came over me. I yelled, "Harder!" In my mind I yelled, *Rape me, rape me!* I screamed in my head; almost certain he did not hear it.

Yes!" he cried. He started to slam my ass. It started to really hurt, but I didn't care. I began to feel subhuman in that instant, getting banged like a wild animal.

After too brief a moment, the poppers wore off. The compulsion died. Enthusiasm dampened. Sobriety returned. It stopped being erotic. But it still was going on.

I felt it was done, or at least I was through. But Adam was not finished. He kept on fucking me. And fucking me. And fucking me. My legs were getting tired. After the poppers had worn off, I felt like I had somehow dropped into this random sex act.

It started to get boring as he continued the repetitive huffing and puffing and thrusting. I had this total lack of desire but keeping me in the game was this need to be desired.

He moved me to his bed and laid me on my stomach. He lay on top of me. All this seemed like an administrative bridge to the next act. In my mind it was rape against my will, he was brutal. Nothing tender, no pretense. But reality was his gentleness and easing me getting back up to speed. The repeated pounding of his cock into my by-now four-lane-highway asshole ceased to hurt and started putting my mind in some strange weird twilight zone space.

He pounded on; I hardly felt anything anymore, but

there was some new feeling of euphoria. It was an intoxication without drugs.

Still, he kept going. I seemed to float patiently for his climax, but it seemed the climax would never come. My mind started to wander. I started thinking about homework that was due. Then it drifted to Casper. And, then I caught a glimpse of Adam's blinking eyes over my shoulder. Looking into his mattress, I saw it was pristine clean. I felt shame. I was dirtying it. Now look at me: just a dumb fuck, much less glamorous than the bitch satisfier. I tried to stop thinking.

Adam must have sensed my attention had drifted because he took the brown bottle out again. A sniff and the world contracted into just sex. I got into it again. Moving my own body back and forth, the erection underneath me was begging for more attention. And then Adam went into animal mode.

"Oh, baby, tighter, tighter, baby!" he pleaded. I tightened my ass, hoping it would bring stronger thrusts to satisfy my own increasingly hungry demands. Without saying anything, he knew and changed his delivery style, now pounding hard, forcing my body to be pushed vigorously back and forth. Adam was like an animal with a single-minded need. I gladly traded the increased pain in my ass for the pleasure on my dick as it shifted under me against the sheets.

"Oh, please, harder!" I moaned.

Then Adam spoke.

"Are you ready?"

"Yes!" And he started to slam my ass. It started to

hurt again, but I didn't care. In that instant, getting banged, I willfully desecrated my images of Tim and Casper. I thought of Tim and what sucking Tim's cock would have been like. I remembered drinking Casper's cum and the sour taste. The thoughts were so repulsive and hurt so badly. I felt an urge to be punished. "Harder! Please! Harder!" I yelled, matching animal call for animal call. I suddenly wanted to be raped more than ever. "Harder!"

He crashed his semen into me, then we both exploded.

At one moment, well after I had cum, Adam laid all his weight on top of me as if he wanted to crush me. But I did not want him to move. I wanted him to completely cover me up and hide my body.

He was sweating. I felt the cold wetness.

He was breathing hard. "Thank goodness, I thought you would never cum," Adam said.

My head was still pounding from the orgasm and poppers. But I then realized he was waiting for me to cum before he would. Adam rolled over on his side. I looked at him and rolled onto my side facing him. Adam looked so grateful. He looked at me with a face that had all the day's stress and anxiety drained away from it. He looked quite beautiful, even. Some emotion, some positive warm nameless emotion, welled up in me. I don't know what came over me. I kissed Adam as if he were the most beautiful man on the planet as my brain continued to swim in this twilight-zone euphoria.

He kissed me back—a soft but aggressive kiss,

making sure a generous amount of his saliva was ejaculated into my mouth. I felt proud for being desired. I pulled away. I smiled broadly. "I love this, Adam." I stroked his cheek, "You're really beautiful. Handsome. Sexy." I said perversely.

"You are a sweetheart, baby," Adam said.

I looked at Adam and felt an urgent need to use the toilet. "I need to use the bathroom,"

I teetered over to the bathroom. I looked in the mirror, and I did not shy away from my messed-up face and mussed-up hair. I embraced what I saw with all my heart and soul. I smiled. I tried to forget the more disturbing aspects of what I had just done. This was my new life: gay sex and proud. I was desired. I was sought after. Casper didn't want me, well someone else did! *Welcome to the Gay Community, James Micaiah Goldberg, the water is warm.*

Variation: Hammerblow III, Dancing in the Lion's Den

January - February 1981

V Rondo-Burleske. Allegro assai. Sehr trotzig.
(Rondo-Burlesque. Quite Fast. Very defiant.)

Chapter 32: Humiliating Hamlet

In the nights that followed, some dark malevolent drive appeared to force me to recreate and create my nightmares. How quickly they stacked up—Casper, Tim, and now Adam. Casper used me, Tim rejected me and my night with Adam was this growing need to be desired and to do that I felt I had to force myself to be used, as if that was all that I was ever good for and the only thing that would make me desirable.

To escape this self-inflicted downward spiral, I restlessly occupied my mind every moment of the day. During work, I relied on the mind-numbing Zen of baking bagels. At home, I sadistically focused myself on studying and when I ran out of homework, I always had the bottomless pit of meanings in Shakespeare's *Hamlet*, for which I was going to be auditioning. To make it even more bottomless, I decided to practice the role of Hamlet instead of the smaller role of Horatio.

I obsessively meditated on Hamlet's troubles and lost myself in his tortured soul. But after a while, even Hamlet would stare back at me and accuse.

I enjoyed Hamlet's diatribe about his uncle's marriage to Hamlet's mother. I was first attracted to the cadence of the words, the rising emotion and indignation. Puffing myself up with Hamlet's sense of outrage, with a noble sense of capturing his emotional outburst I could cry:

> *Carrying, I say, the stamp of one defect,*
> *Being nature's livery, or fortune's star—*
> *Their virtues else—be they as pure as grace,*
> *As infinite as man may undergo—*
> *Shall in the general censure take corruption*
> *From that particular fault: the dram of evil*
> *Doth all the noble substance of a doubt*
> *To his own scandal.*

Over time, though, a different sentence would run through my brain as Hamlet seemed to reject me even as I recited his words:

> *Carrying, I say, the stamp of one defect,*
> *And yet, there is you who—*
> *Never had virtues—nor pure as grace,*
> *As infinite pit of sins—*
> *Shall in the general censure take corruption*
> *From that reputation: the mound of evil*
> *Creating your own scandal.*

The more I studied the play, the more I felt Hamlet to be purer and more worthy than I ever could be. How could I play him except to try and take him down?

I never really knew where I was going with all this until the first auditions.

The first auditions took place in the small theater where Casper forced me to suck him off. The memory added a perverse twist of retribution to the auditions.

Among the others trying out was Ben Geln, thorn in my side. Homophobic Ben, my bully in the Theater Department, was also reading for Hamlet, along with half a dozen other students. One of the best actors in the department, Alec Morgan, was reading Claudius. The auditions were crowded, as everyone in the Theater Department seemed to be reading for something. The auditions were going to take several days.

Before I even started, two students had already given thoroughly convincing readings of Hamlet's pain and bewilderment. Ben gave an amazing, almost sexy, macho reading. It felt useless for me and then came the call.

"Next Hamlet-Horatio pair: Goldberg as Hamlet, Geln as Horatio!" director Dwight announced. As I walked to the stage, Dwight seemed to give me a nod of encouragement.

Ben and I flashed glances at each other: his hateful, mine desperate. Ben's hatred, like Casper's, still stung. I didn't understand what I had done to earn Ben's meanness except being a fag. I knew he would try and trip me up. I was afraid of him, and yet, I felt an odd sense of destructive confidence. Walking onstage, muddled on how to read Hamlet, it then came to me in a flash. I knew exactly how to play him. And the beauty of it was that it would annoy the hell out of Ben, even if the price would be what little self-respect I had left.

Dwight and Mr. Nathan sat in the front row of the small practice room.

"Both of you in the center," Dwight said with an unnerving smile across his pudgy baby face. I never liked the way he leered at me. His smile, though friendly, seemed slimy. "Jamie, you stand in between Ben and the chair there. On the cue, put the chair down between you and Ben. Okay, do the first excerpt."

"Loosen up, have fun with it," yelled Mr. Nathan.

I shot a glance at Ben. He was handsome despite it all. His eyes, deep in the script, didn't see me staring until he looked up. My stare unnerved him.

"What ho, Horatio," I said in a low seductive voice.

"Here, uh …" Ben was surprised by my tone. "S—sweet lord, at your … service."

"Horatio, thou art e'en as just a man, as e'er my conversation coped withal," I said, again trying to sound lascivious. That spooked Ben.

"O, my dear lord—" Ben could barely spit out.

"Nay, do not think I flatter." I approached him, getting closer and closer. "For what advancement may I hope from thee; That no revenue hast but thy good spirits; To feed and clothe thee?" Then u put my hand on his shoulder. "Why should the poor be flatter'd? No, let the candied tongue lick absurd pomp—"

"Get away from me!" yelled Ben backing away.

But I continued my monologue staring right at him—being especially salacious at the words "Give me that man that is not passion's slave, and I will wear him in my heart's core, ay, in my heart of heart, as I do thee."

"Make him stop!" Ben yelled. I went on ignoring his plea and no one interrupted me, much to my glee.

When I came to the end of my monologue, Ben was speechless. Meanwhile, I continued my seduction of

Horatio. I gazed with exaggerated longing into Ben's eyes as his eyes were shooting darts of hatred. How strange, but that fed me! Love versus repulsion.

"For I mine eyes will rivet to his face," as I concluded he turned away, I shouted after him, "And after we will both our judgments join; In censure of his seeming."

Ben was frozen.

"Wow," said someone backstage.

"Ben?" prompted Mr. Nathan.

"Well, my lord: If he steal …" prompted Dwight.

"Well, my lord: If he steal …" Ben began tentatively, then with increasing anger, "aught the whilst this play is playing, And 'scape detecting, I will pay the theft."

"They are coming to the play;" I hushed softly, "I must be idle: Get you a place."

"Stop!" yelled Dwight. I could swear I was about to kiss Ben.

"What were you going to do, faggot?" Ben challenged me.

"It's just a play," I countered.

"That was … interesting," said Mr. Nathan smiling his approval.

"It was not," countered Ben. "There is nothing like this in the text."

"What's the problem, Ben?" asked Dwight.

"He's the problem! Jamie's a fag," Ben complained.

"Ben, you've got to act more professional." Dwight was shaking his fat round curly-haired head in dismay. Dwight leaned over to Mr. Nathan, "But I never saw anything like that in my life."

"Dwight, if you want to direct, direct now. It's certainly not what I expected, but you saw their interaction," said Mr. Nathan softly. Dwight's stare softened on me.

Out of character, seeing shocked faces around me from people awaiting their turn, my heart pounded in humiliation. I braced myself for being dismissed. Ben came up to me. "You don't do that to me again. I'll punch you out—"

"Stop it!" shouted Dwight. Students in the theater laughed, breaking the intensity. Dwight turned to me, "Okay, let's hear you reading Hamlet at reading five. Start from 'Why, what an ass am I.'"

Again, chuckles from the theater.

It was an intense speech, and after the intensity of what I had just done, I was looking for inspiration to deliver this speech. First, I felt my anger at Ben and his threat to fight me. Then, I delved deep into my past. To the murder of Hamlet's father, I applied my own guile in murdering my own innocence; to the anger at his uncle's crimes, my anger at my family's rejection and my powerlessness to do anything about it. It all built up slowly inside, and I allowed it to reach a huge crescendo:

But I am pigeon-liver'd and lack gall
To make oppression bitter, or ere this
I should have fatted all the region kites
With this slave's offal: bloody, bawdy villain!
Remorseless, treacherous, lecherous, kindless villain!

"Thank you, Jamie," muttered Dwight dismissively.

"Excellent," Mr. Nathan nodded approvingly at me. So, one out of two good signs wasn't so bad, I hoped.

"Ben, you read Hamlet, and Alec read Polonius. Reading three," called Dwight.

I was exhausted. Ben sneered at me as he passed and elbowed me for kicks.

"Sorry, chump," he whispered as he passed. He tried to elbow me again but I ducked. "Made ya flinch, pigeon-liver'd," he hissed.

The auditions went on. Almost everyone delivered calmer, more classical readings than I was capable of. I was sure I hadn't a prayer of getting even a herald's part.

The nail in the coffin was Ben's reading of Hamlet's famous monologue. He read with a quiet dramatic intensity, not my more hysterical delivery. I had to admit he was more Shakespearean than I was. Of course, they were going to reject my depraved portrayal of Hamlet.

Chapter 33: A Regular Don Juan

On my first night in Dreamland, Adam was able to reassure me that I was desired and useful. Only the feeling did not last. In the ensuing void my self-image deteriorate I needed to be desired again. On my second night in Dreamland, a cute student named Brian proved I was desirable beyond all doubt—until the next day. The third night started a dry spell with no one wanting me. The sixth night, a homely old man named Craig showed I was loved—until sunrise. Walking away from Craig at dawn, I felt rejected and cast away. Luckily, on the seventh night, all was not lost. I felt abandoned only until three a.m., when, in an after-hours club, a guy named Dan made me feel desirable again. Dan also made me feel cheap as I yet again lowered my standards to sleep with an oafish person, I did not find attractive. The eighth night, I reasoned, would compensate. I would only give in to someone I desired, possibly even loved; however, it got late, and once again, I had to go home with another one who was uglier, fatter, and even more demanding.

The cycle turned into a complex sort of commerce. At first, I would give myself to someone who made me feel desired, which slightly increased my self-esteem. But during the sex act, the loathsome self-hatred would creep back. Afterward, I would realize what I had done and who I had done it with, which dramatically lowered my self-esteem. That meant I had to go back for more sex and more self-esteem, but only to give it away during whatever sexual escapes I had gotten myself into. forever getting deeper into self-esteem debt, requiring yet another night's down payment. Self-image-wise, it was a net loss.

At home, I consoled myself with a new opera to fit my new lifestyle: Mozart's *Don Giovanni*. The Don stood for one thing and one thing only: sex. This made Don Giovanni the patron saint of gay bars. There was no consideration of human vulnerability, emotion, or compassion capable of standing in the way of the Don's sexual needs. Only one minor difference: while the Don's needs were predatory; my needs were to be preyed upon.

Don Giovanni's servant, Leporello, sings a famous song called the "Catalog Aria," in which he lists the Don's sexual conquests. According to Leporello's accounting, the Don had sex with six-hundred-and-forty women in Italy, ninety-one in Turkey, one-hundred in France, and two hundred-and-thirty-one in Germany. But in Spain, he had a thousand-and-three, a feat he managed, like me, as the song attests, by being completely uncritical of whom he had sex with.

I did the math. A sex partner every night for 5.86 years would get me over the Don's record. So, as the very model of the modern homosexual I believed myself to be, I tried for Don Giovanni's record. I even started my own catalogue, complete with statistics. Like the Don, all I had to do was lower my standards and smother my emotions. In return for my efforts, I would find a brief moment of worthiness, grace, and ecstasy.

The nights started blending together: I had to prove I was desirable as my past record was mere history. No resting on withered laurels. The entries in my catalogue multiplied: Adam, Brian, Craig, Don, Eric, Fred, Greg, Hal, Ian ... all engaging in what I thought was the only form of homosexual love.

I was home, sitting on the oval carpet, nursing a painful feeling in my butt, comforting myself with the most heartless piece of music I had ever heard. It was a trio from *Don Giovanni*. Donna Elvira, one of his victims, comes looking for him. She is so conflicted that she is unsure whether she wants to kill him or to marry him.

The Don is glad to see her, only because he wants to screw her maid. The Don forces Leporello to masquerade as Don Giovanni by putting on his clothes and pantomiming his words to lure away Donna Elvira away, freeing the real Don Giovanni to seduce the maid. The heartless treachery counterpointed with misplaced trust spoke to me in how hopeless the situation was for the Donna Elvira's of the world.

> *DON GIOVANNI*
> *(Hiding while Leporello mouths his words)*
> *Come down here, my lovely,*
> *And I will show you,*
> *that you are the one*
> *whom my soul adores.*
> *I truly repent hurting you.*

DONNA ELVIRA
No, I don't believe you, traitor!

DON GIOVANNI
Oh, believe me, or I'll kill myself!

LEPORELLO (aside)
If this goes on any longer
I'll burst out laughing!

Then Dave entered in from the cold. Yet, I froze as if caught in the middle of a terrible crime.

"I am freezing," he said.

"There is coffee in the kitchen," I said as I sipped from my own cup.

DONNA ELVIRA
What a quandary is this!
I don't know what to do!
Oh Lord, please protect my credulous heart.

DON GIOVANNI
I hope she yields quickly!
What a nice little trick this is!
My God, I can do almost anything,
Has anyone seen such a
Fertile talent as mine?

The record ended and the turntable clicked off

"May I join you?" Dave asked as he sat down with me on the floor. "Nice music."

"The music just ended."

"Really? Or did you turn it off?"

"No, it really ended."

"Uh-huh. You seem to always shut off music the moment I come in."

"This time it just shut off, honest." Dave winced when I said the word 'honest.' "I didn't think you liked opera anyway."

"I like anything if it's good." He sat down with me, rolling a joint. "Tell me, how's it going, Jamie-boy?"

He lit the joint and passed it to me.

"Great." I passed it back without taking a hit. With a gesture, he seemed to insist. So, I took a reluctant puff. The mellowness was a welcomed anesthetic to what would surely be a stiff discussion. Smoking also filled in for the awkward silence. Dave was curiously cool. I braced myself for another attack of homosexual panic. I was wondering how he could have found out. After all, I had invented a mythical girlfriend named Chloë.

"By the way, Jamie-boy, I wanted to ask you something."

I braced for the bad news. I held up my hand to his offer of the joint, not wanting to smoke any more. "Ready, aim, fire." Here it came. I decided to try one more valiant attempt to be cool before getting kicked out.

"Chill, it ain't that bad. I am studying child—"

"Oh, by the way, did you hear Chapman is claiming insanity?" I said, at once trying to change the subject to John Lennon's assassin.

"I'm not surprised; he was one weird dude. Anyone who would shoot John Lennon is a sicko."

"The guy even had an obsession with J.D. Salinger's

Catcher in the Rye. Can you believe that?"

"I'd think you'd have an obsession with the *Catcher in the Rye*."

"Me?"

"Yeah, like I was saying, I am studying child ..."

"You mean Salinger in general or just the book?"

"Jamie don't interrupt. I was sayin' that I am studying a course on child abuse with Dr. Farley—I told you, one of my favorite profs. It's pretty sad shit ... but you should check it out. I left a book in the kitchen."

"Me? What's it got to do with me? I haven't harmed a fly." Panic reigned supreme. I knew homosexuals were constantly accused of being pedophiles, but I was not prepared for this from Dave.

"I know that, man. Chill." Dave was getting frustrated with me. "You might want to think about it."

"About what?"

"How do I say this? We're friends right?"

"Yes, of course." I said defensively.

" Yet you act like I am about to hit you or throw you out at any second. Look, the last thing I want to do is to play armchair psychologist with you but ... I'll just say it: were you abused as a child? Physically or psychologically?" His words were like being broadsided by a truck.

"You have to be out of your mind!" I yelled, scarcely believing the anger in my voice. I tried to calm down and throttle the sense that I was fighting for my life. "I had a perfectly normal childhood, and I have completely ... normal ..." My voice trailed off to an almost inaudible. "parents." I felt ashamed for lying. After all, my parents kicked me out of the house. A heavy marijuana high smothered my panic into a deep paranoia that seemed to cut an incision in my heart. I was immobilized but felt I had to run for my life.

"Man, relax, I am just saying, from this book I read, you might want to think about it. You have some familiar symptoms it talks about in the book. Let me tell you, what I mean—" He just rattled this off like he was reading the news, oblivious to my petrified reaction. "To start, you are so hard on yourself … I mean it. You wither like a flower at the slightest sign of disapproval. Shit, you just thought I was accusing you of abusing children just now, didn't you? Am I right?"

"I don't know what to say. I am fine."

"Don't get defensive, we're just talking here. Jesus, you should be called Mr. Damaged Goods."

"Damaged goods?" As soon as he said it, I knew he was right. When I heard the words, it seemed to me such a comforting thought. I thought of the nights I was standing alone at Dreamland unconsciously thinking that very thought.

"Jamie, we don't need to talk about this now, I just thought from our last talk you were …ready."

"Ready for what? I know I am hard on myself, but isn't that just high standards?"

"Cool, but let's face it, man, you're a history of broken relationships."

"Me?"

"I listen to you talk about your parents, your ex-roomie, your dorm mates. Chloë. Nobody really seems to like you. Nobody knows you."

I squirmed at the symptoms. At the moment, Dave seemed like the most hateful thing on the planet. "I can tell you right now, I've never been abused. It never happened. I think I would remember something that important."

"Will you chill? We're just talkin', okay? Just think about it. See if something comes to you."

I fought back the urge to scream, *Fuck you!* "Sure, I'll try … I will. But I am as plain as they come."

"Look, dude, we are a lot of things except plain."

His use of the word 'we' calmed me down. I even felt a surprisingly warm feeling: we were somehow in this together. Then I remembered the words 'damaged goods.' There was something horrifying yet comforting, almost alluring about it because it seemed to explain a lot inside of me. I couldn't think about it too long or a lump would form in my throat.

"Thank you. I don't know what to say."

"Anything but thank you. Look Jamie, I see you struggle, and I wish I could—"

"Well, tha—I'll *think* about it, Dave, but it sounds far-fetched to me. I mean, I lived in a middle-class house." I suddenly needed to get up and put on my coat. "I lived in a middle-class neighborhood, attended a middle-class inner-city school," I said, buttoning my coat, "and I am now attending a middle-class inner-city college, having a middle-class inner-city sex life—education. I mean education."

My need to leave started like an urge to go somewhere and ended like the house was on fire. "Well, I gotta go now, Dave. I'll be back later, so if you see one of your girlfriends, you just use the old rubber band on the door, okay? It's all cool. Bye. You're a great friend, really. I gotta go see Chloë."

I slammed the door shut. I ran. I slowed at the bus stop. I couldn't wait for the bus, so instead, I ran on as fast as I could. After a mile, I was completely out of breath. I slid on a patch of ice and flew to the ground, landing on my butt and back, knocked flat. I heard someone laughing. I lay there. I felt woozy and uncoordinated from the fall and the pot I'd smoked. I felt an ache in my butt. I tried to stand back up. It was only then I realized that Dave wasn't attacking me, as I felt he had. He was being my friend. Feeling like an idiot, I wondered what had I done to project this terrible image of myself to him? I slowly walked the rest of the way to Dreamland.

Chapter 34: The Catalogue Aria

It was early, but I slunk over to my favorite spot on the edge of the dance floor. Swaying my body, hoping someone would notice, I was more desperate than ever for someone. After a drink or two, the bar seemed more like a candy store as it filled up with a wild throng of men just ready to play with me. I learned, I only had to make sure I gave them an inroad to dive in, a look at the bargain that could be had. I swayed to the music. Mostly, I did not need words: my body did the talking, rubbing against others, casually. Once someone made a move back, I suddenly found my lips loosened and my inhibitions tempered. Sometimes, I needed another drink to numb my emotions. Other times, the intended would offer help, and give me a complimentary pill to help with my enthusiasm. I did it all in the name of both adding one more number to my catalogue of self-worth and feeling desired, something I found strangely addictive.

DON GIOVANNI
I can do almost anything,
No one is such a
fertile talent as mine!

I flirted until eventually someone would take the bait.

I was proud of the numbers—look how many wanted me!—yet at the same time, the numbers seemed also to confirm that I was damaged in some way. More numbers were obviously needed. Not enough numbers equaled unwanted. Too many meant I was a whore. Nagging doubts on both sides urged me on. No one can argue with numbers. But what number was enough? What number could obscure the fact that my average stay with someone lasted a couple of hours, overnight if I was lucky? Still, the numbers, the names—it was objective proof, who cared of what.

As the nights flew by, I also had to ignore the disturbing pattern that began to emerge. Though I longed to be used like a receptacle, more and more guys were using me as a human dildo. I didn't like it. I hated the pressure to perform. Number ten in my catalogue was actually a sexy guy. But as I looked forward to being brutally fucked, he was in bed naked on his stomach waiting … and waiting … and waiting for me. I got in bed. I got the hint. I moved on top of him, and he was still waiting. I closed my eyes. I forced myself to fantasize the roles being reversed and it worked.

DONNA ELVIRA
Oh Lord, please protect my trusting heart
You just gonna lay there?

Eventually, by victim number twelve, I'd caught on. Yes, he would just wait there while I did all the work. I was inadvertently becoming what they called a 'top'— the active sex partner. I discovered the gay world was stuffed with bottoms wanting to claim the passive role. The men desired me for something, and I complied. The desire mattered not my enjoyment. I cannot over-emphasize how essential it was that they demand something from me, whatever it was. I never initiated because I wanted to quench their desire for me. My lack of desire somehow absolved me, but of what I did not know. Why was this important to me? I did not know. I only knew it allowed me to function sexually, something I felt compelled to do over and over again.

Around number fifteen, sex started to resemble work. It became rote. Because of the diminishing appeal, it took more sex to feel the same level of desire.

I became insatiable. I now needed daily proof that I was not 'damaged goods.' How ironic that I did this by inflicting more damage. Both damage to me for forcing myself to have sex I did not desire; and damage to the poor sex victim who wanted more than a penis. How could I go deeper in this emotional carnage? This became the challenge. I lowered my standards to meet my numbers; but by then, I had become completely disassociated from what I was doing. It was all just ruthless means to pointless ends.

Walking home after the deeds were done, more than likely drunk or high, I'd yell to myself, "Why? Why?"

By number twenty-five, I realized that regardless of why I did it, I hated myself. But that didn't stop me. I became what the people at Dreamland called generously a 'fast laner' or more ungenerously a 'slut.'

Nevertheless, as my real reputation spread, the pond

of fellow sluts at Dreamland was getting fished out. If I was to make any serious showing of being desired, I needed to lower my standards still further.

At first, I tried more self-destructive propositioning, and when that didn't get the completely desired effect, I tried turning a few tricks in the men's room. I thought that was the infamous center for all gay sex. After many trips to Dreamland's toilets, I was disappointed to learn that sex was not the illicit activity of choice there. Drugs were. Apart from getting dizzy, numb, and stupid there, the bathroom was a disaster.

I still had to find some way to be what I thought was the "ideal" homosexual: wanted, desired, despicable, and damaged. I had a couple of guys take me to the Palmer Park parking lot and suck me off there in their cars. I noticed shadowy foot traffic there late at night. It seemed an airy alternative to the Sassy Cat, with no threat of bumping into Sheldon Kaufman.

In my childhood, I remembered Palmer Park was a place to feed the ducks. Now, as an adult, this same park would feed my hunger to be desired.

At Dreamland, my score had reached twenty-five. At the park, I scored thirty in almost as much time. Some nights I scored two or three times until I found just the right act with just the right amount of damnation in it. There it could go on for as long as my conscience allowed; endurance seemed no issue.

DON GIOVANNI
I hope they yield to me quickly!
What a nice little trick this is!

It was exactly how Don Giovanni did it. Because just as in the "Catalogue Aria" it didn't matter who they were: peasants, manservants, counts, barons, princes, men of every rank, every shape, every age.

In Palmer Park, if I walked by parked cars, I invariably spied someone playing with his cock in his car. With a nod, I just got in, closed my eyes. If the parking lot failed, no worries; I ducked into the woods. I waited. Someone would kneel at my feet or force me down to my knees. Another would kneel and rim my ass at the same time. Occasionally, I was stalked by predators whom I would let them do whatever they wanted, feeling as if I were recreating some kind of compelling hell I had been through before. Including once by this fat curly-haired creep who seemed to come after me when I went into the bushes. I just let him violate me as often as he cared to. I never gave him or the others an ounce of encouragement, I needed unconditional desire.

LEPORELLO (aside)
If this goes on any longer
I will laugh out loud!

But still, I felt compelled to move to go lower and lower, and I wondered how low I could possibly go.

Chapter 35: Atonement Burlesque:
Don Juan in Hell

Then one night, I found out where the bottom was. Needing a few drinks before I could bear debasing myself in the park, my night started at Dreamland. Weirdly, these nights sometimes began by deluding myself into thinking I was turning over a new leaf and was going to find the love of my life at the bar, a love who would deliver me from the life I was leading—my savior with a small 's.' This particular night, I was experimenting with a martini. I loved the form of a martini glass. However, I took a sip; it tasted awful. All the fun went out of it after I ate the olive. Not even two olives, which is what I'd thought made a double martini, were enough to mask the awful taste.

Three medicinal martinis later, there was a presence behind me. The Southern accent was unmistakable, even if it sounded stiffer than usual.

"Hi, Jamie boy. Long time—and no see, boy. If I didn't know better, I'd think you've been avoidin' me."

I turned.

"Jack. It's been a while." *Since you assaulted me.*

"I see you discovered other avenues to damnation besides the men's room."

"Yes, even worse ones." I flushed in shame. Suddenly,

I realized how low I had sunk since I'd last seen him. In the grand scheme of things, what he did to me was no different than what numbers four, eighteen, and twenty-seven 'a' and 'b' had done to me (twenty-seven, 'a', and 'b' I suspected were the same person, but I wasn't sure).

"Worse ones? Do tell," Jack said.

I didn't even want to talk to him, but I was just drunk enough. "I have been going to … the park."

"The park? Palmer Park?"

"Yes. I'd have thought you would approve."

"Too dangerous for my skin. You know that Rags boy. He was arrested in the park."

"Really, your friend?"

"Your trick, honey. You did him, too."

"I did not." Though protesting the point seemed ridiculous given what I had done since.

"Say, interested in a party tonight?"

"Huh? No thanks. I don't like parties."

"Oh, but this one is special—and I think you are in the mood for it, sugar—maybe with just one more martini."

"Definitely not. I hope you don't mind my saying this, but … I don't really want to be around you."

"*Moi?*"

"I can't figure out—"

"What's to figure out? You're the one who makes everything so complicated. I lead a simple life. Just come out with me and get on with it. After the party gets started, we can start right where we left off."

Left off? Was he serious?

"Oh, come on; let your hair down. You know that's what we're all about: men fuckin' like bunnies. And there will be plenty of bunnies where we're going."

"You don't believe in love?" I asked.

"Don't give that crap to me, boy. You don't believe in it. You have a reputation around here. I've heard all about it. Let's get real. The park isn't where you're gonna find the love of your life."

"I don't want to go to the park tonight." I lied just to be defensive.

"Come on, the party will be safer. You'll get more than what you need." He slid his arm down my back to my butt. And I felt an acute sense of hatred for him because he knew how to get me. When he touched me, something clicked, and my self-hatred was getting the better of me. He saw me hesitate. It's hard to hate someone and yourself at the same time. Jack knew exactly how to manipulate me. "Come along, boy. Believe me, my little friend, you will thank me profusely. It's a special house party. Give me your coat check ticket." I did. "Meet me outside. Go on, run along. Outside in front of the door."

I don't remember saying "yes" or even wanting to follow him, but before I knew it, I was outside in the freezing cold with no jacket on, waiting. I felt just stupid enough to start cursing myself instead of Jack.

We drove to an abandoned house. The house was a Detroit classic: a beautiful Victorian, dilapidated beyond hope, brickwork cracked, painting faded and worn, windows boarded up.

Inside, the wood creaked dangerously underfoot. The house roared with loud music and reeked of industrial chemicals and smoke entwined with an acrid human odor. The lights were low, so I could not see well. Couches and floors writhed with uncertain action. At the entrance hallway, I'd been asked to pay twenty dollars. A big mug of a drink that was alcoholic and bitter appeared in my hand. A pill, too.

We are guilty. "What do I do with this?" I asked Jack while the Jewish prayer for atonement started eerily playing in my head.

"Just swallow it," Jack said as he popped it in his mouth like popcorn.

I knew that was not a good idea, but I was drunk enough to do it anyway. I was disoriented for a while. When I got my bearings, I was very quiet. Everything went still. It felt like any inhibition I might have had just melted away, as if I was capable of anything. I started to undo my clothes right there on the spot.

I looked at Jack Devlin, the white Southerner grad student. He suddenly turned into someone else, a tall gangly man. He spoke with Jack's voice and laughed Jack's laugh. "Put my foot in your mouth," he said.

I could see in a recess in my brain an overwhelming loathing for him. Yet, another part of my brain forced me to rush at him like a long-lost love. His hand came to my undone shirt. My remaining clothes fell off me like chicken meat from an overcooked carcass. I was turned around. I walked through a door. Jack disappeared as I entered some kind of sanctuary.

The room was lined with couches. I walked between them; some kind of padding squished underneath my feet. The only illumination came from snowflakes of light shining down in shards from a disco ball. It was difficult to see. Hallowed choruses of cathedral music started to roar in my mind. I gulped down the contents of my mug. Before I could finish, someone took it and spoke to me in a language I could not understand.

A warm sense of wonder overcame me. I stood on the edge of this matted area, maybe for a long time. I stood there thinking I was being watched. I felt a creeping shame. Everyone began to sing with the chorus.

Come, come, pretty boy!
Come, come!
Let me be your flower!
Pretty boy, my loving care
is for your delight and bliss!

Slowly, I could make out through the pulsating music the undulating congregation. They were throbbing and writhing on the floor. My body, too, undulated with the music. Shame seemed to mix with an increasing feeling that God was present. My own seemingly involuntary undulation reminded me of holy men rocking themselves in prayer at the synagogue. Was this holy or was this hell?

Adding to the bizarreness, a tall man in a towel-like prayer shawl entered. It had to be the rabbi of our congregation. The service could begin. From the perimeter near the couches, I followed the rabbi into the center of the congregants. The soft padding under my feet invited me, called me to kneel down and pray. In the middle of a mound of men, passion and piety seemed to burn like an eternal flame. I knelt in this holy place. I had entered the world of atonement as the Jewish prayer again came back to me. The redemption I longed for could be mine. But I knew it would take work. I slunk into the fray, the sweetened voice of the chorus still echoing in my ear. As I knelt, bodies shimmied away, allowing me my space in this pew of sexual redemption. My salvation with an oversized 'S' could at last begin. The *Ashamnu,* the holy Yom Kippur prayer of atonement, ran in my head. I stepped deeper into the sanctuary, naked, and kneeled at its center.

Ashamnu—As I fell to my knees, the room was twisted without a center of gravity. I seemed submerged in a cleansing abyss.

We are guilty—A body glued itself to me. Another pair of hands groped my body, ready to cleanse all that my body had done wrong. Then other congregants joined in. More were needed to expatiate all my guilt. I got a rush of joy; I would get all my sins and all sins of the future wiped away!

We have robbed—Soon, I lost my balance, but I didn't care. The hands kept groping. I stole gropes right back, my hand pulsing with joy at the firm flesh it encompassed. I fell over and landed on the warm damp floor. I laughed so much! I wanted just to dive into the dampness as if it were a swimming pool.

We have spoken slander—I was enveloped by sexy human cockroaches. They creaked and crawled all over my body. I gave myself unquestioningly to these willing predators, their predation purifying my sins and rotten desires.

We have dealt treacherously—This ecstatic hell was burning away my sins. A hand pinched my face. I opened wide and a mouth kissed mine. Random flesh pressed over my eyes. A large nipple crashed against me. A scrotum subsumed me. My brain seemed incapable of acting in any rational way.

We have acted perversely—A cock stuffed itself into my ass and pulled out. I seemed tickled and terrified all at once. Then terror spurred me to strive for a harsher sexual punishment to reach a deeper atonement.

We have acted presumptuously—Despite a feeling of profound lasciviousness, I forbade myself to have an orgasm. I had to serve the minyan. As someone's holy cum splashed on my face, I realized 'they' needed to orgasm, I had to make as many congregants orgasm as possible in order to find my big "S" savior.

We have done violence—Something like a vagina was in my face. I licked it, and it tasted holy. Another appeared. I was not sure if they were vaginas or assholes, whatever I did everything I could to make them cum. I had no idea what gender I was touching or allowing to enter me. Lying on my side, I realized my cock was in someone's mouth, my ass had someone's fingers probing in and out of it.

We have practiced deceit—I could not move. I didn't need to worry about my immobility because others' appendages moved for me. Warm liquids of salvation shot over me, testifying I was ever closer to redemption. Hands violently grabbed me. The extreme feelings were proof I was come closer to the divine.

We have counseled evil—Another body seemed to rescue me, only to shove my mouth over his genitals, and I gleefully obliged. Then that body floated away. Then more supplicants grabbed me. I descended into a fray of faceless bodies.

We have scoffed—It seemed like a hellish heaven. I was overcome with the feeling of not only being desired but also being worshipped, while I in turn cherished, served, and atoned.

We have revolted—There was a devil's chorus groping me, needing me, seeding me, and desiring me. My body seemed to swell more and more in the pulsating ecstasies around me.

We have blasphemed—People seemed to dance wildly around me. Willingly, I threw myself deeper into the swill, now needing to satiate an ecstatic appetite that was otherworldly. Someone kicked my scrotum, and the pain felt purifying.

We have committed iniquity—My eyes finally adjusted; I could see. I saw my soul being eaten by naked serpentine bodies.

We have transgressed—I thought of thirst, and a magic liquid appeared. It didn't quench so I thrust my mouth on cocks hoping to drink the needed balsam.

We have oppressed—I felt another lean and supple body. It felt warm and succulent. This body became more compelling. I felt myself entering its backside, sliding wet and sweaty alongside it.

We have been arrogant—Swaying into this body went on and on and felt so good until the body disappeared. I thought I would explode in rapture.

We have victimized—I seemed to float along in the room until I landed on a damp, spongy couch. I sat. A face turned up between my legs. It disappeared, too.

We have dealt corruptly—At one moment, I found myself pulled on the floor on top of Casper. I was feeling so happy to be on top of him, I thrust wildly, until another Casper put his cock in my mouth at the same time.

We have committed abomination—I was out of control. Thank goodness everyone was Casper. I was howling like a dog, thrusting and bobbing in a way that defied and defiled the laws of man.

We have led others astray—Unable to stand it any longer, I exploded into a wild sexual rapture and ecstasy. *"Gary! Yes, Gary!"* I cried lasciviously. This highest euphoria lasted a split second when suddenly the magic sanctuary disappeared. Bizarre and awful sounds, tastes, feelings, and smells flooded my brain. Then I looked around at what I had touched, sucked and fucked. The hallowed Caspers were random human beings. I felt exposed, defamed, and betrayed by myself.

"No! Gary! No, Gary! Take arms against a sea of troubles!!" I wailed like a drugged-out actor. Where was I? And what had I done in the name of atonement? Where had I gone? How could I ever find myself again?

Everything was ephemeral.

I crashed.

Chapter 36: Let the Search Begin?

Still prostrate in this disgusting throng. Spent. I was conscious of everything I had just done. Another body climbed on top of me and started fucking me. "It's no fun anymore," I lamely cried, and it crawled away. I stood up and everything I had been oblivious to while in the act now came to me in vivid acridity. The people who had just abused me. The ones I let abuse me. The people I abused. I looked at the pit and saw the writhing bodies.

This was the worst possible shame I'd ever felt. I suddenly realized there was this awful loud music hurting my ears. My arms and legs hurt. I was covered in damp lubricant semen-slime. My jaw felt sore. My ass was sore. I touched it, and my hand came away covered with a warm liquid, I looked and there was blood on my hands. I looked around. In the center was sex, while around the perimeter people huddled over needles and candles. Generic dirt covered my body.

I lost all respect for myself. I spoke to myself: "It's over."

It wasn't just another failed ritual; this was *it*. I had completed my task. I could now kill myself in good conscience. My soul had been bludgeoned, murdered. I suddenly, urgently, had to see what a murdered soul looked like.

I pushed my way into a small bathroom to clean up. With strands of toilet paper, I washed up as best I could. I looked into the mirror and saw a face. A face I did not recognize.

I looked at the hollow eyes with bags under them. Were they mine? My cheeks looked puffy. Were they mine? I missed the smooth soft cheeks I used to have. My nose—I used to like my button nose—now seemed bony and obscene. I wasn't really ugly before. I actually used to be quite cute at the right angle. Not anymore. At that moment, looking at that face in that mirror, I saw a pure vision of ugliness. I saw a depraved monster who had to be ruthlessly and brutally murdered; vanished from the planet, before God destroyed the entire world like Sodom and Gomorrah. It wasn't self-hatred; I knew that feeling. This was different: this was a crusade. I looked at this stranger, and I hated him so much. I did not *want* to, I *had* to kill him. Evil incarnate, outside of myself, yet it was undeniably … me.

"O, that this too too solid flesh would melt, Thaw and resolve itself into a dew!" I began to recite. "Or that the Everlasting had not fix'd His canon 'gainst self-slaughter! O God! God! How weary, stale, flat and unprofitable, Seem to me all the uses of this world! Fie on't! ah fie! 'tis an unweeded garden, That grows to seed; things rank and gross in nature possess it merely. That it should come to this!"

"Get out of there already!" yelled someone.

I felt so ashamed. I had destroyed myself through the smothering of my feelings, the inexorable lowering of my standards, the punishing throng of sexuality. My body had turned into a miasma. I had no muscles, no organs of my own, and no soul. I wanted to atone, and the clear answer from the holiest God we could find was, no!

A quiet feeling of hunger tempered my self-hatred. I tried to think. When was the last time I'd had anything to eat? A sudden flood of self-compassion overwhelmed me. I seemed to have been in a spiritual realm, the realization that maybe I had not eaten in days, brought me back down to earth with a crushing crash landing while I stared at myself in the mirror.

"Get the fuck out of there already!"

Chapter 37: Not to Be

I opened the door, and people flooded in. I grabbed a damp towel or perhaps someone's shirt and tried, in that crowded bathroom, to wash every part of my body that I could. I returned, just outside the fray. The orgy was still in full swing. Jack was disheveled but clothed and passed out against the wall. I walked over to a pile of clothes and sifted out mine, along with a reasonable looking pair of socks and underwear. I found my jacket. I had stuffed gloves and a scarf in the sleeve. My wallet was, miraculously, still there. I walked calmly outside into the chilly night. In the cold night, the wind hit my cheeks. It was punishing. I had to fight the urge to tear off my clothes and freeze to death. I forced myself to put the scarf around my neck and the gloves on my hands. I was walking in a poor residential neighborhood. No one was on the streets. I was alone. I walked a long distance. Down the block, I saw a busy street I assumed was Six- or Seven-Mile Road.

I noticed two guys ahead of me. They looked at me. I decided it would be better if I crossed the street. They crossed the street with me. I tried to make it to the busy street, but they met me head-on.

"We need some money, man." The guy wasn't begging.

I vaguely saw both men brandished metal objects in their pockets. Knives? Guns? My race was run.

I took off my gloves. Showed them my empty hands, realizing these were, most likely, the last two people I would see alive. "Oh, dat dis too too solid flesh would melt, daw itself into mush," I said in a weird voice. "No, that ain't right—it's the everlasting something had fix'd his canons to self-slaughter! Oh G-god! How weary, dense, cold, and unprofitable ..."

"I like that." I thought he meant my speech. Instead, he pointed at my wrist. He took my hand and took off my watch with a single sweep of his hand.

"It's my father's watch. It's the only thing he gave me." They did not react at all. "The watch was given to me for my bar mitzvah to celebrate dat ... I had finally become a man." This made them—and me—laugh.

"We'll take care of it for you. What else you got?"

I had no idea what my mouth intended to say, but I shot back softly but with emphasis, "Fie on't! Ah fie! 'Tis an unweeded garden that grows rank and gross!"

The men looked at each other, then at me a little more tentatively. They stepped back. Then I noticed they weren't blocking the entire sidewalk anymore. So, I nonchalantly took a step forward between them. I wondered why they didn't just shoot me or stab me with whatever they were concealing; this was, after all, the supposed murder capital of the world. I took another step. My suicidal effrontery must have unnerved my well-armed friends. I stepped again, inching my way past, moving toward a nearby streetlamp and a busy street.

"Where do you think you are going?" asked the man, mocking my voice.

"I don't care," I said. I suddenly realized, eventhough this might be my last thought on earth, but by not caring a huge weight was off my shoulders. "I DON'T CARE!" I yelled.

I lost my balance and stepped away from them. I muttered, "Oh, that dis tutu solid flesh would melt, thaw itself into doo-doo!"

They both gave a forced laugh, but they looked spooked. I took another small step away.

"Who is this guy?" the other guy asked. I took another step; they did not come closer. I felt I was free.

"Fuck, should we?" one guy asked.

"Are you crazy, man?" the first demanded as I turned my back on them.

"Can I at least buy you a sandwich?" I asked, moving away.

"What?" asked one of them in disbelief.

I was now a couple of steps past them. Testing if this would kill me.

"Can I buy you a sandwich?" I repeated.

"You gotta be kiddin' me."

They were sufficiently put off balance by my offer to buy them a sandwich that the way was now clear, their body language suggesting they'd just as soon be rid of me. Heart pounding, I began to walk faster, bracing myself for the end.

I was farther away and under another streetlamp, staggering into the street. I heard footsteps. I tensed. But the footsteps grew fainter.

I turned around as they ran in the opposite direction. I yelled, "Come on, I'll buy you a sandwich!"

"Fuck you, asshole!" one of them hollered back.

I heard a gunshot. *Hmph, that's louder than I expected,* I thought distantly. A car nearby took the bullet for me.

I ran. I made it to McNichols Road, aka Six-Mile Road. I stepped onto the busy street.

"Yep, there it is," I said to no one as I saw the 'West McNichols Road' sign. On the corner, a small crowd of rough-looking hipsters or gang members—I wasn't sure which—had gathered. I came to a stop in front of Sam's Westside Deli. At this hour, they took sandwich orders, but you couldn't eat in the restaurant. Instead, they had a takeout window, protected by thick Plexiglas. I felt I needed a treat; I had just failed to kill myself—or get someone to do it for me—and I was famished. I walked up to the window. I ordered a pastrami sandwich and a bottle of cream soda. I am not sure what I really looked like, but it must have been strange because the crowd eyed me like I was insane. I saw some guy lying on the ground on the side of the street. So, I asked for a second bottle of soda pop.

I took my order and sat down on the curb next to the man lying in the gutter.

"Here!" I said in a loud voice.

"What?" He looked up at me. I felt gratefully superior to someone.

"You need something to eat," I ordered as if I were his mother. With a pile of napkins from my bag, I gave him half my sandwich. "Cream soda?"

"What? No, man," he said but took it anyway. "Thanks, man."

"Mustard?" I asked, offering a mustard packet.

"It got mustard on it already."

On the curb of the street, I ate half of a pastrami sandwich with my silent friend. It felt good to share. It felt good to help. It felt good to eat. I spilled mustard from the sandwich on my jacket. I tried to wipe it away, but the stain only smeared. Suddenly the clothes I was wearing felt itchy. I looked down. I was not wearing my own pants; these were much shorter. I shrugged, munching the sandwich on the curb. I realized, peacefully, that I had destroyed my life. I was irreparable. I thought of the things I had done. I had sold myself to the lowest bidder. What crazy thought had made me think I would be at some holy place of rapture? How could I brazenly indulge myself to the point of madness, and then feel relieved and atoned? Instead, I just felt wretched.

The only thing left was enjoying my sandwich. I'd never realized how greasy pastrami was. In the cold, the grease warmed my body and comforted my dead soul, a soul that would soon be at peace—endless peace. I gave my scarf and gloves to my new friend. I would brave the cold with the reassuring security that I would do away with myself entirely before anyone found out what I had become.

Finally, I felt I could see clearly the crisis I had been in. James Goldberg had discovered what he was. He wasn't heterosexual. He wasn't gay. He was this disgusting thing who was prepared to throw away all human dignity. And for what? For a duel to the death with an unknown guy named Gary. A duel I'd lost.

I stared out into the void in front of me. I started to recite clearly, "To be, or not to be: that is the question: Whether 'tis nobler in the mind to suffer the slings and arrows of outrageous fortune, or to take arms against a sea of troubles, and by opposing, end them?" I could hardly say the next words because I needed it so badly, but I swallowed and continued, "To die: to sleep; no more; and by a sleep to say we end the heart-ache and the thousand natural shocks that flesh is heir to." I looked at my friend. "You follow me?"

"I follow you, man," he said, returning to his sandwich.

"… that flesh is heir to 'tis a consummation Devoutly to be wish'd. To die, to sleep; … Must give us pause: there's the respect that makes calamity of so long life; For who would bear the whips and scorns of time, the oppressor's … whatever."

My friend had gone away. I was alone. Sitting there on the curb on West McNichols Road, I begged carelessly to any spiritual power that cared to listen for an easy door to go through, a door for which there would be no 'other side;' a door with no exit. After some soul-searching, that door appeared. I had a plan, a final plan.

Chapter 38: Clearing the Path

On the day of my final plan, I dressed myself in the tightest, sexiest clothes I could find. On the day of my final plan, I checked the bathroom and noticed Dave had removed his razor blades from the medicine cabinet. On the day of my final plan, I didn't care about the results of the auditions. But, in some fatalistic last walk through the Theater Arts building, I saw the cast sheet outside Mr. Nathan's office.

Cast Announcement for Hamlet, Theater 831, Winter Term

Set Design   Casper Tyres
Lighting   Eula Meyer
Hamlet   Benjamin Geln
Claudius   Alexander Morgan
Polonius   Frederick Smart
Horatio   James Goldberg
Laertes ...

I could hardly believe what I read. I looked again to see if I was dreaming. This time I noticed Casper's name. It made me assess what I had done to myself since my love for him had first blossomed. How innocent and pure that love seemed to me. How impossibly tarnished

I had become. Unredeemable. Unworthy of any kind of salvation. I could have been something. Now it was too late. Besides, I didn't deserve the part. I would ruin the play for everyone. Just look at the depraved manner I interpreted Hamlet. The whole school would know what a sicko I really was. Moreover, that evening I was not planning to be around anymore, so they would need a replacement for me anyway.

I wrote the following note:

Mr. Nathan,

I think it is in the best interests of all that you find someone else for the role of Horatio. I am sorry, but I can't do it any longer. I have other obligations.

Sorry,
Jamie

I slid the note under Mr. Nathan's door. Resolutely, I walked away. The path was clear.

Chapter 39: Leather Funeral March

The leather gay bar wasn't the horror film I'd thought it would be. The music was different from the music at Dreamland: more aggressive, less romantic. But damn, "It's Raining Men" still made its way to the playlist. The plain wooden bar and benches seemed even more basic; the cigarette haze made grosser by the addition of a flatulent cigar stench. This leather bar seemed disappointingly pedestrian. Still, I had read that these people were murderously sadistic, and I could not think of a better end to my life.

I felt particularly depraved wearing a tight white T-shirt, tight jeans, and a macho black leather jacket I'd bought secondhand for this occasion. I felt as loose as a wooden stick. Luckily, I needed to lure just one sadist into my orbit, and my life would be over.

The trouble was that no one really seemed to want to talk to me no matter how slutty I tried to behave. If it was danger I wanted, this seemed an unlikely place to find it. It was supposed to be a bar where people viciously attacked one another. According that sex ed book I read, these leather bars were "the home of the Nazi SS, the modern-day executioners." I had found in a gay bar newsletter this bar's ad the "premiere leather bar for rough sex." It sounded like what I was searching for. Yet, there was little sign of that here.

I listened to conversations. I listened to how patrons ordered their beers. The talk was banal. Some actually drank wine or sipped sissy cocktails. Who among them was going to give me my final comeuppance? Still, all it would take was one person, one person to take me home and destroy me forever, right?

A few drinks later, in walked two people who I thought were likely candidates. One was overweight. He wore a tight shirt and chaps (leather pants with their naked ass exposed). The fat guy's ass was just sticking out for everyone to see, whether they wanted to see it or not. Wouldn't just such a freak want to handcuff me, take me to some dark place, tie me up, torture me with whips, chains, and knives, and then—when my body was thoroughly mutilated—tie me to a rope and hang me from the ceiling? Blood would drip out of my mouth. Red drops from my mouth would sprinkle his face. He would wipe it away with a starched white handkerchief. He would kiss my bloodied lips, then pause. Wiping blood from his lips, he would finish me off by clubbing me on the head with a two-by-four. Wouldn't he do that?

No. The two guys just ordered beers and walked off without so much as looking at me.

As the night wore tediously on, the only vicious thing turned out to be my fear-inspired fantasies. This was no den of iniquity. What I was looking for did not pan out. Instead of a group of depraved sadists standing around threateningly awaiting their prey for the evening, I found men chatting, drinking, and sporting black leather, bad haircuts, and pungent cigars. Once in a while, a macho muscleman in tight leather pants would show up near me. I would be convinced this was the guy to do me in. But nothing happened.

One guy looked particularly dangerous in his dark leather and mean-looking pointy metal studs—until he opened his mouth to order. "Hon, can you give me a beer?" he asked in a shrill effeminate voice. The voice sounded vaguely familiar. To my surprise, he turned to me, "Hey. Hi. What's-yer-name. I know you."

"I'm sorry?" I got a better look but only vaguely recognized the chiseled face that didn't seem to go with the effeminate voice.

"We've met before, haven't we, hon?" he asked.

"We have?"

"Yes, my name is Kurtz. You're … you're … I know it …"

"Oh, yes. Hi, Kurtz," I replied, urging him on as if I remembered him. I thought I had finally found my sadist.

"Nice jacket," he said.

"Thank you," I said. I looked at his: a black leather motorcycle jacket with steel studs all over it. "I like yours, too."

"You don't remember me, do you?"

"Yes, Kurtz, I'm Jamie."

"I know who you are."

"Of course, we met at Dreamland." He did have a familiar-sounding voice, but that was all I remembered.

"I won't be caught dead in Dreamland. No, we met at a deli … You wanted to be into the scene, didn't you?"

"Yes, desperately."

"I remember you. You seem to have grown into the real thing, boy."

"The real what?"

"Take off your shirt."

"Yes, sir," I said without thinking.

"That's right, boy." He stared directly into my eyes.

I took off my jacket but hesitated with my shirt. Then I saw the fat guy with the ass hanging out. Besides, what was the worst he could do to me? Kill me?

I put my shirt on the bench. My body shivered.

"Cold is good for you, boy," he said.

He took out a chain with two strange-looking pinchers attached to it. He placed one pincher on my right nipple. It hurt. Then he did the left one. The pain crashed against the indescribably sexy feeling emanating from my nipples. Despite the pain, my cock got hard. I'd hit the jackpot: my murderer arrived.

My fantasies started to run ahead of me. What would happen if I went home with Kurtz? He would take me to his house. I knew it. I would be blindfolded, then gagged. Unable to speak, I would be tied up. The scene would get out of hand, just like in the book. What started out innocently would end in my being maimed and then decapitated. Or stabbed through the chest. Or hanged by the neck. Or any number of other ways of being orgasmed to death. I'd finally found the danger I wanted.

"You know, no one knows where I am. Nobody even

cares. Anything can happen to me, and no one would know," I blabbered.

"Huh?" Kurtz looked quizzically at me. Then he frowned. My groin throbbed. I was excited that the end was near, just as I had hoped. Kurtz came very close. He squeezed my crotch. He seemed satisfied with the erection. He squeezed my balls. More pain. More intense erotic feelings. The erotic feelings seem to marry with the pain as if my desire was joining my repentance. I stood there frozen. I could not move.

He had that brilliantly mean look of victory—a vision I had so longed to see. Slowly, he took the pinchers off. As they came off, as blood rushed back, I let out a gasp and then heaved a sigh of relief.

"You want to go home with me?" he whispered.

"Yes, sir," I whispered back.

"You do? Do you know what will happen to you?"

"No."

"Don't you think you should find out first?"

"Why?"

"Why? ... Spread your legs."

I spread them. He kneed me in the crotch. Hard enough that I buckled over.

"You didn't like that, did you?"

"No—I mean, yes." Suddenly, memories of all sorts of things, of this Kurtz, and Gary, started to flood back.

"That's what I mean. We have to discuss what you like and what I like."

"Can't you just do ... it to me?"

"Well, first I don't know what you mean by 'it.'

Secondly, I don't do what people tell me to do. And third, I'm gonna make you so excited, you'll shoot your load on the ceiling. That's what you really want."

He pulled me toward him. He took my nipples between his fingers. He rubbed them gently. It made my erection throb.

"Put your shirt back on, boy. You're gonna be mine before this night's over."

"Have there ever been any accidents?" I asked as I put my shirt and jacket back on, oddly excited to get ready to meet my maker.

"Accidents?"

"Is it dangerous? You know, risky?" I almost pleaded.

"Those two aren't the same question, boy."

"Aren't you ... haven't you ever really hurt someone?"

"Only if they wanted it."

"You never killed anyone?"

"You kidding? Never. It won't be dangerous, I promise that. But yeah, it will be risky. Fetch me a beer."

I went over to the bar. I waited. Then some bizarre fear came over me. I looked to the door. I couldn't go through with it, but I needed to end it all. Then I ran out of the bar as fast as I could. I just ran, and without thinking. I paused at the street corner.

This was it!

Car horns blared. *Put up or shut up,* I started to run, then stopped, but my momentum carried me over the sidewalk, and I stumbled. I was caught before I fell.

"What the fuck is the matter with you?"

I struggled to get out of this person's grip.

"Stop it! Just stop it! I am stronger, and I'm not letting go until you calm down."

"Let me go!" I yelled.

It was Kurtz. He pulled me back into the bar. A crowd came over to me, but no one interfered with Kurtz or his iron grip on my neck and shoulders.

"Let me go."

"You running out of here?"

"No."

"You swear, asshole, do you?" His grip tightened painfully. I thought he would just press a little longer, and I wouldn't be able to breathe. He let go.

"Can we go back to your place, still?"

"Fuck you! You need some serious help."

I am past that now, I thought.

I walked out of the bar. I didn't know what to do or what I was supposed to do. So far, I had blown my chances for an early. After a while, I wandered into an alley. There were a few young guys standing around. One of them approached me.

"You here to trick?"

"What?"

"You here to trick?"

"No. I just want to get home."

"Cool. Those guys back there'll knock the shit out of you if they think you're tricking."

"What should I do?" I asked.

"Buy me a drink."

That didn't make sense. But hoping I would at least

get the shit knocked out of me, I agreed anyway. "A drink, where?"

"The Gas Station is right here." He pointed to the back of the alley where there was a door and no sign. He also waved to the guys in the alleyway, who laughed.

"Okay, what's your name?" I asked.

"I am Bud."

"Hello, Bud. I am Jamie."

We walked into the dive bar that opened into the alley. By now the all-familiar gay bar stench: cigarettes, sweat and other body odors wafted to greet me. Lyrics blasting out of the huge speakers were telling me there was too many men and too little time. Bud looked so sad to me. He looked perhaps the same age as me, but prematurely aged. He might be homeless with his ragged clothes. He had stringy blond hair, tattooed muscles, and a scarred face. But he seemed oddly attractive. Thoughts of Casper came back to me. It seemed like such a joke to me now. My aspirations for Casper reduced to a street person. Still, something inside me told me from experience that this, finally, was the right one.

"Hey, how about that drink?" he asked.

We walked over to the bar. He ordered a beer and a few shots. I ordered only a beer, realizing I didn't have that much money. I took out my wallet and paid for the drinks. He stared at my wallet like a starved lion. *Don't worry, it will all be yours when it's over*, I thought.

"Here, try this." He put a pill in my hand. I looked at it. I didn't know what it was but knew it was just what I needed. I couldn't stand another humiliation like the one with Kurtz. So, I murderously popped the pill in my mouth.

After a while, sipping my beer, I could barely place the glass down on the bar. The bar seemed to be swaying, this pill was having a stronger effect than I'd expected.

Not knowing what came over me, I was compelled to kiss the guy. I moved my face close to Bud's. He flinched and I kissed him. His face looked like it had sucked lemons. But then he came back at me and kissed back, briefly, a tight kiss on my lips. I was confused.

"I know you from somewhere, don't I? You don't recognize me? Jamie … Goldberg? Jamie Goldberg? Your name is Gary, isn't it?" I slurred.

"No, man; I said my name is Bud."

"Ever go to Dreamland?" I got a blank stare. "How about Palmer Park?"

I impulsively put my arm on Bud's shoulder. I felt weird, as if he had a compelling attraction. I needed to be with him. Bud pulled away. My arm was slow on the reaction and tried to hold on.

"Oh, I am, sorry; I didn't mean to offend you." I felt ashamed of being too forward, unsure why I was behaving this way. *I need him, but how is he going to kill me?* I wondered. "I am sorry. You're a nice guy. You don't want anything to do with me."

"Man, I can't understand a word you're saying. It's cool. Not many people are nice to me." He smiled; a few teeth were missing. He took my hand and put it around his shoulder. I looked at him and he looked different. Now, he had soft eyes. His shoulder was tender to the touch; his clothes were soft. He didn't smell as bad as I thought he did at first. I had somehow been groping him. This time he didn't seem to mind. I marveled that he was such a good human being, because I was sure he would be so sickened by me that he would kill me.

"You're nice, Gary," I said.

"I am not Gary, man. I said my name's Bud."

"Oh, yeah, sorry. You seem like a nice guy, person," I said, avoiding his name. I was afraid that what I thought I was saying was not actually coming out between my lips.

"Thanks. You're not like the others around here," said Bud.

"Do you like me?" I asked.

"You can't tell?" Bud asked back.

"Are you gay?"

"Why else would I be here, man? Maybe you come back to my place?"

"Sure. Now?" I asked eagerly, thinking that just like Kurtz he would kill me as soon as I went home with him.

"Nah, I can't go home yet. I gotta make some money. Let me turn a couple tricks and see you in a minute?"

I withered. A prostitute? Did he want to go home after work or as the last trick of the day? Why did it matter, and what happened to my suicide? That seemed very unlikely to me anymore. And after this drug I felt a compelling affection for Bud.

"I don't want to be rude, but I don't … you know"

"It's cool. I just need to work before I can go home

with someone I want to be with, okay?"

"Sure, whatever works for you," I said.

Bud left the bar. I was there alone.

Time passed. I was getting bored, but I felt stuck. I felt obligated. He was coming back for me. He didn't want any money from me. As time went on, I began to doubt if he was coming back, but I was just uncertain enough that I decided to stay until the bar closed. Plans for my suicide seemed long dead.

Around one in the morning, still bored, frazzled, and drunk, I spontaneously decided to go home.

I was about to ask the bartender for a taxi when he approached me with a drink.

"Tequila." He proffered the glass.

"I didn't order it."

"A little whore friend did," the bartender said uncharitably. I looked around, but I didn't see anyone at the other side of the bar or anywhere.

"A whore?" I asked.

"He is, but he's buying *you* a drink."

"Oh, this is the guy I know."

"What is it you're looking for, buddy?" The bartender stared and sized me up.

"I don't know; I want to make him happy.."

"I'd forget it," said the bartender, who then disappeared.

"Hey, hi." I didn't recognize Bud, but who else could it be? Drunk and drugged, I was pretty out of it, but there was this strange compelling need to make someone feel good.

"It's late, guy ... Bud? Go?"

"Let's go." He was unconvincing and a little too happy. I couldn't help thinking of the bartender's warning. In fact, the whole scene started to lose its allure altogether. But Bud wasn't as ugly as I remembered. His soft features had sharpened. His smile seemed wry, his eyes bright. He didn't look either as friendly or as attracted to me as he had earlier.

"Follow me," he said. "Let's do it. I think you're hot. Come here." He motioned me to follow him.

Unaccountably, I followed. But he only took me to the men's room. He pushed me into a stall and shut the door. He grabbed me and whispered, "Just relax. You make me so fucking horny. Here." That's when I realized he wasn't Bud.

The next thing I knew, he held a brown bottle that reeked of a familiar industrial waste smell. The bottle was planted under my nose. I breathed in. The poppers revealed he was the sexiest man in the world. I had to trust him completely.

"Tell me what to do," I begged. He smiled.

He shoved the bottle under my nose again and kept it there. The pounding desire for sex overpowered me, and I became sexy and wild. My heart started pounding.

"Give me your ..." he started, but before he could finish, I had pulled down my pants and knelt down on the concrete floor, my naked knees touching the damp floor. I unzipped his pants and fished around, trying to pull out his cock.

"Get up, man!" he hissed.

What happened then is a little foggy. It seemed like the guy and I were in the middle of some very intimate moment. The guy became larger than life. I was feeling great … until he shouted at me, louder than was needed.

"What the fuck are you doing, faggot? Give me your money!"

As I looked up, to make his point, he took out a switchblade. My heart was pounding even harder. Life switched from near sex to near death. The end of my life seemed truly near. The thing I feared but wanted most. I yelled at the top of my lungs, "Gary, kill me!"

I was still on the ground, unintentionally frustrating this guy's plans to rob me. Even as I got up, my wallet was in my pants on the floor. I looked up and staggered to my feet in this claustrophobic toilet stall.

"My wallet is on the floor!" I yelled so he could hear.

I barely bent over. I fell against the side wall. I was groping the floor for my pants. I just lifted my head enough when the stall door flew open it hit me on the head. In a flash, Gary came back to me: but a trip down memory lane was not on order for the moment. I looked up, and I noticed a green bathroom stall door in my face, and looking down, my pants still on the ground. I heard this kid being dragged away. I pushed the door closed. Disoriented, I said something brilliant like "What the fuck?" I got up and pulled up my pants. I realized it smelled bad in there, so I staggered out.

I heard what sounded like a violent thud.

"Hey, leave him alone!" I heard my voice say faintly.

"You're eighty-sixed, Todd!" yelled the bartender.

I played the remark, "You are eighty-sixed, Todd," over and over in my mind. I zipped up my pants and then, proud I could fold my belt into its proper loop, decided to peek behind the door. The bartender was walking off with a baseball bat in one hand and 'Todd' in the other.

I was too woozy and stupid to feel scared. But I had to get out of the foul-smelling men's room and find my way home. Once out, I sat down on a bench against the wall of the bar. I looked up. I noticed a gas station pump. I looked around. The Gas Station bar was actually decorated with gas station paraphernalia all over the place. "Only in Detroit," I said to myself.

"Let's go," said a familiar voice. Bud was sitting next to me.

"Oh, there you are, Bud. I am okay," I said.

"What?" Bud asked. I stood up and looked at my pants.

"Oh, fuck, I gotta get home," I said, looking at my damp pant leg.

"Come on. Come back to my place." Bud gazed at me with such a friendly look.

"No, sorry, man. I have to get into a bed."

"I know, come on. I'll help you."

I thought it was awfully nice of Bud to take me back to my house. Together we staggered out of the bar.

Variation: Path to Redemption

February - March 1981

VI Andante con moto
(Slowly with fluidity)

Chapter 40: Small 's' Savior

"I don't want to die," I slurred to Bud. I thought this was a very important pronouncement, but Bud just ignored it. Bud helped me to his car. It was the dirtiest car I had ever seen. It was huge as a boat, and the grime-smeared seats had not been washed in years. The smell of grease and something like paint reeked from the car. The seats were strewn with papers, torn envelopes, hamburger wrappers, and empty beer cans. I was so shaken and tired, I didn't care. I plopped right down on everything amid squooshes, squishes, and squeaks. I had no way of getting home. Helplessly, I watched Bud drive the wrong way to my house. All I managed to say was "Thanks, Bud." It was an attempt to soften him up in case he was mean like Todd.

We drove for a long time. We ended up way out on the east side and pulled up to a once-beautiful Victorian turned slumlord special. The porch was piled high with tires and rusted auto parts. The floor of the porch was soft and creaky. Inside the house, it was too dark to see. There was nevertheless a suggestion of junk everywhere. It smelled of mildew, beer, and cigarettes. We moved in the dark, banging and kicking odd things on the floor. Once through the living room, we climbed some stairs.

At the top of the stairs, Bud opened a door and turned on a light. I walked into his bedroom. The room was austere but surprisingly clean. At last, a bed.

The severity of the plain room endeared him to me. A single bed. A wooden chair. No desk. No books. No clutter. A dingy, low wooden dresser. I finally understood the warm sensation I felt with this stranger. What I thought was love was actually sympathy. I knew somehow, I would be okay. All I had to do was lie down and close my eyes and love him, or at least pretend did.

Before I could take a step, Bud stepped in front of me.

"You got a twenty, dude?" he asked in an uninviting voice.

I felt ill but now wide awake.

"It's not for …" he looked to the ground. He looked ashamed. I felt both preyed-upon and predator as we both became unwilling parties to this affair.

"You need the money," I said, trying to finish his sentence. "Bud, I don't have any money. I spent it all. But if you can give me a ride home, I can at least give you all I've got left." I stupidly took out all I had—some bills and change. I held them shakily in my hands. He grabbed them.

"Where's your bathroom?" I asked.

"Just next door to the right."

I walked like a zombie to the bathroom and bent over and tried to smell my pants to see if they stank. Then I fell over and bumped my head on the floor. My head hurt. I pulled myself together. I got up, washed my hands and face, tried to get ready—but for what, I could not imagine.

"Let's get undressed!" he chirped, trying to sound happy. I was just tired and exhausted. So tired that killing myself seemed like more effort than it was worth. I just wanted to go home. But I was trapped. We stripped. I piled my clothes in a heap on the bare wooden floor. His were neatly folded on the dresser.

Awkwardly, we both stood naked. No longer the sexy guy I had thought he was, he looked like a scared scrawny young guy more permanently lost than I'd ever hoped to be. Something urgent welled up in me; it was a feeling of complete worthlessness and total adoration and sympathy for Bud.

He lay down on his bed, face up. I looked at him. He looked like he was bracing for the worst.

"You still want me to do this, Bud?"

"Fuck yeah."

"Well, okay."

There was his vulnerable naked body. I knew the look. I knew the posture. How did he become the victim I wanted to be? Lying there, he became so beautiful, so vulnerable.

"Come on, get on top; I'll suck you," he said again, chirpy yet with no trace of desire. He was losing his patience. "And pull out before you cum, dude."

I can't do this, Bud. I can't. Keep the money. I'm going home, I thought. But there was no way to get home except by satisfying Bud.

"Come on, baby," he pleaded. "Like you love me."

My moral compass had no needle. I had no idea what he really needed or what I really wanted except to go home.

"What can I do?" I asked.

"Sit on me, dude. Come on."

I got up on the bed, sitting beside him.

"Dude, come on."

I straddled his chest, my knees on either side of his neck. He propped his head up with some folded towels for pillows. He moved his mouth toward my groin.

He put his hands on my butt, pushing so I would get the idea of what I was supposed to do. I started to rock. He put his mouth around me. I looked down at him, and I saw myself. I felt like I was face-fucking myself.

Unlike me, Bud was indeed an expert. As exhausted, repulsed, and shocked as I was, he got me hard and moving in no time. He knew all the moves and tricks to get me working quickly. It wasn't until I started to feel that extreme ecstasy that I shook myself out of my reverie and realized I had forgotten to pull out. Interrupting the ecstatic rush came a flood of guilt. "Oh, shit, I am coming. Sorry, sorry; I'm coming."

I pulled out halfway through my ejaculation. Bud drew his face away from my groin with a disgusted look on his face. My penis continued to pulsate sperm onto his face. It landed like the worst mistake of my life. It wasn't the hot moment porn stars would have you believe it is. Instead, it looked as if I had completely and totally dehumanized Bud. To finish it off, he turned, looking as if someone had shot poison in his mouth, and spat out my sperm. Then he took a towel from behind him and with an old-cleaning-woman-like drudgery wiped my semen off his face.

I'm so sorry, I thought.

"I told you to pull out, dude," he said with arresting softness.

"I'm sorry; I wasn't thinking."

"Right, dude; I heard it before."

I dismounted and stood next to the bed and looked away. "I just want to sleep," I whispered to myself.

Just then, we were interrupted by the sound of a slammed door and someone shouting obscenities.

Bud jumped out of bed and turned off the lights. He then held me tightly from behind. His naked body pressed against mine had an odd calming effect. Until he put a hand over my mouth.

"Oh, shhh! That's Michael. He owns this place," Bud whispered, keeping a painful muzzle on my mouth. "Don't make a sound. He said he wasn't coming home. He just got out of jail. If he hears you in here, he'll go berserk."

Fear aside, I didn't know how to tell him this painful grip on my face was totally unnecessary.

Meanwhile, outside the room, the movements were heavy and boisterous. Inside, the pain of Bud covering my face grew fierce. My jaw locked as he dug his fingernails into my cheeks.

Terrified, I wanted to break free and run for it.

Bud must have sensed it because he grabbed my arm with his other hand.

"Don't move, man."

After what seemed like hours, Bud released me. Blood flushed my cheeks, and I heaved a sigh of relief.

"Shhh. He might be in his room. The noise died down below," he said—a terrible choice of words. "Just be quiet, baby, please. Please let me …"

"I have to … I gotta go home."

"Don't freak me out," Bud said. I turned and faced him.

"I have to go, buy you're beautiful. You're absolutely beautiful," I whispered. Bud turned beet red. I caressed his cheek. "Are you okay?"

"Yes, of course. Why are you asking, man?" Bud whispered.

"You are a special person. I am very lucky. Thank you for tonight."

"Right."

Not knowing what else to do, we kissed silently. His lips were surprisingly supple. We stood embraced.

Eventually, I sensed a lengthy silence that suggested Michael had gone to bed.

I clumsily got dressed in the dark.

I was about to leave, and then some weird sense of obligation came over me and I said, "Goodbye, Bud. You deserve love." I kissed him again.

"You're the nicest person in the world to me. Take care. I think Jesus brought you to me tonight."

"He did?"

I thought for a moment I had to stay. I mean, Jesus Christ was a pretty heavy card for a gentile to play. I looked at Bud. What had I done that was worthy of such impossible gratitude? Me, the lowliest sinner—yet I apparently did something right.

"Look, I gotta go. Bye! You are really lovable. You have to know that you are lovable, and you're not damaged goods no matter what anyone says. God—Jesus loves you." I put on my leather jacket. I frantically blew him a kiss and stealthily crept out of the room.

All was dark. I could barely see the stairs. I wanted to be silent, but the floor creaked as I walked. It was hell and seemed to take forever as the symphony of creaks and cracks from the stairs reverberated like the "Ride of the Valkyries" at triple volume. At the foot of the stairs, there it was—the door.

It was locked.

I could not figure out how to unlock the door. How complicated could it be? But there was no latch. No secondary lock. No lever, nothing, and the door would not open.

"Shit!" I hissed.

"What the fuck is going on down there?" I heard a large threatening voice. A light went on from above. *Lord have mercy!* My eyes darted to a back door. It had a bolt lock. I crept quickly to it. I reached the door, turned the bolt lock, and the door opened. I heard footsteps behind me.

I bolted out of the house. I ran like a crazed maniac zigzagging down the street, running away from my presumed pursuer and presumed imminent gunfire. Quick, turn right! I continued running and running from death itself. Quick, turn right! I kept thinking, *No one is running after me.* But I kept running. Quick, turn right, *I'm freezing cold!* I started to feel exhausted. *No one was after me.* Still running, I noticed the street was starting to look familiar when I tripped on a pothole as a car approached. As I fell, the car screeched to a stop in front of me. I looked up: it was a police car. It was the pigs. They were coming to arrest me. I braced myself as the police officers stepped out of the patrol car.

Their guns were out. "Hold it there, buddy," shouted one. *Here comes the end. Armed police officers are going to kill me. They don't know I don't have a gun. It's over! Goodbye, God! Goodbye, world!* In the street, in my leather garb, the moment I had always known was going to come had arrived. The death of my cousin Harold came to mind.

"What are you up to, kid?" shouted one of the police officers. "Hey, Ralph, look at this guy."

The police officers looked at me quizzically. Both lowered their guns.

"Buddy, you okay?"

"I just want to sleep," I cried.

"Where's home, kid?"

"Amsterdam Street, near Detroit State—but I love East Detroit, really." Afraid of telling them where I really lived, I gave the address of the bagel factory.

I was afraid to stand up and show what I was wearing, certain I would get beaten up for being a leather queen and tossed aside for dead.

"Get off the ground, kid. You know where you are?"

"Not really. Someone brought me here and then he took my ..." I thought better of finishing that sentence, "...then I ran away." It was enough to satisfy their curiosity.

"This is not a neighborhood to be out walking home, kid. Jesus, what do we do?" asked Ralph.

"I don't want to leave him here," said the other cop. "Hey, up by Detroit State, isn't that where you and Julie were looking for a house?"

"Yeah, the place isn't far from there."

"You want me to check it out?"

"Sure."

"Okay, kid, we'll take you home. But we're not a taxi service, you get it? You're lucky his wife is looking at a house over there. Frisk him, Ralph. Then stuff him in the back."

Ralph patted me down. He gave me a Kleenex.

"You can hold that on your cheek," he said.

I did. Then I looked at the tissue. There was blood.

I climbed into the back seat of the police car. They reported into the station using some cryptic language.

Apparently, not all policemen were pigs. I had been saved. Sitting in the back of the police car, I fell asleep.

I awoke to discover myself babbling uncontrollably, neither officer replying to anything I said until we reached Amsterdam Street.

"Just pull up to the bagel factory. What can I say, officers? I just love you!" I gushed.

"Great, you don't know how that makes our day."

"No, I mean it. You saved my life. Thank you.

Thanks for bringing me home."

"Home? You live at a bagel place?"

"Yes. Thanks."

"Okay, great. Get out of the car, buddy."

"You guys are the best. Good night."

"Nice to be appreciated," said Ralph. I had no sooner closed the door than their car peeled away.

I never did learn the other officer's name.

The police car disappeared from view. I crouched by the door of the empty bagel factory in exhaustion. I thought I could sleep if I just closed my eyes long enough. I'd been there for a while when I thought I heard noises from inside.

I turned and noticed a light was on. I rang the bell.

A rustling sound came from within, and then an oblong form approached the door. Sheldon opened it.

"You're here early; I am just settin' everything up." Shel then glanced at my scraped face with bits of bloody Kleenex dangling from it, the torn leather jacket, and the knee-size holes in my pants. "What the fuck happened to you?" he demanded.

"I fell?"

"Well, come on in," he said. "Let's get you cleaned up. Didn't I tell you not to be a fuckin' moron?"

Chapter 41: Dancing with a Crumb

My head was throbbing. I walked up the stairs to the apartment I shared with Dave as if every step twisted the dry sponge of my brain in a hopeless search for a drop of thought. I was dead tired from binge drinking, getting my head smashed and from working all morning in the bagel factory. A sickly hangover bloomed inside my brain. I looked to where my watch used to be and realized how close I had come to actually getting killed.

I was about to put the key in the door when I saw it: the rubber band. He can't mean it; it was one in the afternoon. I listened at the door; Dave was serious.

I sat down on the stairs outside the apartment. It was cold, and as my ass made contact with the concrete step, pain shot through it. The stairwell had an ammonia-like scent I'd never noticed before. That made sitting there extra excruciating. I held my head in my hands. I stared at an ant crawling on the wet cement. Staring at the ant, I felt jealous. It was carrying a gigantic crumb. *How happy it must be to be an ant*, I thought. I stared at the steps. The ant seemed so happy; it was dancing with the crumb.

I counted my losses. My parents and Casper, of course. Tim. Then, the only thing I did right in twenty-one years, winning a role in a very competitive audition—but then quit. I pissed off Mr. Nathan, my only source support.

I folded my arms over my knees and put my head down. Suddenly Dave was calling me.

"How long have you been here?"

"Just since midnight."

"Come on in. The coast is clear."

I stood up, stretching my aching body. My back was sore from leaning against the edge of the steps. My legs were stiff and tight. My head ached. I felt like shit.

Dave stared at my face. "What happened to you?"

"I fell."

"You fell?"

"Yeah, I fell … and I got hit in the head with a bathroom stall door."

"You lead a varied and interesting life, my man. Come on in. Sally and I were just gonna have a joint."

"After sex?"

"Why not?"

"Oh. I don't know. I am really tired. I need to sleep."

"Oh, fuck, dude, you're banged up. You need a doctor."

"I'll be all right if I can just sleep it off."

"Suit yourself."

I took a step toward the door and almost lost my balance. I grabbed Dave. He didn't flinch. "You're fucked up, man."

"I know. I haven't been to bed all night, and I just

came in from work. I'm sorry for being a mess like this."

"You don't need to apologize to me."

"Oh no? I feel like I have to apologize to the entire world." Then, feeling shooting pain from a bump on my head, I shut up.

I walked in, the smell of sex and marijuana unmistakable. I didn't smell so fresh myself. I blushed as I saw a naked girl, who must have been Sally. She wore her bare skin like a casual suit. She was predictably in a lotus position on the shag carpet.

"Hi, I'm Jamie."

"Oh, hi. I heard a lot about you. What happened to your forehead?" the naked girl inquired. "Oh, and your face?"

"He got hit with a toilet door."

"You did?" Sally studied my face for a moment. "Well, far out."

"We gotta hear the lowdown, man," said Dave.

"Just a minute," I said. I had to go to the bathroom, but before I could go, I saw a letter addressed to me on the table. I picked it up. "What's this?"

"I don't know; some guy brought it by last night."

Letter in hand, I zombied over to the bathroom. I sat down on the toilet, exhausted. I noticed my groin itched. I scratched it a little. The itch became more urgent.

The envelope indicated the note was from Mr. Nathan. I opened it. Inside was my note, torn to pieces. There was also a card. "I never got this. See me Monday morning at seven a.m. SHARP! — Arthur"

"I am not worthless," I sobbed. I scratched and

scratched my groin, crying. I was so relieved Mr. Nathan was not just going to abandon me. I kept scratching. *It must be some mosquito or spider bite*, I thought. I scratched some more and looked at my finger. There seemed to be something transparent on my fingertip— like a minute fleck of cellophane. Then the fleck began to move.

Curiously, I wondered what it was. I looked at it closely for a moment.

"Aaaahhhhhhhh!" I let out a piercing scream. "Help me! Help! I am dying!"

The flimsy door lock broke and the door of the bathroom burst open.

Dave entered, looked at me in horror, then calmed down when he saw I was just sitting on the toilet staring at my index finger.

"Are you out of your fucking mind, Jamie? What the fuck is the matter with you?"

"There are animals crawling on me!" I screamed, showing him my finger. Dave stared at me, then looked down at my finger. Sally rushed in to see what the commotion was about. I felt horribly embarrassed. Dave and a naked woman were staring at me on the toilet, and all I could think of was these animals crawling on me.

Then Dave laughed. "Oh, man, you just got the fuckin' crabs. Get a bottle of A-200 from Sentry Drug and you'll be fine."

Chapter 42: The Path Begins

"I am never having sex again. I am never having sex again. I am never having sex again. I am never having sex again. I am never having sex again. I am never having sex again."

"Will you stop it? Just take a fuckin' puff and chill." Dave stuck a joint in my face. For what seemed like an hour, I had been repeating the one solitary sentence like a mantra from a crazed monk. I lamely took the joint I did not want, puffed on it, and passed it to Sally. I thought Sally, now draped in a robe, gave what I thought was a compassionate sigh, but she was just taking a deep toke on the joint. My shoulders started to shake. Dave put his arm on my shoulder and the shaking stopped.

"Calm down. Maybe just tell us from the beginning what happened," urged Dave.

We sat on the carpet in our lotus positions, and I suddenly had this safe feeling—not safe exactly, more like confidence that I could talk to Dave and his girlfriend about whatever I needed to say. Maybe because he was with a girlfriend. Maybe they would judge me, but I could take it. If Dave did kick me out, I'd find another place to stay. But I knew he wouldn't.

"I can't tell you."

"It can't be that bad," said Dave.

"The cops."

"The cops did this to you?"

"No. I did."

"You did?"

"I'm a liar! Oh, God, I am a liar! I lie to everyone and everything. I have lied to myself for so long, I don't know the truth anymore."

"Calm down, man; you're trippin'."

"Don't you see? I've been lying to you."

"Lying to me?"

"And myself. There is no Chloë. I don't have a girlfriend."

"You don't?"

"No, I don't."

"You don't."

"No, I don't."

"Stop this broken record," drawled Sally.

"So, who's Chloë anyway?" asked Dave.

"I can't look at you and tell you this." I drooped my head to the floor.

"Yeah, right. Sally, can you do me a favor? Go to Sentry Drugs and get this kid some A-200?"

"And miss the story? Okay—okay, sure Davy-wavy. Be right back."

"Davy-wavy?"

"It's her pet name for me—She thinks it's cu—cool."

"You were gonna say cute."

"No, I wasn't, man."

"Yes, you were."

"Who is Chloë?"

"Be back in a few," said Sally, coming back camouflaged in a thick winter coat, hat, gloves, and scarf.

"Thanks, gal. So, tell me, who's Chloë, Jamie?"

"You won't throw me out?"

"Of course not."

"You will. Let me just go. Can you give me a couple days, though—"

"Jamie! I am not throwing you out."

"I'm gay."

"Oh, that."

"You knew?"

"Chloë never existed, then."

"You knew that, too?"

"I think you called her a half a dozen different names before you settled on Chloë."

"Oh, I did?"

"You also changed the pronunciation a few times."

"Oh, I did?"

"Chloë, Cloe, Chlo, Shloe, I think Cole a couple times …"

"I am going to be okay, then? Thank you, Dave I can't tell you how grateful that makes me feel … I just can't tell you what I have been through."

"How bad can it be? What, you're out in the parks fucking anything that moves?"

"Who told you?"

"You just did. How many?"

"Uh … er … forty-one … maybe forty-three or so,

including the last few nights."

Dave whistled. "Ah, I see. That's quite a number, even for me. You should be proud of yourself."

"That was the intention, but it didn't work out that way. But I was almost halfway to Don Giovanni's total number of sex partners in Turkey."

"Oh, really."

"All the while I did it, I pretended I didn't care." I looked down at the ground, ashamed. "Oh, the things I have done! The people I let use me. I was just taking my self-hatred out on me, myself, my body, my brain ... I am just unlovable—I thought I would prove I was at least desirable. So, I did this and the truth is ... I'm damaged goods, just like you said. I am damaged. Unlovable. I'll move out. I'm hopeless."

"Look, just because you hate yourself doesn't mean I have to. Let's keep the damaged goods for another day. Just tell me what happened last night."

"Where do I start? I was almost killed. The strange thing is, I thought it was what I wanted all along. But then when I was cornered, I prayed. I prayed to God like a devout nun. I turned into a withering coward."

"Whoa, man, you survived."

"I didn't die. I'm still here. I'll move out."

"Will you stop with that shit. You don't need to go anywhere, man; you're having a bad trip."

"I can't handle this. Can't you see? A male prostitute beat me up!"

"He hurt you; I can see that, man. It's fucked up if anyone hurts you. You're my friend."

"I am?"

"Yes of course; you're my friend, man."

I relaxed. A feeling of love welled up inside me. *I have a friend*, I reminded myself. "Well, actually, now that I think about, I wasn't beaten up. It was kinda my fault. I was a little drunk already ... No, I wasn't. I was blitzed and high ... on something. This guy gave me something that made me really high in a strange way. Like I felt an obsession to be with someone. I felt this weird need to cuddle people who looked ... lonely and dangerous."

"What were you on?"

"A pill or pills."

"Pills?"

"This guy gave me—well, he took one, too—I thought it was okay. I was already a little tipsy when he gave it to me ... I don't know what it was. In fact, he disappeared after I took it ... or I did."

"Cool, happens to me all the time. But maybe I have better friends than you. They usually tell me what something is before I go poppin' it."

"Anyway, I thought this guy was taking me home."

"Who? This prostitute?"

"I don't know who he was. Oh, yeah ... Todd—no Bud. How could I forget? Instead of getting to his car, he takes me to a toilet stall. Anyway, it happened so fast, I was kind of bewildered in the toilet stall and ... and then somehow during all this, I pulled down my pants. You think I am sick, don't you?"

"You think this type of thing doesn't happen in

straight clubs?"

"It does?"

"All the time. All the fuckin' time, man. Nothin' new under the sun. Go on, your pants were down."

And then it all came out—the whole ugly story. Dave listened while I poured forth in lurid detail. And then he said, "Oh, that's all."

"A police car almost ran me over," I added.

"They run you in?"

"No, they saved my life."

"Lucky you, everybody's saving your life."

"Yeah. Then they drove me—to work all the way from way out on the east side. I was never so grateful to anyone. I even told them I loved them. Can you believe I said that?"

"Of course. They saved your life. They sound like pretty nice guys to me, man."

"They were. You're not angry?"

"Why would I be angry?"

"I thought you hated the cops?"

"Me? I'm certainly no fan, but I don't go around callin' the cops pigs like you do."

"You don't?"

Just then, Sally returned from the cold with a brown paper bag. "I got the A-200 for your crabs, and look," she took out some candy bars, "some peanut butter cups for the soul."

Dave and I devoured the candy like lions eating red meat.

"Jamie, let Sally massage you with the A-200. She's

studying to be a nurse—"

"I am not!" Sally interjected.

"Sorry, sorry, Sally. She's studying to be a doctor. I keep forgetting. Anyway, let her do it for you."

"Oh, that's okay; it isn't necessary."

"It's cool. It's better I show you anyway," said Sally. "It's no big deal, nothing I haven't seen before.

"Shit, take a fuckin' hit and relax."

"Okay. Dave, I have another confession. Please."

"Yeah, sure, kid; go ahead."

"You were right about something."

"What?"

"Never mind—I am not in poli-sci."

"I see. Not in the Democratic Party either?"

"No. Fact is … I was … am … was … I was a political activist since age four, thanks to my mother. Anyway, I am not in poli-sci. I was, but I transferred to theater. If I'm lucky, I might even be in a school play, *Hamlet*. I'd be really happy if you—and Sally— would come see it in a few months."

"Of course."

"I'd love to see you; I am sure you'll be great," said Sally. "But now, strip, young man, and let's kill those dirty crabs."

Chapter 43: Redemption

On Monday morning, I hesitated in front of Mr. Nathan's office. I desperately needed to talk to someone. How could a professor be that person? Yet who else was there? I had no confidant, no father confessor. I knew there was only one person left in my life to whom I could tell the truth: the one person forcing me to talk. That is why it was with fear in my heart that I leaned into the crack of an opening in the door to the benevolent Mr. Nathan's office.

Peeking into the small office, the first thing I saw were books everywhere: lining the walls and piled on his desk. Not a neat pile of books like most professors but dozens of books laid flat and open with a hairdo of bookmarks and slips of paper. Mr. Nathan was visible through a break in the horizon of books on his desk. He seemed to have underlined the entire book he was studying. Deep in concentration, he was obviously trying to absorb every word. And though I wanted to run away, I took a step in. The wooden floor creaked as my foot fell into the office, he looked up. He smiled, recognizing me. This made me feel so much more ashamed of myself.

"Jamie!"

"Hello, Mr. Nathan. You wanted to see me?"

"Yes, James. Come in. Take a seat."

He had two hard wooden chairs in front of his desk. I walked over and sat on the one closest to the door. He walked to the door and shut it. He scrutinized my body. Mr. Nathan took the chair next to me.

"You're looking a little the worse for wear."

"I know … I had … a bad … I had a real bad night."

"I see." Mr. Nathan looked right at me. He maintained his optimistic tone and non-confrontational posture. His voice sounded as if he was going to ask me if I wanted an ice cream. "Your note had me confused and, I dare say, even angry."

"I am sorry—"

"We don't have much time, Jamie. You have an hour. An hour to convince me of two things. First, you have to convince me you are not a quitter, and second, you have to convince me you really want a career in theater. There are two things at stake. One is the cast sheet on my door; the other is this letter."

He held up an envelope from his desk. "This is a letter of recommendation. Last Friday, I was about to send it to a dear friend of mine in the drama department at UCLA, stating why they should accept you as a transfer student."

"What? Really? Me? Los Angeles?" I sat up in my chair. "Wow, I didn't know."

"Start by telling me what the note was about."

"The note? It's not so easy. I am sorry I wrote it. I never wanted to quit."

"You're not getting off that easy. You did write it,

and you left it in my office. Can you tell me why?"

"The whole story?"

"Jamie, trust me. Nothing bad is going to happen, but I need to know, why."

"Uh … I was trying to commit—no, I have to go pretty far back."

"I have an eight o'clock, so you better get started."

"Of course, you know better than I do what I'm doing here."

"Right, time for the train to leave the station."

I didn't know where to start. I thought only of something my roommate Dave had said to me: "Damaged goods," I sighed.

Mr. Nathan examined my bruised face.

"So, I gathered. What damaged you?"

"I thought I was saving myself but really destroying myself. 'Strange how in the name of salvation, we seek out our very damnation.' I heard that from somewhere."

"You heard it from Parsifal. I know the quote well."

"You do? Of course. Well, Friday night—no, I have to start earlier than that." I heaved another sigh. "I've never done this before. I can't do this. I can't upset you like this."

"Jamie, what's been going on?"

"You don't want to hear this. You're my teacher, not my—"

"That's the broken record you've been playing. Jump the needle over the skip, and let's hear it. Go on. You've got my permission."

"I do?"

"Yes," Mr. Nathan said softly.

"It's not easy piecing it all together."

"I imagine not."

"It's not very pretty … Okay. I thought the way I did Hamlet in the audition, everyone would think I am … I am …"

"Depraved."

"You thought so, too?" I asked. Mr. Nathan nodded his head. "Well, you put it much more … kindly than I would have."

"I know what you really meant," Mr. Nathan switched to his dramatic voice, "you felt like shit!"

"Yes!" I laughed an encouraged laugh. "I thought I'd be kicked out for that reading … but to explain that reading, and why I did what I did afterwards, I have to back in time, back to when I played chess."

"Chess?"

"A long time ago. I want to say I just remembered it, but I always knew it, only now I stopped fighting it and I remember that it was sort of … sexual abuse—kinda—when I was … younger." The feared words fell from my mouth like damnation.

"Oh Jamie, I am so sorry," came Mr. Nathan's compassionate response. Life seemed to get easier.

"But it's just the label they give it. Rape is another label, too."

"Rape? By whom—"

"Neither happened, but both did, but not the way you think. Or the way I thought. But that's where it started. They told me it was abuse, though it wasn't really abuse because I wanted it, you see?" I looked to the ground, ashamed. "It's really my fault. I truly am … depraved."

"I am so sorry, Jamie. I had no idea it was this. How old were you?"

"I was raped when I was fifteen or sixteen, but for the rest I know I was really much younger—maybe seven at most." Tears were welling in my eyes.

"I beg your pardon, you were a teenager?"

"No, I that's when I might have been … raped or whatever."

"Might have been?"

"A doctor said I was. You know this isn't what … Labels aren't what they say they mean. A real rape means you're jogging in a park and get attacked. Child abuse means some horrible predator ties you up and does whatever. Or some sadistic leather man ties you up and … those things never happened. That never happened. I am to blame for it myself, really. I feel like Benedict Arnold or Judas for just saying this."

"Jamie, you're making no sense. Just start from the beginning, and don't worry what it's called. Remember, I am not here to judge you; I am here to understand."

"It started when I was eight years old."

"And again, when you were a teenager?"

"I'll get to that in a moment." I took a deep breath. "Why is this so hard to say? It was …" My throat seemed to rebel and prevent me from talking until I forced a swallow. "… Gary." I suddenly felt guilty of the worst form of betrayal known to man, the crime of the century. "For saying that name, God forgive me ... Gary. A friend of Steven's." Sob-less tears rolled down my cheeks.

"Who was Steven?"

"My brother."

"Your brother?"

"Steven's my brother, but Gary is the only person who ... loved me or even cared about me."

"I see." These were the two most important words of my life at that moment. It meant he really heard me without the feared judgment, without the dreaded chiding or telling me how my parents must have loved me and how horrible this guy must have been. Now I could say it.

"Gary loved me until my mom or my dad, one of them anyway, threw him out. I hated my parents for it. I guess I still do. Not that they kicked him out to save me from anything—they never knew—it was their stuff they cared about."

"I am sorry, Jamie, I am not clear on this. How did you get to know this Gary? What do you mean by love?"

"I knew Gary when I was six or seven. You see, when I was younger, my brother used to give me marijuana ... to smoke ... with his friends. I was the life of the party, you know, the 'watch the whacked-out little kid' thing."

"I've never heard of any such thing."

"But that really had nothing to do with it. Steven didn't know."

"So, this started when you were just a child?"

"The smoking did. Smoking pot with Gary and my

brother, sometimes others. When I smoked or drank too much—"

"Drank?"

"Yeah, now that I think about it, they made this punch from wine and fruit juice. Sometimes they would let me drink some. If I drank too much, the room would spin so I would lie down on the floor watching the room spin. But it was me, stupid for drinking. They thought it was funny … I think I was eight when *it* started for real. I'm grossing you out."

"I can take it. You're not telling a professor; you're telling a friend."

"That makes it harder. Let me try again. Steven had this friend, Gary."

"How old was he?"

"Old. College age. My brother was going to high school at the time, but this was an older friend of his. He sold him his … stuff … Back then, my brother sold marijuana to his friends. But to me, Gary was kind of my substitute parent. He paid attention to me when my own parents wouldn't. One time he even saved me from getting beat up at school. He chased some bullies away. He was a hero then. In my brother's room, after they all did the 'get the kid high' bit, Gary got to know me. He'd take me back to my room, put me to bed … and talk. He took an interest in me. Really, he seemed way more interested in me than my mom or dad were. He would listen to me talk about music or history—no one else did. Gary asked me about stuff and really listened. He took me to ball games and let me sleep overnight at his house … at first, an oasis from my house … No one at home did this for me. My mother was too busy at work. My father had a very hard-working job. Steven thought I was a nuisance. But Gary was interested in me. He was physical … in a nice way, patting my head, stroking my cheek, putting an arm around my shoulder … It made me smile. For my eighth birthday, he gave me a present, a chess set. We played chess together. He taught me how to play. But I wasn't any good."

"That's a pretty tough game for a child."

"I enjoyed it. He took the time to teach me. I was grateful to him. But during the game he would touch me, differently. He would tell me to concentrate on the game, and he would stroke my back or my belly or … elsewhere. But when I lost … he wanted stuff from me like I'd lost a bet. Simple stuff: a quarter, a baseball card."

I looked at Mr. Nathan, searching for some sign of disapproval or revulsion. There was just a nodding head, encouraging me to go on. I tried to wipe the tears off my face; they were just replaced by new ones.

"It made me proud. This father-like guy actually wanted something I could give him and that would make him happy. It made me feel important … loved."

"Loved. I see. Yet he wanted stuff? Why was that?"

"I don't know. But it made me feel really good that he wanted something I had. I liked giving him things I had. He would ask for stupid … stuff." I stopped. Mr. Nathan looked intently focused but did not show any emotion. I cringed thinking about what I would say next.

More tears trickled down my cheeks. "Mr. Nathan, I am sorry; I can't look at you and say this. I can't … I don't know how."

"One syllable at a time, Jamie."

I put my head in my hands, looking to the ground.

"Tea-ching me chess … was-n't for free. Lo-sing wasn't free either. Everything had its price. If I wanted to play, I had to … had to pay the price. I had to give him something—a keepsake. That was the bargain. No one held a gun to my head. He never even suggested playing. I did. And I knew what that meant. He'd leave otherwise. Do you see? No one forced me. Gary always reminded me of that. It was my choice. His demands started out with something stupid like a simple baseball card, then it became my favorite baseball card … or something else I cared about … If it was something I wanted to keep, I was given an … alternative. At first, it was a joke. Then I didn't dare to because it was too scary. Then he wanted things like a *Mad* magazine, a comic book, an article of clothing—these meant something to me. But I still wanted to play. So … I asked for an alternative. I think I knew what I was asking for. He didn't threaten me. I did this myself. He just said that we wouldn't play chess together anymore. I was afraid he'd disappear if he did that. I didn't want th—that. So, I did whatever I had to do to keep him coming back. Finally, I … let him do things, but I had to ask for it. Not many facts, eh?"

"Jamie don't worry; I get it. It's okay you can stop here—"

I bent over and cried as silently as I could manage.

"Jamie, here, take a Kleenex."

I tried to straighten myself up, wiping the tears and runny nose.

"He liked me. He did nice things for me. Gary would show me his underwear, like it was a game, except now it was a … price or it was a game. Dare to touch it. Dare to kiss it. Dare to … take something off, but all during chess—like a by-the-way kind of thing. And his touching got more … intense while playing. Touching me below the waist and such. And this price, the game, the I-don't-know-what, kept going up. That's when it really started. Gary pulled down his pants and underwear. I'd never seen an erect penis before. It scared me. He told me what to do. I did what I was told. I closed my eyes. Opened my mouth and counted to ten. Gary did the rest. You see—I didn't say 'no.' It was my fault. But that made me feel incredibly guilty. I suddenly felt like I was cheating my parents in so many unforgivable ways—and I could never tell them, but I needed help."

"Where was Steven during all this?"

"Everyone thought Gary was just … pallin' around with me. And for a few years, he was. When it changed … Oh, but I am making him seem like a monster. He wasn't. I loved him. Did I say that? Anyway, I didn't say 'no.' I asked for it. So, I wanted it. It was my fault."

"You were just a small child. He took advantage of that. Didn't you call it sexual abuse?"

"Abuse? He helped me do this better. Helped me to learn to enjoy it. I found that as long as I did that with him, I could do anything. Was that so horrible? Was that, really?"

"You're the only judge of that."

"Other stuff muddied everything."

"I see. This all took place in your house?"

"No, not always. For a treat on a weekend, he'd come pick me up. My parents were glad to be rid of me—no, that's not fair. They thought it was okay; they didn't suspect anything. But I went sometimes to his pad, abandoned playgrounds, or empty rooms … somewhere. But what I really lived for was the nights we would go out. Gary would tell my parents he'd buy me a malt or something—how I loved the way he fooled my parents. I worshiped him. He just fooled them, for me, so I could have a good time. Gary made me happy. Until …it stopped. Until I did betray my mom. I gave Gary something … from my mother. Did he ask for it? I don't remember—might have been my idea. I think he needed money. His own parents died, a restaurant burned down, something terrible. So, he needed … But my … my father caught me giving it—a ring—to Gary. My parents didn't know anything about anything except the theft. The look of hatred, absolute hatred … Oh, dearest God, my mom was so angry. My father, my emotionless father, hated me. I begged them. I begged them on my knees, saying it was my fault. And they didn't fucking care!"

Mr. Nathan hugged me. For a moment, I thought it was compassion, and then I realized I was about to fall off the chair. I steadied myself. Mr. Nathan let go carefully.

"Take it easy, Jamie. Steady."

"My mother—" I stopped. "I can't."

"Wait, Jamie," Mr. Nathan said. "Take a deep breath. You're going to be just fine."

"How can that be? Anyway. that was the horror I tried to block out, never think about. But never forgot. I never told my mom or dad. They could never find out what really happened I felt so ashamed. So the ... so the darkness descended. So, instead of facing *it*, I felt this incredible guilt about everything. I felt horrible, but *it* disappeared. *It* never happened—so I told myself."

"Never told anyone?"

"Until now, no, not even myself. I am surprised how much and how vividly I remember things. I never thought about this so openly until recently. Yet it seems I remember being afraid of this memory my entire life. No. So I just blocked it out of my mind. Do you see what a horrible person ... what a—"

"What a frightened little boy you must have been. You should try and be easy on yourself; you were just a child."

"Then the rest, well the rest just followed. I then learned how damned I was when my parents gave me a sex-ed book—a terrible one. The book described how gay men would be condemned to having sex in toilets ... I couldn't become that. That was the first time I tried to ..."

"Tried to kill yourself?"

"I couldn't bring myself to do it, and I thought I could get someone else to do it for me. That's when I met a boy, a little older than me. He turned out to be a male prostitute. This guy took me to a terrible rundown house and he … he didn't kill me, but he … raped me. Or at least that's what the doctor called it. It was against my will, but I don't know if that guy knew that. I told myself it was another botched suicide. Damaged goods. What drew me to *Hamlet,* I guess, is that I imagined Hamlet was tormented like I was."

"I could tell that."

"You could?"

"Oh, I didn't know this—not any of it, Jamie. But you suffered as Hamlet did, of that I was sure. Your reading was … whatever it was, but you nailed that character."

"You know, Gary—it seems like such a dirty but sacred name to say out loud … and then that confrontation with the guy and sex made me sick. Just revolted me … until I … fell in love … with a student. Of course, you know but you can't tell anyone."

"No, I won't."

"That is about to get harder, sir."

"Keeping a confidence usually involves a burden I am used to bearing."

"I fell in love with Casper."

"Casper? Our Casper?"

"Yes."

"He's quite the ladies' man, I hear."

"I didn't know that. All I knew was how beautiful he was."

"Yes, he is," Mr. Nathan quipped. I wondered if he

understood me better than I realized. I relaxed.

"He was different. His beauty taught me that love was a good thing. I felt so … inferior, and he was so sublime. Maybe this gay-curse can be a beautiful thing. But Gary turned out to be a jealous god. I loved Casper, but I let it turn into something terrible—self-abusive sex. I wasn't really ready for that, but I didn't tell Casper. I just did it. Humiliated myself in front of the last person I wanted to see me like that. Guess he was more than just a ladies' man. I just forced myself to do it like I had done it … way back. But I was older and better at it. I told him I was a virgin, a pure-white virgin—and there I was sucking him off, like a real pro—oh sorry I didn't mean to say that. But that must be why he hates me now. He knows all about me."

"He can't possibly know, Jamie."

"Maybe Gary goes to school here?"

"By your account he'd be way too old to be in school now, right?"

"Well, anyway, Casper left. Abandoned me, like Gary. He left me and wouldn't talk to me. I never really knew why; I went into a tailspin. Making it worse was your theater course. Unlike music and literature, where I could fly into a fantasy, theater made life more real and more visceral to me. Instead of dreaming life away, it started to confront me. I had to suddenly live with it on a …"

"An honest level."

"Unmercifully so. Characters in plays went through things like I went through. They recited my darkest secrets to everyone. How could I ignore it then? *Equus,* the play *Equus*—substitute Gary for the horse—and it was the same thing. And Hamlet's suicidal struggles, 'Pursued in my revenge by heaven and hell. Must, like a whore, unpack my heart with words, and fall a-cursing, like a very drab, lowest form of human life.'"

"Not exactly the quote but good enough." Just then, there was a knock on his door. "Timing. Hold on a moment, Jamie." He walked to his door. It was Ben of all people. "I know I was supposed to see you but come back during my office hours, Ben. Sorry, but I am in the middle of something here." The door closed. Professor Arthur Nathan came back. "A good chance to catch our breath. So, I gather, after you had put Gary out of your mind, now you started to deal with it."

"Now I dared to think about it, allow myself to admit it. Slowly, in bits and pieces, like a kaleidoscope, it all started coming back. Gary, the other boy, stealing, and everything I had done. But not in any coherent way. Pieces that seemed to go together I couldn't put together: the fun chess game, the frightening climaxes, the price tag, theft, love—real love—and the base betrayal."

"Betrayal?"

"I betrayed … I betrayed … look at the backlog of betrayals: I betrayed him. I betrayed my parents. I betrayed God. I betrayed myself. I am betraying them all now by telling you."

"Just remembering, just admitting the truth, you undo betrayals."

"About the time we studied *Equus,* I started to admit

the truth. And then the worst was when in this convoluted Shakespearean English, someone talked as if my heart were on display for all to repulse. It was all there in *Hamlet*. His mental torment, the suicidal thoughts, and even … even love. Love of a failed Ophelia and a requited Horatio. Still, unlike Hamlet, I felt so … polluted, I couldn't allow myself to have normal sex. I had to be a … a sex receptacle or a … service. I did stuff to make reality fit that image. Instead of going to school, I went on a rampage, trying to either punish myself with sex or drown my feelings in it or both. Anything to stop my remembering the details. The worse the things were that I did to myself, the more I would remember; the more I had to forget, the more I ended up hating myself. So, then I had to punish myself more and more by giving out more … services—you can probably imagine the things I let people do to me—" I ended with a statement of fact, without a sob or a tear. "I am so ashamed, Mr. Nathan, just so ashamed."

"You're doing a courageous job of it."

I straightened up and gathered myself to get to the point.

"But it was all a useless fight, because—eventually— I remembered it all. All of it. All of the past and all of the present. Gary. My asking for it, my loving him, and my hating him. I wanted to obliterate Gary, but I couldn't. So … I tried to obliterate … myself."

"You wanted to kill yourself again."

"Yes. That's the moment when I wrote the letter to you because I knew you'd need a replacement. Because

I knew that … I wouldn't be around. I saw what I was and what I was becoming … but I couldn't be that. The last nights were meant to … kill me. But I didn't die. No matter how low I went, I didn't die."

"But judging by your face, it looks like you made a pretty good attempt."

"I slid on the street in front of a cop car. They saved my life. This weekend, I got a chance to end it all, more than once, but I couldn't pull the trigger. Not that I had a gun. Other people did. They would have obliged, but I bailed out. Ha!—A guy I thought would kill me saved my life. Yeah, I did a lousy job of dying but a pretty good job of damaging myself. I am an expert at that. I managed to lose … all respect for myself, like everyone … You must have lost all respect for me, too. Ha ha. At least that's one thing I did earn. So here I am at the bottom, sir. There is only one way to go now, only I don't know how." Then I looked into Mr. Nathan's eyes, searching. "I need your help. I have nobody, only you. And now you know everything. That's it. End Jamie's confessional. You didn't need to hear all this. But I need your help, and if you did want to help me, I couldn't bear keeping anything from you, especially anything that would embarrass you—any more than I already have. But I have become despicable, so please don't feel ob— obl…" I stopped talking.

Mr. Nathan said nothing but looked at me in a fond manner. I was going to come out of this alive.

"You've got my enormous respect, Jamie. That took a lot of guts, Jamie. You just took an enormous risk."

"I did? I just wanted to make this Gary go away. He wasn't even good-looking." I let out a nervous laugh. "When will he just go away? Anyway, I am sorry to be dumping all this on you—"

"Jamie, I like to pride myself on being approachable and understanding. I will say this has been very challenging to hear, but I do my best. I hope I have been helpful. So anyway, it makes perfect sense that you came to me."

"I feel stupid and ashamed."

"Be ashamed. Feel guilty too, Jamie, it's part of you. Only don't be ashamed or guilty about one of your most powerful traits."

"Powerful?"

"You're talking with a theater professor, not a therapist, not a priest—nor a rabbi. A ruthless honesty is required to be a good actor. Your experience gives you insights to play roles with a vitality that few actors possess. You don't know what I am talking about?"

"No, I guess I don't."

"Am I so bad a teacher?"

"You're the best."

"Apparently not if you don't—take the role of Hamlet." He switched to his theatrical voice that mimicked my own: "'The pangs of despised love, the law's delay, The insolence of office'—it's the climax of one of Hamlet's most important monologues. You nailed it better than anyone else, better than some of the students who are far more experienced. You did that because you lived those lines, and they hadn't."

"Yes, but that's because I am depraved."

"That's exactly my point."

"What?"

"Jamie, your experiences will help you leap over anyone else playing Hamlet. Or Alan Strang. Remember how you read Alan? How you knew Alan like the back of your hand? Eula, too."

"Eula?"

"Yes, she's a bit more public about it than you are. Because each of you in your own way have been where Alan and Hickey and Brick and of course Hamlet have been. In your own way, like all of them, you tried your innocent best to make sense of it."

"Innocent?"

"Get over these labels. You're not innocent, you're not guilty, you're not garbage, you're not a saint. But yes, you acted innocently. It doesn't get more innocent. You unwittingly built a little world around this Gary, as Alan did around horses. But that is just one of many, many plays in your life. Your problem is that your Gary play keeps playing over and over. Time to bring the curtain down for a while, as the curtain will come down on *Hamlet*. When you walk off stage, the part disappears. Only resign yourself to the fact that this Gary play of yours isn't going away. You can't burn the book, you can't censor out the parts you don't like, and you can't ban the play."

"I can't?"

"It's part of your integrity."

"Oh. That's so disappointing, but it explains a lot,

like why my integrity has been impossible. I kept trying to hide it. Do I have to tell everyone?"

"You are already telling everybody by your behavior."

"I am a freak."

"Throw away all those labels you've got plastered all over yourself. You are just you. Come on, you know that. You did the report on Sartre's *No Exit*. Wake up, Jamie. You are not as special as you think you are. There is a perverse side in all of us. It's there in you and me and every actor who aspires to play roles like Hickey in *The Iceman Cometh*."

Mr. Nathan's voice then switched to a guttural theatricality full of hatred and anger: "*'Christ, can you imagine what a guilty skunk she made me feel! If she'd only admitted once she didn't believe any more in her pipe dream that someday I'd behave!'* We actors have that in us, Jamie. That same pursuit of peace you tried to get through sex, Brick sought in alcohol: *'I have to hear that little click in my head that makes me peaceful. Usually, I hear it sooner than this, sometimes as early as—noon, but—Today it's—dilatory.'*

But you also have a Tom Wingfield in you." Mr. Nathan then sounded like he was imitating my voice. "*'Oh, Laura, I tried to leave you behind me, but I am more faithful than I intended to be! I reach for a cigarette, I cross the street, I run into the movies or a bar, I buy a drink, I speak to the nearest stranger— anything that can blow your candles out!'*" He stared at me. "You can't lead a sheltered life and hope to do any of that. That's us. That's all of us."

"That's a good thing?"

"It's a good thing to have lived life, Jamie." Mr. Nathan stared at me suddenly with a scowl. A disapproving scowl, even as his voice remained light. "Now on to something really serious. You know me well enough by now to know that I won't judge you. You are the ultimate judge of whether your life is worth living or not. But do you understand how many people are counting on you?"

"Oh. I never thought—"

"I went out on quite a limb choosing you over students far more experienced than you for Horatio. So, I need to know right now if I can count on you."

I couldn't believe what I was hearing, I'd been cringing, awaiting a condemnation, and instead, I was going to be okay.

"How do I say 'yes' so you can believe me?"

"Say 'yes' if you realize how many lives will be *totally screwed up if you die*. And that you are willing to give that priority over your own self-pity."

Ouch. "I will do anything and everything I can to prove it. No more self-pity!" Hearing 'self-pity' issuing from Mr. Nathan was my long-needed wake-up call. What did Nietzsche, one of my heroes, hate more than self-pity?

"Okay, whose lives will you fuck up if you die?" he asked blithely.

"The entire cast of the play and you, especially if you recommend me."

"Oh, come on, your world is so much larger than that."

"There are more?"

"You'll traumatize an entire school. Every friend you ever had, every acquaintance, and all your relatives will feel the guilt for the rest of their lives. Your parents will never forgive themselves—especially if they've screwed up somehow, which I dare say they have. Other lives you will destroy? Anyone else who's counting on you to succeed? Aunts? Uncles? Cousins? Neighbors? Schoolmates? Casper? Eula? Gary? In short, anyone who knows you will regret the day they met you. Is that the legacy you wish to leave behind on this planet? Is that why you were put here? I certainly don't want you doing that to me—"

"Stop it! Please! I'll show you I am worth it. I promise. I promise." Shame suddenly mixed with pride. "You know somebody else once told me, 'You are not a disease'—I thought it meant being gay was not a disease, but now I realize what he really meant."

"Good. I'll believe in you then. You have a second chance. Take it. I'll keep this letter for now. After the *Hamlet* run, we'll talk about UCLA again. Don't get me wrong, I am not going to be happy until I see you are a successful actor. But first, you have to kick ass in *Hamlet*. Make Horatio come alive as he never was before—but do it by taking risks, for God's sake, because if you have proved nothing else, you have proven you know how to take risks and survive them."

Chapter 44: Family Aid

Each step felt as if Daniel was taking a step deeper into the lion's den, even though it was just a stupid restaurant. I walked into Sam's Westside delicatessen. It felt awful as if I were returning to the scene of a crime. I hadn't been to the deli since that night I took the big dive that evening, I'd been drugged, sexually abused myself, I was shot at, threatened with a knife, and almost run over. I was now back at the scene to get some business done. I saw my brother Steven sitting in a booth. I walked over to him.

"Hi, Steven," I greeted him stiffly as I sat down.

"Hi, Jimmy." Steven had a contemptuous edge to his voice whenever he spoke to me. I tried my best not to take it personally.

"How's Mom?"

"Just fine," he said sarcastically.

"Dad?"

"Picture of health. Getting fatter, actually."

"You're not doing so bad yourself." I noticed he seemed to have put on some weight.

"You would say that. Yeah, I gotta lose weight. Look at you; you're skinny as a rail!"

"Yeah, I have a fast metabolism," I said, trying to

skip over the fact that I had been starving myself the past week. There was a pause in the conversation. "You got it?" I asked.

"Yeah. All I could get you was five hundred bucks. Remember, it's a loan. I need it back. Here." He gave me a wad of twenty-dollar bills. As he handed over the money, he said to me, "Look, why don't you just tell them it was all a joke?"

"Lying."

"You lie to your roommate, why not them? You haven't exactly gone very far with this so-called truth, have you?"

"Lying to prevent people from knowing I am gay is different from lying to people who already know," I said. "Besides, I am not lying to my roommate anymore; he knows."

"I see. Okay, then at least see that shrink Mom and Pop want you to see. How horrible can that be?" I couldn't believe he was suggesting this, and my face showed it. "Fuck, why do you have to be the asshole all the time? Just try it. D'you wanna stay a fag all your life?"

"You were doing good there for a while, Steve."

"Do you? Is that what you want? You want to be some fag?"

"I guesso," I muttered.

"You piss me off; really, you do. I help you because you're my asshole brother, and I feel sorry for you—"

"Well, thanks for that ... Should I call them?"

"Better not call them, not till you see that doctor ...

Dr. Baker. I have his phone number." He handed me a business card. "Just call him and see what he's got."

I looked at the card: "Dr. Jonah Baker, Psychiatrist, Men's Academy, Provo, Utah."

I handed the card back to Steven.

"I am not going to call him."

"Why not? What have you got to lose?"

"This guy is in Utah. Come on, you expect me to go there?"

"They have a rep here, and he's Jewish … What's wrong with that if he's gonna cure you?"

"Baker … Jewish? Come on. He's a Mormon."

"Jonah, that's a Jewish name," said my brother.

"I fought too hard for this. You don't understand: this is me; I am gay." He winced when I said the word. "I fought for this. You get it? It's who I am," I said, repeating myself even though I was not exactly thrilled about the fact.

"That's spoken like a real trooper. You fought too hard for *this*? What is *this*? To be a fag? Big fucking fight. You've been kicked out of the house. You got spit on by your best friend. They kicked you out of your dorm. What is the this you worked so hard for?"

"To be honest." It made me nauseated to admit it, like I was picking a sexual perversion over my own parents.

"Honest? You were lying to this cockamamie roommate you have. Lord knows, you are probably lying to me right now."

"With Dave it's different; I needed a place to stay.

Besides, I told you, he knows now."

"Yeah, not the last time I talked with him … You need a place to stay and, well, don't you need a mom and dad too? Can't you at least lie to them? Show them the same consideration you showed to that stoner roommate of yours?"

"Too late. I'm not going back in the closet. It's who I am, who I always was. You know that. Or should I start lying to everyone now? Is that what you want?"

"I don't care. I don't like being in the middle of all this. Don't look at me like that. Harold was like a brother to me, so don't give me the *I don't understand* crap. I understood him too well." Talking about our dead cousin was a shock for both of us. He suddenly changed his tone. "What are you gonna do?"

"I don't know. Learn Faggot 101: Survive."

"Survive?" Steven's contemptuous smile was better than none.

"Survive the best way I know how. I applied for a student loan for next year. In the meantime, I got a job baking bagels at Brooklyn Bagel."

"You're working at a bagel factory? You know, you're killing Mom and Dad. Dad already has a heart condition, and Mom's stressed out."

"I am not killing them."

"No? You should see them. They want you back, but they want you back normal. That isn't too much to ask. Look at yourself. You need me to support you." I wished I could throw the money back in his face. "You're miserable. You can't possibly convince me you're happier being this ... fag business. And you know that's true. Okay, just supposing you're right. Supposing you're not killing them. If Dad has another heart attack and dies, you will feel guilty for the rest of your life. Do you want to risk that? Do you? Feeling guilty for the rest of your life?"

"That's impossible."

"What do you mean?"

"I will already feel guilty for the rest of my life. Steven, give it up; I know what I am. You know you're right-handed, and I know I am gay."

"Done any drugs?" he asked. I was wondering if marijuana qualified as a drug. But my hesitation was enough for Steven. "I thought so!"

"I am not like Harold. And like you haven't done them." I stopped myself from pointing out that I knew he was dealing drugs.

"Not so loud, moron," he hissed. "Besides, pot isn't like heroin. Harold did major heroin. And I'll tell you the truth: He didn't overdose. That's bullshit. He killed himself."

"How did you know that?"

"I know. Believe me, I know."

I was uncomfortable with him talking about my cousin. But it put a welcome pause in the conversation.

"He dressed up in women's clothing?" I asked.

"He did all sorts of shit."

"Why? Why did he do that?"

"He was a fucking head case and a queer with a mother who couldn't ... never mind. He was fucked up."

"Did he wear women's clothes?"

"You saw the picture in the newspaper," said Steven. There was indeed a graphic photo of part of his dead body wearing what could have been women's clothing.

"But did he wear them all the time like everyone says he did? Come on, you know?"

Steven shifted. He didn't like this turn in the conversation.

"No, I never saw him wear them before—well, once … but it was … a joke." A smile came to his face. I wondered what the joke was.

"I remember when I was a little kid," I said, "when Mom and Dad were away, and I stayed with Aunt Louise. I used to sleep with Harold in his room. He played all sorts of games with me. He made time for me. He'd listen to my stories."

"He was cool."

I bit my tongue. I was grateful for the money, so I refrained from saying, "It was more than you ever did."

"You didn't know about him being gay?" I asked.

"Of course, I did … You're not going to see Dr. Baker? It ain't electro. He tries other ways."

"But he'll use it as a last resort, right?"

"You don't know that."

"So, then I will have to lie to him to not get electrocuted. What's the value in that?"

"You don't know that. He's an okay guy."

"You met him?"

"Yeah, he wanted to meet the whole family. He thought your case would be easy to cure."

"He did?"

"Yeah, he did."

"You're lying; you're a fucking liar. The guy's in fucking Mormonland. You didn't go there." I swore when I got angry.

"Come on, this is the eighties; they don't do electroshock therapy like they did in the Neanderthal period."

"I can't believe—I really can't—" I was beside myself.

"What have you got to lose? Seriously. This is your chance to be normal, and for what? What price? What do you risk?" he asked, gesturing at me.

He knew how to hit the shame button. Shame and guilt made my face flare up in heat. I could feel the creeping self-hatred coming along with it. Steven knew the right buttons to push.

"What have I got to lose?" I mindlessly repeated.

"Exactly. You've already lost everything, but now ... but now you can gain it all back. Not many people get a second chance in life. But you do if you do this. You can do this. We'll stand right by you the entire time."

"I've lost everything? Wait. What do you mean? Did they throw away my stuff?"

"I saved a few boxes."

"You got my winter coat?"

"I don't think so."

"I have nothing. I really have nothing? They hate me?"

"They don't hate you ... they hate ... this gay business."

"It is me; I am gay. You can't cut it out like it's cancer."

"I hear there's a gay cancer now."

"Fuck you … I have nothing."

"Nothing's an overstatement."

"Right, three boxes," I said bitterly.

"Yeah, they're in the back of the car if you want them. Come on, kid, what have you got to lose? Just try to be cured."

"I'll tell you what I've got to lose …" I said, struggling against the creeping self-hatred. I racked my brain, but I had nothing to finish my sentence with. I wished more than anything I could spit in his face and storm out.

Then suddenly it began: I started feeling sorry for myself. I didn't have a home anymore. My parents didn't want to talk to me. I felt ready to implode and explode.

"I see a cripple in front of me. Look at yourself. Is this anything like you used to be? You can't tell me you're proud of this because I see right through you. You lost everything Mom and Dad gave you. You're wallowing in filth. What made you think you were a homo anyway? Were you out hustling on Seventh and Woodward?"

"You know about that?" I asked. The moment it jumped out of my mouth, I realized what I said was open to two meanings, but I felt powerless to correct him thinking I was a prostitute.

"Everyone knows!" he shot back. "Everyone does; you're a disgrace." He pounced on the misunderstanding, and in my weakness, I accepted it as the truth. By then, I felt low, really low, as low as a prostitute. Some-how he knew it. It hung there: Me as a prostitute. Me as a whore teasing an innocent Parsifal. Me covered in slime, defiling everyone I touched. The idea started to even appeal to me. How low could I go? I reminded myself that I had tried that already with pretty bad results. Then I realized in this reverie that Steven was still talking. I waited. Eventually, he stopped. When he stopped, he seemed happy. Or at least satisfied with himself. I stood up.

"Thanks, Steve. I appreciate you doing this for me. I'll pay you back as soon as I can. I gotta go back to school."

"What do I tell Mom and Dad?"

"Whatever you like."

I had to leave quickly. Walking out the door, I was stranded again. I'd counted on a ride back to school from Steven. Now I had a long hike in front of me. Walking down Woodward toward downtown, I saw the streets were empty. Alone, I silently sobbed to myself. The sound grew louder, and then it bubbled out of my mouth and felt strange. I realized, despite the tears in my eyes, I wasn't crying. I was laughing. Laughing through my tears, I thought, *I pulled it off. I have five-hundred bucks to keep going to college.*

Chapter 45: Enlightenment

I was sitting high on an examining table. The doctor was on a low stool. Still, I felt him looking down at me.

"I heard you are recently out of the closet, is that right?" asked the doctor. I nodded. "Then, congratulations. But with this freedom comes responsibilities, young man. Have you ever considered having sex with a condom?"

"No, why would I want to do that?"

"Well, because—"

"Is it like with a doll with a condom in it? I think I've seen those at sex shops or something like that. I thought those were for—" This sent the doctor into hysterics. "What's so funny? You said sex with a condom."

Tears were falling down the doctor's cheeks. "Sorry, but that was about the funniest thing I have heard all year." He tried to catch his breath. "No, I mean have anal sex with a condom attached to you or your partner's penis. You know, the one who will stick it inside." He continued laughing. I felt the heat off my blushing face.

"Oh, I see. You're joking, right? I'm not worried about getting a guy pregnant."

"Preventing VD is more the problem, considering all the things you got."

"All the things I've got? What do I have?"

"Well, let's see," he said glancing at his chart. "Gonorrhea, syphilis, anal warts, strep throat, and the sore on your penis, which is probably herpes."

"Warts? Gross."

"I can only guess that you are leading a fast-lane lifestyle."

"Fast lane?"

"How many sex partners have you had?"

"Forty-one—though maybe forty-three."

"How many in, say, the last two months?"

"Forty-one—forty-three."

"I see. Getting all that pent-up energy out of your system?"

He made it sound so much better than trying to destroy yourself or smothering your feelings, or any of the other reasons that came to my mind.

"That must be it."

"Have you ever taken drugs intravenously? You know, with a needle."

"I've never taken drugs with a needle."

"Good. Look, run your life the way you run your life. I am just advising you to take some precautions to protect yourself, especially from these scarier diseases. Okay?"

"Scarier diseases?"

"There are also some strange diseases going around; maybe you've heard about them?"

"Gay plague? But I don't live in San Francisco or New York."

"First, I prefer the term Gay Related Immune Deficiency Syndrome. It is rare, and you're right, it is mostly centered in San Francisco and New York, but it will only be a matter of time before it comes here, too, if we're not careful. Think about using a condom, please."

"I have it. Don't I? I'm gonna die. I have GRIDS and probably AIDS, too."

"I wouldn't count on it. First of all, they're the same thing, second, you don't really know until much later, and—look me in the eyes." I looked into his eyes; they were warm and friendly. "Venereal disease is a germ, not a moral pronouncement. Having sex is fun, also not a moral pronouncement. But use common-sense caution. You're not the victim. In fact, you're lucky. These diseases we can treat—except the herpes. And even that will probably seem to go away by itself, though you'll always have it. One more thing before I give you your shots: how many people did you infect?"

"What?"

"How many people did you infect?" he asked as he gathered a couple of syringes and began to fill them with serum. "How many people do you think you could have given this to? The people you fucked, or they sucked you, and all that—before your last VD checkup?"

"Forty-three?"

"I've heard higher scores," he said while placing each syringe on a metal plate. "You should tell them, or as many as you can before they unknowingly infect others."

"I have to?"

"You know what I say? And this is just me personally.

For me, if I do something, I take responsibility for it. Sometimes, it means I have to clean up a mess I left behind. It's how my mother raised me. It's my integrity if you will. Now bend over and pull down your pants."

"That's what got me in this spot to begin with." We laughed.

It's my integrity if you will, were words that would haunt me. It was as if my atonement, my penance, my way back was shown to me. He spoke like a priest. And I followed his words like a true believer.

"Hello? Is ..." I'd forgotten the name already. I looked down at my little catalog booklet. "Fred there?"

"This is Fred," said the voice on the telephone.

"This is Jamie." I was sweating for the tenth time that day. No reply. I glanced at the initials in my catalog by Fred's name. It was *JS*. "I mean Jimmy Stewart."

"Oh, hi ... mister movies from Dreamland?"

"Yep, that's me."

"Thanks for calling, sweetie. Hey, I can't tell you how glad I am you called. I have been thinking about you."

"You remember me, then?"

"Of course, I do, Jimmy. We met at Dreamland a couple weeks ago?"

I glanced at my catalog of crimes against my own humanity. "Actually, three weeks ago this Tuesday."

"Sweet. You remember, too. We had the chemistry, didn't we?"

I blushed. I glanced again at the catalog. I saw the symbols by his entry. "Oh, yes ... I see, we had quite a time, didn't we?" *Gr-A, Fr-p, Rm, Sl-T*: I fucked him, he sucked me with a small 'p' meaning I didn't cum in his mouth, and one of us rimmed the other, the participant suffix was missing, and we also slept together the entire night.

"You were really sweet, Jimmy. I was hoping you would call. Did you want to get together again?"

I wished I remembered who this was. Not knowing who it was didn't make the impending humiliation any easier, especially because this appeared to have been someone nice.

"Sure, but the reason I am calling you is ... is ..." *Just say it and get it over with.* "Because you should probably get tested for VD if you haven't been lately."

"What? Why is that?" His question was so naive and vulnerable.

"I have reason to suspect that I gave something to you." The way I said it, it sounded like a Christmas present.

Silence. "Really? What? ... Did you give me the clap?" The quarter dropped. He switched over to anger like the rest.

"The good news is you were probably early eno—" I glanced at Fred's position, but it was way down the list. "Oh, never mind. I got my test results the other day, and I have VD."

"Whoa. You gave me VD?"

"Not on purpose."

"What did you have?" He hated me now.

"Gonorrhea ... and syphilis ... and herpes ..." I

couldn't bring myself to say the other things. But I had to, so I took a deep breath. "And anal warts."

"Jesus fucking Christ! Did you sleep with the entire city? You sleazebag. If you gave me herpes, I am gonna kill you!"

"Sorry, I didn't—" *Click.* "Hello? Hello?" I didn't even get to the crabs. But that wasn't so important because he would have known that by now.

Great, another person hates me. I guess we were not getting together again. At least he hates me for a good reason, not an imagined one, like Casper.

Strange, but this unrelenting negative feedback was not damaging my self-esteem. Quite the opposite. I felt I was undoing the damage and regaining my integrity. Funny how much more effort it took to regain my integrity than it took to lose it.

Because they were faceless, I didn't remember how ugly, abusive, or abused these people were. I thought I was the abused. But now I learned that what I'd set out to do—smother my emotions—meant trampling on the feelings and the health of others. True, some didn't care. A few even tried to pick me up again. No one was grateful for the news I brought them. It was lonely work repairing the damage from trying to destroy myself.

I realized many entries in my catalog had no phone numbers. I braved a few visits to Dreamland and the park for some equally uncomfortable confrontations. No one hit me. No one splashed a dramatic drink in my face. People tended to be more polite in person. And, yes, I did find one person who was grateful.

"Really? Anal warts? Is there anything I didn't get?"

"That about covers it."

"Rick—what's your real name again?"

"Jamie."

"Jamie, you slept around?"

"I guess so."

"How many people did you have to tell?"

"Forty-three."

"You know the exact number?"

"I kept a … a catalog."

"You kept a catalog? What number was I?"

"Twenty-eight."

"Woo," he whistled. "We never had a chance, did we?"

"No. I'm sorry if I said so."

"You didn't. I just hoped all on my own. Yet you bought me a drink to confess all this to me?"

"Yes."

"I am beginning to feel a little sick to my stomach right now, but that shows a lot of class, Rick."

"My real name is —forget it."

"I remember your name, Rick Goldman, right?"

"Yeah, sure."

"Well, Rick, thanks. I'll be sure and get checked out. But why are you doing this? You must have some feelings for me?"

True now, but I didn't then.

"Well, my apologies again."

"Thanks, you are a cutie, Rick. Wanna go back to my place for a little repeat action?"

"Thanks. I don't sleep around anymore."
"You got a boyfriend?"
"Yes. Finally."
"What's his name?"
"Jamie."
"Jamie is a lucky guy, Rick."
"Yes, he is a lucky guy. He gave me a second chance."
"Good for you, I hope Jamie sticks by you. You're worth it."

About the Goldberg Variations

Although *The Redemption of the Damned* is intended to stand alone, it is part of a multi-volume work called *The Goldberg Variations.* It is the successor volume to *The Rites of Passage.* This series follows its main character on a journey of self-discovery through an odyssey of trials, errors, and the occasional moment of grace leading this main character, Jamie Goldberg, on his elusive journey to discovery, redemption and self-actualization. This journey takes him to many places while meeting a diverse cast of characters along the path to his own surprising, quirky self-discoveries.

Acknowledgements

I would like to thank the man whose presence looms large in this book, my husband the late Dr. Morris Taylor. In the artistic creation of this book I must thank Michael Arent (the amazing cover designer), Rene Capone (the artist of the compelling front cover image) and Steven Brookings of the ArnoLand Press our trusty book designer who won the battle for Futura. I also must recognize the ones who have read, proofread and sweated with me over the book, I thank Lawrence Brown, David Siegel, Bob Cooper, Linda Watanabee McFerrin and Peter Paulus my guardian angel at ArnoLand Press.

About the Author

Jonathan A. Taylor is a San Francisco-based writer and designer who was born and raised in Detroit, Michigan (with a not inconsiderable interim stay in Amsterdam in the Netherlands). He is a leader in the LGBTQI+ alternative sexuality community. He is also a leading designer for creating user-friendly technology and has worked for companies such as Google, Nokia, and General Electric, as well as for the Dutch design bureaus Informaat and Keen Design. Jonathan has published two books on software design. *The Rites of Passage* was the first installment of *The Goldberg Variations* series. *The Redemption of the Damned* is the second novel in the series.

Jonathan's passions include theater, opera, history, social justice, studies in human sexuality, and cooking. All of these passions figure prominently in his writing. Jonathan can be reached at his website www.jonathantaylorauthor.com.